D0029743

# Lady Thief

Kay Hooper

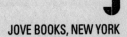
JOVE BOOKS, NEW YORK

**THE BERKLEY PUBLISHING GROUP**
**Published by the Penguin Group**
**Penguin Group (USA) Inc.**
**375 Hudson Street, New York, New York 10014, USA**
Penguin Group (Canada), 90 Eglinton Avenue East, Suite 700, Toronto, Ontario M4P 2Y3, Canada
(a division of Pearson Penguin Canada Inc.)
Penguin Books Ltd., 80 Strand, London WC2R 0RL, England
Penguin Group Ireland, 25 St. Stephen's Green, Dublin 2, Ireland (a division of Penguin Books Ltd.)
Penguin Group (Australia), 250 Camberwell Road, Camberwell, Victoria 3124, Australia
(a division of Pearson Australia Group Pty. Ltd.)
Penguin Books India Pvt. Ltd., 11 Community Centre, Panchsheel Park, New Delhi—110 017, India
Penguin Group (NZ), Cnr. Airborne and Rosedale Roads, Albany, Auckland 1310, New Zealand
(a division of Pearson New Zealand Ltd.)
Penguin Books (South Africa) (Pty.) Ltd., 24 Sturdee Avenue, Rosebank, Johannesburg 2196,
South Africa

Penguin Books Ltd., Registered Offices: 80 Strand, London WC2R 0RL, England

This is a work of fiction. Names, characters, places, and incidents either are the product of the
author's imagination or are used fictitiously, and any resemblance to actual persons, living or dead,
business establishments, events, or locales is entirely coincidental. The publisher does not have any
control over and does not assume any responsibility for author or third-party websites or their content.

LADY THIEF

A Jove Book / published by arrangement with the author.

PRINTING HISTORY
*Lady Thief*: originally published by Dell Publishing / July 1981
"Masquerade": originally published by Jove Books / February 1994
Berkley Sensation trade paperback edition / March 2005
Jove mass-market edition / May 2006

ISBN 0-515-13941-6

JOVE®
Jove Books are published by The Berkley Publishing Group,
a division of Penguin Group (USA) Inc.,
375 Hudson Street, New York, New York 10014.
JOVE is a registered trademark of Penguin Group (USA) Inc.
The "J" design is a trademark belonging to Penguin Group (USA) Inc.

PRINTED IN THE UNITED STATES OF AMERICA

10  9  8  7  6  5  4  3  2  1

# Contents

# Lady Thief

*In loving memory of Mary Sue Price,*
*my Aunt Sue, who kept the faith,*
*and who did not live to see*
*the realization of my dream*

# Chapter One

Dominic Vernon Ware, Duke of Spencer, swayed easily in the traveling coach, making no attempt to hold to the strap even when the wheels struck a bad rut in the road. He was deep in thought, remembering what one of his friends in the War Office had told him.

Richard Standen's face had been grave, his eyes worried. "I just don't know what to make of it, Nick. Vital papers turn up in the wrong files or, worse yet, are simply found lying on someone's desk. Last week an entire bundle of military papers was left on the doorstep of the Office—and no one knows how long they'd been missing. The next day, Conover was found near the coast; he'd been shot."

"Any speculation?"

"Of course. The most popular idea seems to be that Conover was a spy trying to get the papers to France, and that the Cat stopped him and returned the papers to us."

"The Cat? But the Cat is a thief."

"True. She is also something of a legend. After all, how many female highwaymen have there been?"

"You have a point. What do *you* think, Richard? Do you believe the Cat is trying, in a rather unorthodox manner, to locate and eliminate spies?"

Standen shook his head, puzzled. "There's something deuced odd about the woman, that much I'm sure of. She seems more concerned with jewelry than money, and yet . . . Nick, do you remember how old Farrell ranted and raved a few weeks ago about how she took his signet ring?" As Spencer nodded, he continued. "I saw him the other day and he was wearing that ring—not a copy, but that very ring. When I questioned him, he said that he had misplaced it."

"Perhaps he did."

"Nick, that ring hasn't been off his finger for more than thirty years. No, I believe the Cat took it from him—and I believe that she returned it to him."

Spencer frowned. "But, why?"

"That, my friend, is the question—why?"

Spencer was brought abruptly back to the present as his traveling coach ground to a shuddering halt. There was an ominous silence, and he began to reach for the pistol that he kept in the coach. But before his hand touched the handle of the gun, he changed his mind. With a faint smile on his lean face, he folded his arms and settled back in his seat.

The door of the coach was suddenly flung open, and a calm feminine voice said, "Step out of the coach, if you please—and don't do anything foolish."

Spencer slowly climbed from the coach, realizing that his team was perfectly quiet and that his coachman sat rigidly in the box, eyes fixed on the imposing figure of the Cat's henchman. The large man was masked and hooded, and held two pistols in his capable hands—one pointed at the coachman, one at the duke.

Spencer straightened and turned his gaze to the woman sitting at ease on the back of a huge, powerful black stallion. Dressed like a man, she was outfitted entirely in black and, like her cohort, wore a black hood and mask. She seemed a figure carved from the night, save for her strange eyes, which glittered like the eyes of a wild animal. One black-gloved hand held a pistol pointed squarely at the duke's heart.

The stallion stamped one hoof suddenly, his eyes glaring redly, and the duke wondered which was wilder—the woman or the beast she rode. "So," he murmured, "you are the Cat."

"Indeed." Her voice was cool and mocking. "And you are His Grace, the Duke of Spencer." A small leather pouch was tossed to land at his feet. "Your money and jewelry, if you please. And, Your Grace—don't try to be a hero. My silent friend there would like nothing better than to shoot you where you stand."

The duke smiled and slowly bent to pick up the bag. He heard the large man shift slightly in his saddle, and knew that both guns were trained on him. As he began to empty his pockets, he casually remarked, "I count my life worth more than a few trinkets—tell your silent friend to relax."

A soft chuckle came from the Cat. "I felt sure that you were a reasonable man." She watched as he deposited his money and jewelry into the pouch, and then held out one black-gloved hand. Carefully, the duke tossed the pouch to her, and watched it disappear beneath her cloak.

At that moment, the moon came out from behind the clouds, and he felt curiously light-headed as he saw clearly the strange wildness in the Cat's vivid eyes. He was conscious of his heart thudding in his chest, and had to force himself to concentrate on what she was saying.

"You have friends in the War Office, do you not?"

"Yes."

She smiled coldly. "Tell your friends to look within their ranks for the spy. That is where he'll be—unless I find him first." With that, she wheeled her horse and disappeared into the forest, her henchman at her heels.

Spencer stared after her, his mind bemused by her eyes and by her words.

"Your Grace?" The coachman sounded hesitant. "I beg pardon, Your Grace, but it all happened so fast." He fought to control the suddenly restless horses, glancing worriedly at the silent duke.

The duke stirred slightly. "Never mind, Owens. There was nothing you could have done."

"It were the queerest thing," Owens muttered. "That black devil jumped out of the woods with nary a sound. Stood right in our path, he did, with fire in his eyes. The grays stopped like they'd run into a wall—an' stood there as calm as you please. It weren't natural. Your Grace, them standing so quietlike when they're generally wild as be-damned. That black devil bewitched 'em; or that female on his back did."

Spencer prepared to climb into the coach, a faint smile on his face. "So you think they were bewitched, do you? I don't suppose it would do any good to tell you that there was nothing unreal or unnatural about either the girl or the horse." He wondered absently if he believed his own words.

Staunchly, Owens responded, "Talk till doomsday, Your Grace, I still say the pair of 'em weren't spawned on this earth. Demons, that's what they were. Why, that black devil did just what she wanted him to—and she never picked up the reins."

"Which only proves that she is an excellent horse-woman."

"Proves she's a witch—and that black devil's her familiar."

Spencer sighed. "I can see that your mind is made up. Let us be on our way—before you conjure up Satan himself." He climbed into the coach, leaving Owens to stare about nervously.

Owens allowed the fretful horses to continue on their way. The duke could think what he liked—Owens could recognize a demon when one appeared beneath his very nose. He shivered as he recalled the red glare in the horse's eyes, and the wild glitter in the eyes of the woman. With another nervous glance at the dark, silent woods, Owens urged the team on.

The huge black stallion galloped swiftly through the forest, weaving easily between the trees as he responded to the light hand on his reins. After nearly an hour's ride, he reluctantly obeyed a signal to halt. They stood at the edge of the forest as the woman on his back listened tensely for any sound of pursuit. After a moment, she urged the horse toward a small inn just across the road from the woods.

The two riders dismounted at the rear of the inn. The large man reached for the stallion's reins, dodging a lashing foreleg. "Here," he grunted, "I'll take 'im—you go on inside. Have a care—there may be strangers about." He led the horses off into the darkness.

The woman slipped silently through the back door of the inn. The door opened into a kitchen, where an older woman sat at a table, her face turned anxiously toward the door. Her eyes softened as she saw the black-clad figure. With a relieved sigh, she rose and turned up the lamp on the table. "There you are, dearie! Had me worried—you've been gone for hours."

The Cat drew off her hood, and then her cloak, revealing a slender young woman with raven hair and strange golden eyes. Smiling, she said, "There's no need to worry about us, Annie—we came off without a scratch! John's putting the horses away."

Annie clucked anxiously. "I hope you know what you're doing, dearie. That no-good brother of mine should be shot for letting you ride all over the place, dressed like a man and shooting at people!"

"Hush, Annie." The younger woman sat down at the table, her eyes bright. "You know how John tried to talk me out of this. I won't have you abusing him. He only rides with me so he can watch over me."

Annie sat down across from the Cat, her plump face worried. "Missy, why don't you stop this? It's too dangerous—and you are little more than a babe."

The Cat gestured impatiently. "Annie, I'll stop when I find the talisman ring and not before."

At that moment, the door opened and the large man came in. He pulled the hood from his head and looked inquiringly at the Cat. "Did the duke have the ring?"

Annie let out a scandalized gasp. "Oh, mercy! You never robbed a duke! John, what were you thinkin' of?"

John grunted and lowered his considerable weight into a chair. "T'weren't me that picked the duke—missy did."

"You should have stopped her, John. "

John's weathered face creased in a wry smile. "I never could stop her when she got some fool notion into her head. Trouble with her is, she was never broke to bridle. Wild as be-damned, she is."

"Will you two please stop talking about me as if I weren't here." She pulled the leather pouch from her belt and upended it on the table. Aside from a rather large amount of gold coins, only a tie pin and an emerald signet ring rolled from the bag. She smiled wearily. "Well, Spencer doesn't have it. Or, if he does, he doesn't carry it with him."

John gave the Cat a thoughtful glance. "A right knowing one, the duke—unless I miss my guess," he said slowly. "You'd best stay out of his way, missy."

The young woman got to her feet, smiling. "I fully intend to stay away from him, John. After all, what chance have I to meet a duke way out here in the country? You know Sir George rarely allows me to attend any of the local balls—and a Season in London is out of the question. It isn't very likely that I will see His Grace again." She swung her cloak about her shoulders and picked up the hood. "Put the money and jewelry in a safe place, John." As he turned to go, John spoke again.

"You'll see the duke when you take his jewelry back to him."

She turned back to stare at his expressionless face. "So I will."

"Be careful, missy. If anybody learns the truth, it'll be the duke."

"John, you must be getting old." She smiled and added, "You worry too much." With that, she slipped silently from the inn.

Annie stared after her. "John, why didn't you go with her? It's an hour's ride to the manor—she shouldn't be out there all alone."

John sat back and regarded his sister with a tolerant smile. "She'd only lose me in the woods. She doesn't like to be followed."

"But, John—"

"Oh, woman, never mind. Why do you think they call her the Cat? She always lands on her feet."

The Cat drew her weary mare to a stop and gazed at the dark windows of the large manor house. It was a beautiful old house, dating back several generations. Surrounded by formal gardens, it sprawled gracefully at the edge of a large game preserve. Many generations of Courtenays had lived and died beneath its roof, and the girl felt a surge of rage as she thought of the man who now ruled the manor with a despotic hand.

With a smothered and very unladylike curse, she urged her horse toward the stables, vowing silently to throw Sir George out the moment she turned twenty-one. Her father had left the house, along with the majority of his fortune, to his only daughter. Unfortunately, he had chosen his neighbor—Sir George Ross—to be her trustee. A scant two years after her husband's death, Mrs. Courtenay had become Lady Ross. Sir George had it all now. For another year.

Once inside the stables, the girl quietly rubbed the mare down, erasing all traces of the midnight ride. With a silence born of long practice, she made her way through the gardens to the house. Warily, she moved to the west wing, where a large tree grew beneath her bedroom window. In moments, she had climbed the tree as easily as a boy. She slipped through the open window and carefully closed it behind her. Only then did she heave an unconscious sigh of relief.

She drew off the black hood and flung it onto the bed, her movements swift and restless. She lit the lamp on the bedstand before picking it up and carrying it to the dressing table. For a long moment she stared fixedly into the gilded mirror above the table.

A beautiful, raven-haired, golden-eyed young woman stared back. The shining black hair was drawn away from her face and wound in a braided coronet about her head, exposing the delicate bones of her face. Her nose was small and straight, and the gently curved lips seemed more inclined to a smile than a frown.

But the most outstanding feature of all was the golden eyes. They were enormous, with long, curling lashes. Catlike, they had a slight upward slant. There was no serenity in their golden depths, only wild, restless emotion.

She continued to stare into the mirror, remembering with a bittersweet pang how her father had always teased her about her eyes. He had told her that one day she would meet a man who would calm her restless spirit and tame the wildness in her soul. She had flung back her head and told her father that no man would ever master her.

Her father had smiled and gently touched her cheek. "He won't master you, kitten. If he's smart, he'll just love you." His calm golden eyes had been warm with love. "And if you love him, you'll find peace of mind."

She leaned against the dressing table and stared down at her clenched fists. "I haven't found him yet, Papa," she whispered. "I don't think he exists. Oh, Papa, why did you have to die? Everything would have been so different." For a long time, she stood silent, telling herself fiercely that she wouldn't cry. She could only remember crying once, years ago, when her father had died. Never before, never since.

Suddenly, there was a soft knock at the door. She stiffened, her heart thundering in her ears.

"Jenny?" It was almost a whisper.

Jenny relaxed and went to open the door. A slender wraith in a pale pink dressing gown slipped through the doorway. A stray blond curl had escaped from her nightcap, and her blue eyes were wide with fright. "Oh, Jenny," she whispered breathlessly, "Father wanted to see you, but I knew that you were riding tonight, so I told him that you had a headache. He was furious!"

Jenny went to turn up the lamp and then turned to face her stepsister, her expression grim. "Was he drinking, Meg?"

Meg sat down weakly on the bed. "Oh, yes. He was ranting and raving. Jenny, he said that you had refused the Earl of Stoven! He was *furious!*"

Jenny's wild eyes darkened with rage. "I don't care how angry he was. I will not marry that pompous, self-opinionated *ass*. He has a red face and sweaty hands, he's fifty if he's a day, and fat as a pig besides." She began to pace restlessly around the room. "Your father only wants me to marry Stoven because he's rich. Well, he can just forget it. I won't marry him."

"But, Jenny—" Meg hesitated. "He—he won't live forever! You could have a fine house and beautiful clothes, and you could spend the Season in London."

"I can't, Meg."

"But, why? Oh, Jenny—at least you could get away from Father."

Jenny turned to Meg, her eyes blazing. But, when she saw the innocence in her stepsister's eyes, her anger melted. Gently, she said, "Honey, I *can't*. You don't understand—I can't bear to have the man touch me."

Meg's face pinkened. "Oh! You—you mean the way he holds your hand and puts his arm round your waist?"

Jenny managed to smile faintly as she sat down beside Meg. "There is a little more to it than that. A husband and wife are—intimate. They sleep in the same bed and they—hold and touch one another."

Meg went scarlet suddenly. In a small voice, she said, "You mean when they make a baby?"

"Yes. I just couldn't bear to let Stoven touch me that way. The thought of it makes me ill."

"Jenny, will I—will I feel that way about the man I marry?"

"Oh, my dear, of course not. If you love him, you'll want to be close to him."

Meg's blue eyes widened in sudden fright. "Oh, Jenny— what if he makes *me* marry Stoven?"

Jenny gave her stepsister a gentle hug. "You're only sixteen—not even your father is monster enough to marry you to a man like Stoven."

"I hope you're right."

"I'm sure I am. Meg, anytime your father tries to make you do anything against your will, just tell me. I'll stop him, or get you away from here."

Meg smiled. "I know. You've always protected me from Father's temper." Her smile died as she looked gravely at her stepsister. "But, Jenny—who will protect *you*?"

Jenny stood up abruptly. "It's late. You had better get to bed."

Meg slowly got to her feet, blue eyes concerned. "You didn't answer my question, Jenny."

Jenny smiled brilliantly. "I'll protect myself. I always have and I always will."

Meg suddenly looked older than her sixteen years. "Jenny, you can't stand alone forever. You need someone. Someone big and strong. You need someone to rely on occasionally."

"Well, if that's so," Jenny responded lightly, "then I think I met him tonight."

Eagerly, Meg asked, "Who? Jenny, who is he?"

"The Duke of Spencer. He's tall and strong—he's even handsome."

"A duke. Just think—you could be a duchess." She sighed rapturously. "It's like a fairy story."

Jenny, no stranger to her stepsister's romantic nature, smiled wryly. "Don't get your hopes up, Meg. To Spencer, I'm just a strange woman in a black mask, a woman wanted by the Runners, a woman who robbed him." Rather grimly, she went on. "I can't let Spencer—or anyone else—find out who I am. If the Runners catch me, I'll hang."

Meg went white. "No. Oh, Jenny, please don't go out anymore."

Seeing the fear in Meg's eyes, Jenny hastily spoke. "Now, why do you think they call me the Cat? I have nine lives. Don't worry about me, Meg—they'll never catch me."

A sob escaped Meg. "I never thought how—how

dangerous it is! It seemed so romantic—like a fairy tale. But, now . . . Jenny, even if they don't catch you, you could be shot. Please, *please* don't go out anymore."

Jenny shook her head. "Meg, I *can't* stop. Don't you see that it's the only way I can hope to find my father's murderer?"

"But, Jenny—"

"Hush. I'll be fine—really. Only you, John, and Annie know who the Cat really is. And that's the way it will stay." She led Meg to the door. "Now, you go to bed and get some sleep."

Meg paused in the open doorway and whispered, "Father—what if he beats you?"

"I'll just stay out of his way until he calms down. Good night, Meg."

"'Night, Jenny." She silently made her way toward her own bedroom.

Jenny closed the door and leaned against it wearily. After a moment she straightened and prepared for bed. She undressed and donned her nightgown, then sat before her dressing table. Unconsciously avoiding her mirrored image, she took down her hair and began to brush the long silken mass that hung below her waist.

She hid her masculine clothes in the locked chest she had had since childhood. After blowing out the lamp, she crawled into bed. She lay sleepless until dawn, her ears echoing with the memory of a deep, resonant voice.

# Chapter Two

Sir George Ross had never been noted as an even-tempered man. Although sympathetic voices maintained that he had suffered a severe disappointment in his youth, those who knew him well could say, with complete honesty, that Sir George was a hard-drinking, evil-tempered man who kept his wife in a state of cowered obedience and terrified his daughter. As for his stepdaughter, no one was quite sure what her feelings were toward her mother's second husband.

Miss Jenny was a lovely young woman of twenty, with cool manners and a quiet, well-bred voice. She bore no resemblance to her mother, either in looks or temperament; Lady Ross was a faded woman with a fluttery manner and nervous eyes.

It was Miss Jenny, rather than her mother, who tended the sick and injured among Sir George's tenants. It was she who interceded, on the tenants' behalf, whenever Sir George's harshness escaped the bounds of reason. It was she who kept the manor running on an even keel. Many of the numerous servants had been heard to say that they would not remain above a day in the employ of Sir George were it not for Miss Jenny.

The local gentry had mixed emotions regarding Jennifer Courtenay. The gentlemen all said that she was an uncommon beauty and a bruising rider; their ladies agreed that she was lovely, and added that she did not give herself airs or put herself forward unbecomingly; and all the young bucks of the district had been, at one time or another, hopelessly in love with her.

But no one had been able to penetrate the shell she had erected about herself since her father's suicide eight years before. She was always calm, always polite. And yet, more than one person had become very uneasy after gazing into the strange wildness of her golden eyes. She was an enigma.

Jenny had managed to avoid her stepfather for the better part of the day. She had no wish for a confrontation. She was still rather weary, and lacked both the strength and serenity to deal with one of Sir George's famous—or infamous—rages.

She was slipping quietly past Sir George's study, her arms full of linen, when she suddenly found herself jerked into the room. The linen went flying in all directions, and it cost her a severe inner struggle to keep from swearing.

She turned to see her stepfather leaning against the door, his clothes mussed and wrinkled, his eyes red-rimmed from drink and lack of sleep.

"Was there something you wanted, Sir George?" Her voice was cool and calm.

"You're damn right there's something I want," Sir George answered harshly. "I want to know why you refused Stoven."

Jenny clasped her hands before her and regarded him expressionlessly. "I have no wish to marry a man who is old enough to be my father. There are other reasons, of course, but that one will suffice."

Sir George stepped forward, swaying slightly. "You fool. He's rich."

"I have no need of a wealthy husband."

"You need what I say you need! And I say that you will marry Stoven!"

Jenny carefully gauged his mood and knew from the menace in his eyes that he would fly into a rage no matter what she said. "I will not marry Stoven. I will not, in fact, marry anyone while I remain beneath your guardianship." She smiled coldly. "You will get nothing from me, Sir George. You will not benefit from marriage settlements, or anything else."

Sir George clenched his fists, his face going red with fury. "You'll marry him!" he bellowed. "I'll not stand for any more of this willful disobedience! You'll do as I say!" He took another step forward. "When I get through with you, miss, you'll be glad to marry Stoven." Suddenly, his hand lashed out to strike her across the face.

It was a heavy blow, with the entire weight of his arm behind it, and Jenny reeled. Her eyes watered from the pain, and she reached up a shaking hand to wipe a trickle of blood from the corner of her mouth. She raised her eyes just as Sir George drew back for another blow, and something in her gaze stayed his hand.

Sir George stared into the deadly fury of her strange eyes and felt a chill run down his spine. He had never before seen such a look of hatred in her eyes.

In a voice devoid of all human emotion, she said, "I won't stand for any more of this from you. The next time you lay a hand on me, on Meg, or on my mother—I'll kill you."

Sir George's hand fell to his side and he let out a laugh

that, even to his own ears, sounded strained. "You wouldn't dare. You don't have the stomach to kill a man."

"Would you care to bet your life on that, Sir George?" She smiled coldly. "I am a much better shot than you are. And I mean what I say. I *will* kill you."

Sir George forced another laugh. "I'll get you out of my hair one way or another. If I have to, I'll have you arrested for threatening my life. What do you say about that, miss?"

"I say, Sir George, that you would be the laughing stock of England if word got out that you were afraid of a mere girl—and your stepdaughter at that. No, you won't have me arrested. Who would believe you?" Her voice was mocking. "But you and I know the truth. And we both know that I mean what I say."

She moved toward the door, scorn in her eyes. "Stay away from me—or you'll be sorry."

Sir George found himself almost nervously moving out of her path. He watched her leave the room, his brow dark with anger. One of these days, he thought, I'm going to give that young lady exactly what she deserves. On that dark thought, he flung himself into a chair and splashed whiskey into his glass.

Jenny slowly climbed the stairs, one hand against her bruised cheek. Her expressionless face concealed a rage as great as any she had ever experienced. Not even the memory of her father's death had the power to arouse such fury in her.

She halted by her mother's door and, after a moment, knocked softly and went in. Her mother was reclining in a lounge chair by the window, bundled in shawls and blankets, and holding her smelling salts in one slender hand.

Lady Ross looked up as her daughter entered. In a fretful voice, she said, "Jenny, you know how I hate to be disturbed. I need my rest."

"Mama," said Jenny, ignoring the petulant voice, "I cannot remain in this house."

Lady Ross frowned. "What nonsense is this?"

Jenny lowered her hand, revealing the bruised cheek. "If I stay, Mama," she said quietly, "you'll be widowed for the second time."

"Oh, Jenny," her mother murmured, "what have you done?"

"I? What have I done? Mama, how can you ask such a question? When did he ever need a reason to strike me?"

"You must have done something to cause your father . . ."

"That man is not my father. Mama, how can you continue to defend him? He treats you despicably."

"Jenny, he's my husband. For heaven's sake . . ."

"He's an animal. He doesn't deserve your loyalty. Mama, I mean what I say. If he touches me again, I swear I'll kill him."

Lady Ross sighed tiredly. "Stay away from him, Jenny. When this year is up, you will be your own mistress. Until then, just stay out of his way."

Jenny studied her mother thoughtfully. "You didn't seem at all surprised when I threatened to kill him. Why, Mama?"

"Because," Lady Ross replied with a twisted smile, "you are exactly like your father was—strong enough to do whatever you feel you have to do."

"You never talk about Papa."

"I do not want to think about him. He killed himself, Jenny. Do you think I want to remember that night? I do not! All the good memories of our life, our years together, were wiped away by what happened that night."

"Mama, he *didn't* kill himself. I was there—I saw him murdered."

Lady Ross shook her head wearily. "You were only a child, Jenny. You saw what you wanted to see."

"I didn't want to see him murdered."

"You didn't want to see him kill himself."

"Mama—" Jenny sighed in defeat. "Never mind. You refuse to believe me, no matter what I say." Turning to go, she continued quietly, "But one day—one day you'll believe me." She left the room as Lady Ross watched with troubled eyes.

Meg rode through the woods, giving her horse his head. She didn't really feel like riding, but it was the only way she could escape from the manor. Sir George was still drinking and Meg was afraid to be near him. She was terrified that he would try to force her to marry Stoven—no matter what Jenny said.

She thought of Jenny and sighed. Meg loved her stepsister; she couldn't bear it if anything happened to her.

Deep in her reflections, Meg failed to notice that she had left the woods and was now crossing a field near the road. She also failed to notice a hare in her path. The tiny creature, frightened by the huge horse, darted toward the woods. Meg's gelding shied violently, and she was thrown to the ground.

The next few moments were a confusing blur to Meg. Finding herself suddenly on the ground was enough of a shock, but then, to look up and see a large chestnut bearing down on her with a blond-haired gentleman on its back was too much. She fainted.

Moments later she came to, and gazed up at a strange face with concerned deep blue eyes. With a murmur of confusion, Meg sat up hurriedly. "Oh! What happened?"

The gentleman sat back on his heels and continued to look concerned. "You were thrown from your horse. Are you all right?" His voice was deep.

Meg smiled shyly, feeling oddly breathless.

"Oh, yes. I'm fine—really. But why did my horse shy?"

The gentleman smiled and nodded toward the woods. "I believe there is the culprit."

She gazed in the direction he indicated and saw a small brown rabbit looking at them inquisitively. "Well! I never thought that Prince would be so timid as to be frightened by a hare."

"Perhaps he was startled." The gentleman rose to his feet and offered her a hand.

As she allowed him to help her to rise, Meg thought what a handsome gentleman he was, and wondered why she had never seen him before.

Retaining her hand, the gentleman bowed low over it. "Robert Collins—at your service, ma'am."

She blushed and smiled. "I'm Meg—Margaret Ross."

Robert gazed down at her with a bemused smile. "Are you certain that you are all right, Miss Meg?"

"Oh, yes. I've taken tumbles before, you know." She made no move to withdraw her hand from his grasp. Starry-eyed, she smiled up at him and said, "Do you live around here? I've never seen you before."

"I am visiting a friend. I live in London."

"London. Oh, how I envy you. I would like, of all things, to live in London."

"Why? It's nothing special, you know."

"It is. All the things to do and places to go. The parties and balls—and the *theater*!"

He grinned at her, amused by her enraptured voice. "London is cold and wet in the winter, and hot and dusty in the summer. The traffic is terrible and the busybodies are worse." He sighed dramatically. "Society watches your every move; if you step out of line, you're ostracized for life."

"Oh." Meg looked sympathetic. "Did that happen to

you?" She blushed suddenly. "I'm sorry. That's none of my business."

He chuckled. "That's all right. Actually, my father was the bounder. He gambled away most of his fortune and left me without a feather to fly with."

"How terrible for you."

"Not really." He chuckled again. "I do well enough. But society has a long memory, so I receive the blame for my father's sins."

She frowned. "That doesn't seem fair."

"Society never claimed to be fair. In any case, it's rather fun to be considered a bad sort. At least the matchmaking mamas don't cluster round me like bees to a honey pot."

"Then—then you're not married?"

"No, but don't let *that* frighten you. I promise I won't bite you."

She laughed. "How absurd you are."

He smiled at her. "I made you laugh, anyway—and a very pretty laugh it was."

She blushed slightly. "Well, no matter what you say about London, I'd love to go there."

"Why don't you? It's only about forty miles or so."

Her face fell. "I—I can't. My father won't allow it." She pulled her hand from his grasp and turned toward her patiently waiting horse.

Robert stepped forward. "Wait, I'm sorry—I didn't mean to upset you."

Meg reached for her horse's reins and then smiled at the concerned young man. "You didn't upset me. But it's late and I really must go home."

"May I call on you?"

"Oh, I—my father wouldn't allow it," she said in a low voice.

Robert frowned. "But I *must* see you again."

Meg looked up at him shyly, her cheeks rosy. "I—I could meet you someplace."

He shook his head, a spark of anger in his eyes. "It wouldn't be right. I want to court you properly."

"Oh, Robert, I want the same thing. But Papa—he'd be furious. He'd send me away."

Neither of them was aware of the exact moment that their relationship had changed from mere acquaintance into something deeper; they only knew that it had changed.

Robert reached out to take her hand. "There must be some way of convincing your father to allow me to call on you."

She smiled suddenly. "I know. I'll ask Jenny—she'll help us."

"Jenny?"

"My stepsister. She's the only one who isn't afraid of Papa. I know she'll help us."

"Do you think she can persuade your father to allow me to call?"

"If anyone can, it will be Jenny." Meg laughed and said softly, "And if she can't talk him into it, she'll find *some* way of gaining his permission."

Robert smiled wryly. "She sounds like quite a lady."

Meg glowed. "She is."

"Will she be willing to help us? She may not approve of me."

"Oh, yes, she'll help us. I'll ask her and then we can meet here tomorrow, and I'll tell you what she said."

He frowned slightly. "I don't like it, but it seems the only way I'll be able to see you again. Very well then, we shall meet here tomorrow. May I escort you home?"

"Oh, I'd like you to—but no. If Papa should see you . . . The manor is just through the woods there. I'll be fine."

Robert helped her to mount her horse, and then gazed up at her with a smile. "Until tomorrow."

Breathlessly, Meg responded, "Until tomorrow." She turned her horse toward home. At the edge of the woods, she gazed back at him, lifted a hand in farewell, then quickly rode on.

Robert stared after her. His face bemused, he turned finally and began to make his way toward the road, his horse trailing along after him.

It was a full half hour before he remembered to mount his horse.

# Chapter Three

Jenny wound her way through the forest, her mind considering various ways in which she could leave her stepfather's house. Not that it *was* his house—not really. But for the next year it might as well be his house. Lady Ross wasn't about to stand up to her husband—even for her daughter's sake. She would go on turning a blind eye to Sir George's tyranny because it was easier for her to do so. She lacked her daughter's strength of will.

After considering and rejecting several plans of escape, Jenny finally abandoned her unproductive line of thought. Oh, she could leave the manor easily. She had faith in her ability to take care of herself. But Meg was another matter entirely. Jenny had no intention of leaving Meg to Sir George's tender mercies. Leaving the manor would mean a hand-to-mouth existence at best, and Meg was simply not suited to such a life.

Jenny sighed and brought her mind back to the reasons

why she was riding out on such a depressingly cold, damp day. John had sent word that there was someone waiting for her at the inn. Someone, that is, waiting for the Cat. She had a strong suspicion that it was Jason. If it was indeed Jason, Jenny hoped he had chanced across another spy.

She could not be certain, of course, that her father's killer was still in the business of selling information to enemies of England, but that still seemed her best chance of finding the murderer.

Jenny stopped her mare a hundred yards or so from the inn and dismounted. She tied the horse to a tree, then pulled on her hooded mask.

Moments later, she slipped silently inside the back door of the inn—so silently, in fact, that the man sitting at the table leaped to his feet and made an instinctive grab for his pistol when he looked up and saw her. He lowered his gun and glared at her. "For God's sake, woman—d'ye have to creep about like a cat? I could 'ave blowed your brains out afore I knew what I was about!"

He was a hard looking man of medium height and middle age, wearing patched and frayed clothing. His boots were cracked with age, and a greasy muffler was wound about his neck. For all his tattered appearance, he contrived to give an impression of dignity and, even in the short time she had known him, Jenny had learned to respect this man—this highwayman.

She stepped forward, amusement in her golden eyes. "Sorry, Jason. I had to make certain you were alone."

Jason laid his pistol on the table and continued to look irritated. "Sure, and who would I have with me? Me, that's wanted by the Runners almost as bad as you are."

Jenny chuckled and sat down across the table from him. "Never mind that, Jason. Why did you want to see me?"

He resumed his seat and stared at her. "I wish I knew why a lady like you would take to highway robbery."

"I told you why. I am searching for a spy."

"I remember what you told me. But I've got a few wits left, and I know there's more to it than that. You're too fine a lady to end with your neck in a noose. You ought to leave robbery to them that knows it best."

"Like yourself?"

"Bloody right!" He frowned at her. "This spy of yours— why is he so important?"

Jenny clasped her hands upon the table and leaned forward slightly. "Jason, correct me if I'm wrong, but isn't there an unwritten rule against one thief asking another thief awkward questions?"

Jason scowled. "I take that to mean you ain't going to answer me."

She smiled brilliantly. "I'm glad we understand one another. Now, if you wouldn't mind telling me why you wanted to see me . . . ?"

Jason grunted. "If that's how you want it."

"It is."

Obviously out of charity with her, he pulled a packet from inside his coat and tossed it across the table to her. "Took that off a gent the other night. Thought it might interest you."

Jenny slowly picked up the packet and stared at the official seal. After a brief struggle with her conscience, she broke the seal and opened the packet. There was a long silence while she flipped through the papers. "Jason, who did you take these from?"

"Don't you consider that an awkward question?" he asked with a sneer.

"Don't be difficult, Jason. Who was it?"

He shrugged. "Damned if I know. Just a flashcove with a fat purse and no taste for playing the hero."

"Meaning that he didn't shoot at you."

"Aye." Jason laughed. "He whimpered and moaned like

I was the devil 'imself. Nearly broke his neck, he was in such a hurry to hand over his purse and them papers."

"Can you describe him to me?"

"Don't be daft, lass—it was as dark as pitch."

Jenny smiled wryly. "Sorry. I forgot that you refuse to ride on a moonlit night."

"You'd do the same if you had any sense. One of these 'moonlit' nights, some cove's gonna figure out who you really are; then the cat'll be out of the bag for sure, if you'll pardon my choice of words."

Jenny laughed. "Perhaps. But, never mind that now. You were right about these papers—they interest me very much. I'm much obliged to you, Jason, for bringing them to me."

Jason shrugged again. "No skin off my nose."

Jenny tapped the packet against the table thoughtfully. "This will have to be returned to the War Office as soon as possible." Her golden eyes were grim. "I *must* discover who was carrying these papers." She gazed across the table at her highwayman friend. "Jason, was the coach traveling toward the coast?"

Jason nodded. "Aye. 'Twas on the road to Dover."

"Was there baggage strapped on?"

He looked thoughtful. "Now that you mention it the top of the coach *did* seem a mite bulky. Happen the gent was planning to cross the Channel."

Jenny slammed the packet down on the table, her eyes flashing angrily. "Damn. Sometimes I think that half of England is spying for the French."

Jason shrugged. "It's profitable."

"It's also traitorous."

"Well now, lass, not everyone can be as loyal to England as you and me." He grinned at her. "What's in the bundle of papers anyway?"

Jenny continued to look angry, but her voice was calm as she replied, "Dispatches."

"Dispatches?"

"Yes. From Wellesley. He plans to invade Southern France by crossing the Pyrenees. You can bet the French would love to know that."

Jason looked suitably impressed. "Aye, they would at that. But, who could 'ave stolen the dispatches? Seems to me they'd be kept under lock and key."

Jenny sighed. "They should have been, but things are very confused at the War Office these days."

He cocked an eyebrow. "And how would *you* know that, lass?"

She smiled easily. "You're asking awkward questions again, Jason."

Jason leaned back with a grunt. "If that ain't just like a woman. Here I am trying my poor best to help you catch this spy of yours, and you won't even answer a simple question."

Jenny relented with a rueful smile. "Well, don't get in a huff. I know what goes on in the War Office because I keep my ears open, that's all."

He looked irritated. "You could 'ave said so in the first place. You didn't 'ave to be so bloody mysterious about it."

She chuckled softly. "You should watch that temper of yours, Jason. It'll get you into trouble one of these days."

"Never mind my temper. What do you mean to do about those dispatches?"

She shrugged. "Return them to the War Office." With a thoughtful frown, she continued slowly. "But I think I'll hang on to them for a few days at least."

"Why?"

"I'd like to be able to tell them who stole the dispatches."

"Aye." Jason responded wryly, "I can see it now. You just walk up to the War Office (wearing your mask, o'course), knock on the door, and then tell whoever answers that you're the Cat and that you'd like to give them back some important dispatches that was stolen. Then you tell 'em who *stole* the dispatches, and leave." He shook his head. "Not bloody likely. They'd 'ave a noose 'round your neck afore you could open your mouth."

Jenny smiled faintly. "That wasn't *quite* how I planned to do it, Jason."

"*Any* way you plan, it is wrong. The Runners want you, lass—they want you bad."

"*Damn* the Runners," she responded irritably. "I'll do whatever I have to do. If they catch me, they just catch me."

"Now, lass—"

"Stop calling mc lass."

"Then tell me your Christian name." He glared at her. "What am I supposed to call you if I don't know your name?"

Grudgingly, she replied, "Jenny. My name's Jenny."

"*Jenny*, then. You've made fools of the Runners for more than a year, but your luck won't hold out forever. Sooner or later they *will* catch you, and then this spy of yours will be free to go on selling information to France. If you mean to catch the spy afore the Runner catch *you*, you got to be careful, la-er-Jenny."

"Jason, I have every intention of being careful. I don't *want* the Runners to catch me, I assure you. But my most important task is to discover the identity of the spy." Beneath her breath, she muttered, "I only hope he's the right one."

As low as the words were, Jason caught them. With a quizzical tilt of his head, he asked, "What do you mean 'right one'?"

Jenny shrugged. "Nothing. Forget it."

After a moment of frowning silence, Jason's air of puzzlement vanished. Slowly, he said, "You ain't looking for spies—you're looking for *one* spy. Who is he, Jenny? Why is he so important to you?"

Glaring at him, she responded, "I said to forget it. It isn't important—and it isn't any of your business."

"Jenny . . ." He hesitated, and then continued gruffly, "If I knew *why* you're looking for this spy, why he's so important to you, I mean, then maybe I could help."

For a long moment, Jenny was silent. Then, slowly, she said, "This particular spy is also a murderer. He killed someone very dear to me. I intend to see that he pays for it."

"Who did he kill, lass?"

"My father."

"I'm sorry, Jenny." He shook his head slowly. "I guess maybe you want this gent pretty bad."

"You guess correctly." Her voice was grim. "He'll hang for what he did—or I'll put a bullet in him myself."

Jason studied the young woman silently. He could not see her face—had never seen it—but he knew that she was very young—too young to devote her life to guns and masks and violence. He guessed from the tone of her voice and manner of speaking that she was gently born, and he had wondered from the first moment of meeting her why she had chosen such a violent life. Now he knew. But his curiosity about her remained strong.

He smiled inwardly as he remembered his one attempt, weeks before, to see her face. He had thought, mistakenly as it turned out, that he could wrest the mask from her by force. The attempt had gone sadly awry. He had found himself looking over the barrel of her pistol into a pair of coldly glittering tawny eyes—this before he had even begun to carry out his plan. She had an uncanny ability to seemingly read his mind.

She trusted him, but only to a certain point. He respected her for her caution; in fact, he respected the lady herself. She was quite a woman.

Jenny stirred slightly beneath his intense scrutiny. "Jason, will you please stop staring at me."

He grinned suddenly. "You're no thief. I always wondered about that. You come into the world hosed and shod—you've no need for thievin'. Now I see what it is. You want to find this gent that killed your father, so this is how you hunt for him."

She shrugged. "I didn't have much choice."

He shook his head slowly. "By choosing this way, though, you've gotten yourself in a pack of trouble. You have to watch every move you make because of the Runners. And if some gent gets lucky and finds out who you really are . . ." His voice trailed off. After a moment, he continued slowly, "You'll hang. Lady or not, you'll hang."

Jenny smiled wryly. "That's one of the qualities I like about you, Jason—you're always so cheerful."

"You know it's the truth."

"Of course." Her eyes were grim. "I'm well aware of the fact that I've broken the law, and I don't expect any special consideration because I'm a woman. But, no matter what happens, I intend to find the man who killed my father. If the Runners try to catch me before then, they'll have to kill me to do it."

Jason frowned. "Your father's dead, lass. No matter what you do, you can't bring him back."

"No, I can't," she agreed. "But, perhaps I can help him rest a little easier."

"He won't rest easier if you're dangling at the end of a rope—or bleeding to death on some deserted back road," Jason replied starkly.

Jenny winced slightly.

He looked irritated. "You've got to face facts, Jenny. You can't help your father—and you've got your whole life before you. You're too young to waste it on some wild notion of revenge."

"It's not a wild notion. Jason, the man is a traitor. He's also a murderer and I mean to stop him."

Jason sighed in defeat. "Well, since you're hell-bent to get yourself killed, I'll ask about and see if any of my friends have heard anything about a traitor. Maybe I can find out something."

She smiled at him. "Thank you, Jason—I knew I could count on you." She looked thoughtful. "Why don't you meet me here tonight?"

"I can't find out anything *that* soon," Jason objected.

Jenny nodded. "I know, but I thought that you and I could try to spot that coach you held up the other night."

"Oh, you did, did you?" Jason looked glum. "And I suppose you mean to stay out all night hunting for that damn coach?"

"Now, Jason—you *said* you wanted to help."

"I ought to be shot for what I said," he grumbled.

Jenny grinned and rose to her feet. "Eight o'clock, Jason. See you then." She lifted a hand in farewell and then slipped silently through the door and disappeared.

Jason stared after her. After a moment of frowning silence, he rose and prepared to leave. He had much to do before he met her at eight o'clock.

# Chapter Four

It was a dark, gloomy night; the rain that had been falling steadily since morning seemed determined to continue. It dripped incessantly from the trees, falling softly on the dead leaves below.

The huge black stallion standing just inside the woods pawed the ground restlessly; he was unaccustomed to standing still for such a long time. The woman on his back soothed him with a gentle hand, then turned her gaze to her companion. "You're very quiet, Jason. Something wrong?"

Jason drew his cloak tighter about his shoulders and glared at her. "What could be wrong? You drag me out on a night like this—a night not fit for man or beast—just so I can catch my death."

"Don't fuss, Jason. You have to identify that coach for me."

"What makes you so bloody sure the coach will even be out tonight? The gent's probably at home hiding under his bed after being robbed the other night."

Quietly, she responded, "Jason, I—may not have much time. I must look for the man every chance I get."

"What do you mean by that?" He frowned at her.

"There are—problems. Problems that may force me to go away for a while."

"What kind of problems?"

She sighed softly. "Family problems. Never mind that now, Jason, just hope that the 'gent' had somewhere to go tonight."

Jason continued to frown. "An' if he ain't got somewhere to go? What then?"

Jenny uttered a very unladylike word. "Jason, will you *stop* asking me questions that I cannot possibly answer? If I do not find him tonight, I shall continue my search. I have no other choice."

Deciding that a good argument might serve to warm his chilled bones, Jason deliberately set out to anger his young friend—a calculated risk, her temper being what it was. "Don't be a fool. You 'ave another choice," he said.

Icy yellow eyes regarded him expressionlessly. "I should be delighted to hear," she remarked with awful politeness, "what that other choice is."

"You can stop your thievin' an' go back to bein' a proper young lady like your papa wanted. You ain't helpin' your papa, lass—an' how would he feel if he could see what you was doin'? D'you think he'd be proud of his little girl? No! He'd be grieved to see you actin' like a common thief."

It was a long speech, especially coming from the normally taciturn Jason, and Jenny stared at him rather blankly. Instead of taking offense, as he had intended for her to do, she merely seemed concerned.

"Jason, are you all right? You do not sound like yourself."

He sighed. Addressing the heavens, he said, "Ain't that just like a woman. They never act like you expect 'em to."

"Jason, what are you talking about?"

"Nothin', lass."

She stared at him for a moment and then shrugged slightly. He was, she decided, in a very peculiar mood tonight. She spared very little thought for it, however, as her ears caught the sounds of distant hoofbeats. Both the horses shifted restlessly as their riders' tension communicated itself to them.

As the coach rumbled past, Jenny strained her eyes to see if there was a crest on the panel, then turned a questioning gaze to the highwayman. He shook his head silently.

When the coach had disappeared into the darkness, Jenny swore softly and jerked off her hooded mask. "That makes the fifth coach tonight," she exclaimed irritably. "I am beginning to agree with you, Jason—this was an idiotic idea."

At that moment the moon made a brief appearance and, before it hid again behind the clouds, Jason was treated to the sight of Jenny's unmasked face. Astonished by the beauty he had been given a fleeting glimpse of, he was moved to say sharply, "For God's sake, woman, put that mask back on!"

Jenny shrugged and carelessly responded, "It's all right, Jason. I trust you."

"More fool you," the highwayman said darkly. "There's quite a price on your head; I *could* inform against you."

"You could," she agreed. "I could also inform against you." Her smile flashed white in the darkness. "I don't want to be brutal, Jason, but ask yourself who the Runners would be more likely to believe—you or me?"

Immediately struck by the truth of this question, Jason grinned at her. "You have a point."

"Of course."

He chuckled softly. "Now that we've cleared *that* out of

the way, are we goin' to sit out here in the damp for the rest of the night?"

Jenny sighed in resignation. "I don't suppose it would do any good."

"Now you're being sensible."

The two riders turned their horses toward Maidenstone and rode back to the inn. They parted there, and Jason merely nodded when Jenny reminded him to "keep an eye out" for that coach.

Jenny stabled the black stallion and saddled her own mare for the ride back to the manor. Her vain attempt to discover the coach that Jason had held up caused her to feel deeply depressed, and the long ride back to the manor only increased her depression.

By the time she was safely back in her bedroom, Jenny desired nothing so much as a hearty bout of tears. But she did not cry. She lay silently in her bed and cheered herself with the thought that tomorrow night she would visit Spencer to return his jewels. On that pleasant thought, she fell asleep.

Jenny performed her routine household tasks the next morning, until an odd restlessness drove her to saddle her mare and go for a ride. She could not understand herself; knowing that she had a long ride ahead of her that night, she should not have been restless. Nonetheless, she had to escape from the manor—for a little while at least.

She wandered rather aimlessly through the woods near the manor, her mind on her coming meeting with Spencer.

This pleasant occupation of Jenny's mind was very lucky for Meg—otherwise Jenny would have been far more angry than she was when she came suddenly upon her stepsister locked in a passionate embrace with a blond stranger.

Jenny reined her mare to a stop and calmly gazed at the red-faced pair. Lifting an eyebrow, she remarked casually, "I am surprised at you, Meg. I really think you could have found a more discreet location for this—assignation. Who is this gentleman?"

Her calm acceptance of what was definitely a compromising situation deprived Meg of speech for a full minute. Finally, she recovered enough to say weakly, "Jenny, it—it isn't what you think!"

"Isn't it really? Then if it isn't what I think, Meg, perhaps you had better explain to me what it *is*. And, I repeat, who is this gentleman?"

Having by this time regained his composure, Robert stepped forward. "My name is Collins, ma'am—Robert Collins."

"How do you do?" she responded politely. "I am Jennifer Courtenay." With an economy of movement, she slipped from the saddle and tied her horse to a tree. Facing the worried couple, she said pleasantly, "You still haven't told me what the situation is, Meg."

When her stepsister remained silent, Jenny regarded the young gentleman with a measuring eye and remarked outrageously, "There is no need to be afraid of me, you know—I certainly cannot reproach you for your behavior toward Meg. However much you may deserve it, the feat is beyond my capability—you're too big."

Robert blinked at the remarkable young woman and said hastily (for he had the distinct feeling that the feat she spoke of was *not* beyond her capability), "I assure you, Miss Courtenay, that my intentions toward Meg are strictly honorable."

"Are they indeed? And just what *are* your intentions, Mr. Collins? Or shouldn't I ask?"

"I want to marry her."

Meg entered the conversation at this point. "I meant

to tell you, Jenny, but you've been so busy the past few days that I never got the chance. Robert and I want to be married."

This dramatic pronouncement brought not the slightest change in Jenny's calm expression. "Really? This is rather sudden, is it not, Meg?"

"We've known each other for days."

Jenny fought to control her amusement. She had no doubt that Meg was completely serious. Only a slight quiver in her voice betrayed her when she murmured, "Days! That is—er—quite some time. And yet you have not applied to Sir George for his—er—blessings?"

"Well, of course not!" Meg exclaimed with pardonable annoyance. "What a perfectly bird-witted thing to ask. Jenny, you *know* Papa."

"Meg, do I really need to remind you that you are under age? You cannot possibly be married without Sir George's approval."

"Yes, well—that's where *you* come in, Jenny."

Jenny felt a sense of foreboding. "I? What can I possibly have to do with anything?"

With an angelic smile, Meg answered, "You can win Papa over, Jenny—I know you can."

"Meg, your father and I aren't even on speaking terms at the moment. Or have you forgotten Lord Stoven?"

Meg's guilty expression proved that she had, indeed, forgotten Jenny's rejected suitor. "Oh, dear. What can we do now?"

"Well, for one thing, you can explain to me how you came to do such an improper thing as to meet Mr. Collins in the woods."

"Jenny, where else could we meet?" Meg's voice was pleading. "You couldn't expect us never to see each other just because of Papa. We want to do the right thing, really we do, but we must see each other sometime."

"I understand that, Meg." Jenny sighed. "It will do no good to talk about it now, however. You and I must return to the manor before Sir George discovers that we are missing." She turned her gaze to Robert. "Mr. Collins, with all due respect to young love, I must ask you not to meet Meg in the woods any longer. The next time you two meet, you will be duly chaperoned—by me."

Jenny was completely aware of the absurdity of the situation. The Cat, a notorious thief, was calmly advising—no, commanding—a young couple to obey the laws of respectability.

She also realized, though, that Meg was far too innocent to understand the dangers of such a situation. But Jenny understood, and she had no intention of allowing Meg to destroy her reputation. One hoyden in the family was quite enough.

"But, Jenny—"

"Say good-bye to Mr. Collins, Meg. And don't look so upset. I promise that you two will meet again."

With Jenny's eye on them, the young lovers contented themselves with a handshake and an exchange of intense looks. Robert assisted the ladies in mounting their horses and watched as they rode off toward the manor.

All the way back to the manor Jenny listened as Meg praised Robert to the heavens. Yes, he was certainly a handsome young man. Yes, he seemed to be a perfect gentleman—ignoring the obvious strike against that particular virtue. Yes, his voice was certainly pleasant. Yes, his profile almost exactly matched that on a Greek coin.

Once at the manor, Jenny was able to escape from her stepsister's raptures. Pleading a headache, she escaped to her room for a few moments of well-earned rest.

Lying on her bed, she found her thoughts turning to Spencer, and scolded herself sharply for her selfishness.

She should have been trying to think of a way to solve Meg's romantic problems.

Pushing the duke from her mind, she carefully thought about Meg and Robert. Immediately, the expression in Robert's eyes when he looked at Meg rose to her mind. Hard on the heels of that mental image came wistful thoughts of the duke.

With a silent curse, Jenny rolled over on her stomach and firmly thrust the duke from her thoughts once again. She was only thinking about him because of their coming meeting, she told herself. It was absurd to think that her recent exposure to young love had anything to do with her preoccupation.

# Chapter Five

Spencer gazed broodingly into the fire, thinking of wild eyes and a cool, mocking voice. He wondered irritably how a woman with such distinctive eyes could be unknown. From her manner of speaking, she was gently born and well-educated. Yet more than two weeks of discreet questions and careful search had failed to discover a single young woman with wild, glittering eyes.

He propped his long legs upon a footstool and released a weary sigh. Devil take the woman. She was nowhere to be found.

"Good evening, Your Grace."

He jerked his head around, staring toward the window. It was her. She sat upon the windowsill, hooded and masked as before, negligently holding a pistol in one black-gloved hand.

Involuntarily, he said, "I have been searching everywhere for you."

"I cannot imagine why—unless you wished for the return of your property." Her free hand tossed a small leather pouch to land near his chair. "Your jewels. I regret that the money could not be returned as well. Unfortunately, it was needed elsewhere."

She turned to go, but Spencer said, "Wait. I—would like to talk to you." He knew instinctively that if he made a move to rise, she would disappear into the night.

Her golden eyes studied him intently. "I see no reason for a conversation between the two of us, Your Grace," she said coolly.

He smiled. "Humor me. I wish to get to know you. You are, after all, an enigma."

"By choice, Your Grace," she responded dryly. "A well-known thief tends to have a distressingly short career."

Again he smiled, genuinely amused by this strange, bold young woman. "You have nothing to fear from me, I assure you. Even if I knew your true identity, I would disclose it to no one."

Birdlike, she tilted her head to one side. "That is a very strange statement, Your Grace. I am a notorious thief; it is your duty as a loyal subject of the king to do your utmost to aid in my apprehension."

He leaned his head back against the chair and studied her speculatively. "I am not entirely certain that you are a thief."

Small white teeth gleamed in a brilliant smile. "Have you forgotten that I robbed you?"

"No. And yet tonight you returned the jewels."

"But not the money."

"Which you said was needed elsewhere. I have talked to most of the people you robbed and they all told me that, without exception, all of their jewelry was returned to them. Hardly the behavior of a common thief."

"I never said I was common, Your Grace."

"What are you searching for?" He saw her stiffen in surprise, and continued quietly, "The only answer I could formulate is that you are searching for a particular article of jewelry."

"Astute of you," she responded abruptly. "And the money?"

"I can only assume that you have need of the money."

"Why not assume that I am simply a thief—greedy for riches?"

"There is still the matter of the jewels. If you were greedy, you would not have returned them."

Her golden eyes narrowed. After a moment, she said softly, "You *think,* Your Grace. That can be very dangerous in a man."

His eyes locked with hers. "It can be even more dangerous in a woman," he responded smoothly.

For a long moment, a silent battle of wills took place between them. Then the Cat began to smile. With a soft chuckle, she said, "You would be a formidable opponent, Your Grace."

His eyes were grave. "I have no wish to oppose you; I would like to help you."

She seemed surprised. "I believe you mean that."

"I do. If you would tell me what you search for, perhaps . . ." His voice trailed off as he realized that, although she was still smiling, she had withdrawn from him.

"Thank you. I am very grateful for the offer, but this is something I must do alone."

There was a tinge of regret in his gray eyes. "You do not trust me."

Her smile twisted wryly. "My trust in my fellow man was never strong, Your Grace; it has deteriorated sadly during the past few years."

Quietly, Spencer said, "Some tragedy pushed you into this strange career. Something in your past. I feel that."

For a moment, she was silent. Then, in a rather mocking

voice she said, "You are an incurable romantic, Your Grace; I am sure that your friends have often remarked it."

"Perhaps." He smiled faintly. "But I have always trusted in my instincts. In this case, my instincts tell me that you are not a thief, or a murderess, or even an essentially violent woman. I believe that you are simply a woman who searches for something which is very important to her."

He waited tensely, hoping desperately that she would confide in him. He had the distinct impression that she *wanted* to confide in him, but something held her back.

After a long moment, during which she stared at him gravely, she stirred slightly and said, "If I hear anything concerning the spy, I'll contrive to send word to you."

As she made a move to go, he said sharply, "Wait! Is there some way I could send a message to you, if need be?" There was a thick silence, and the duke, seeking to allay her distrust, spoke calmly. "I may hear something at the War Office concerning the spy."

Her wild golden eyes probed his serious gray ones. "Do you remember where I held you up?" she asked quietly.

"Yes."

"Just before you reach that point, there is a large hollow tree on the left side of the road. It is very distinctive; it was blasted by lightning and now leans heavily on another tree. Place a message within the tree. If you hear nothing from me within two weeks, you will know that I am unable to reply."

Spencer thought fleetingly of the various reasons *why* she would be unable to reply—a gunshot wound, a hangman's noose. He forced a smile. "Thank you."

She threw one leg across the windowsill and then paused, an alarming coldness creeping into her eyes. "Do not betray me!" she said intensely. "If a trap is set . . ."

"There will be no trap," he responded quietly. "I give you my word."

The coldness slowly faded from her eyes, to be replaced by a faintly wondering expression. "Strangely enough, I believe you. But make no mistake—I am not bound by a code of honor. If I am betrayed, the price will be great. I will do whatever I must do to survive."

Spencer inclined his head gravely. "I understand."

"I hope so, Your Grace. I do indeed hope so." A moment later she was gone.

Spencer was left to stare after her, feeling both disappointment and elation—disappointment because she had not confided in him, elation because she had given him a means to contact her. And he had every intention of contacting her. He had a very definite desire to learn all that he could about this young woman called the Cat.

Jenny drew her cloak more closely about her shoulders, and gave the stallion his head. After a year of skulking through the back streets of London, the horse knew the quickest and safest route home as well as his mistress did. He picked his way through the quiet streets, leaving Jenny free to turn her thoughts to her visit with the duke.

She was somewhat angry with herself for giving the duke a means to contact her. She could not remember ever having made such an incautious move before, and her reasons for having done so now worried her. It had been a purely instinctive, feminine reaction to a handsome and charming man. It had not been the reaction of a thief who feared the hangman's noose.

She could not remember ever having been drawn to anyone the way she was drawn to this stranger. She had had an absurd impulse to confide in him—to tell him why she had become a thief. When she had overcome that impulse and refused his help, when he had looked at her with regret in his eyes—regret and perhaps something more—she had been conscious of an absurd desire to cry. She felt strangely afraid to ask herself why she had reacted that way.

It wasn't as if Jenny had never spent time with a man; she had been the object of masculine attention since she had first put up her hair and let down her skirts. The young men of neighboring estates had flocked around her for more than four years. But that was different somehow.

The young gentlemen had been pleasant company. They had been very anxious to please her, taking her riding, dancing with her, writing poems in praise of her beauty— the list was endless.

She had never had the desire to confide in any of those pleasant young men, had never been tempted to express the pain that she felt whenever she thought of her father, or the resentment—even hatred—that she felt toward Sir George.

She had never felt breathless when they looked at her or oddly confused when they smiled at her. And her heart had never tried to leap out of her breast when one of those nice young men exclaimed that he had been searching everywhere for her.

A man's voice had never tingled along her nerve endings like pleasant music, stirring impossible dreams in her mind. A man's eyes had never seemed to light up the entire room, had never made her see herself through his eyes.

A man's face had never haunted her dreams or stubbornly intruded on her thoughts. A man's broad shoulders had never inspired her to relinquish burdens that she had carried for years, burdens too heavy for her own narrow shoulders.

But, most of all, a man's simple presence had never stirred in her such a vivid awareness of her own womanhood. A man's gray-eyed gaze had never set her on fire with a burning desire for something she had never experienced, something she could not even put a name to.

Until she had met the Duke of Spencer. This man—this

stranger—had managed to do all of these things. His smile caused thoughts to fly from her head like chaff in the wind. His calm gray eyes made her feel, for the first time in her life, like a woman. His face haunted her dreams, her thoughts. His voice echoed in her mind. She wanted to confide in him, to lay her burdens on his strong shoulders, and to give her heart into his keeping.

They were usual thoughts of a young woman on the verge of falling in love. For Jenny, they were dangerous ones as well.

Jenny frowned, considering the matter. She tried to understand what it was about the man that had caused her to react as she had. He was certainly a handsome man, with his dark hair and gray eyes. He had the look of nobility—with high cheekbones, an aquiline nose, and a firm mouth.

He was tall and broad-shouldered; his voice was low and pleasant. In short, he was everything she had always dreamed of in a man.

Sternly, she reminded herself that dreams were dreams—vague, insubstantial things—and that reality, though not always as pleasant, was a great deal more important. She could not afford the luxury of being attracted to a man at the present time—not any man.

Having come to this conclusion, she resolved to put the Duke of Spencer out of her mind. It was a very firm and carefully thought out resolution. Unfortunately, it did not take into account Jenny's undoubtedly feminine nature. Even though she could outride, outshoot, and outswear most men, she was still very much a woman.

Halfway back to the manor, Jenny realized that she was still thinking of the duke. She swore under her breath and urged the stallion to a gallop. She had to find some way of putting Spencer out of her mind, once and for all. Perhaps the brisk gallop would do it. Then again, perhaps it would not.

# Chapter Six

Jenny paced restlessly in front of the young couple. She still had quite a few reservations regarding their intended marriage, and she wanted to be very sure before she tried to help them—which was why she was up and about so early in the morning, and why she was wearing a path on the rug of a private parlor in a small posting house near the manor.

She halted suddenly and faced Meg and Robert. "I think you're both fools. Even if you had Sir George's approval, you're both too young to set up housekeeping."

Quietly Robert Collins said, "I'm twenty-six, Miss Courtenay—old enough to know my mind."

"For heaven's sake, call me Jenny." She smiled suddenly. "Since you seem bent on becoming my brother-in-law."

He smiled in return. "Only if you will call me Robert."

"Very well—Robert—you are twenty-six and Meg is sixteen—"

"Nearly seventeen." It was Meg, her voice firm.

Jenny nodded. "Seventeen, then. The fact remains, Meg, that you are barely out of the schoolroom. And to marry a man you have just met . . ?"

"Jenny, I *love* him. I don't have to know him for years to be sure of that."

Jenny sighed. "I know that, honey. I only want to be sure you aren't getting married only to escape from your father—if you will forgive my plain speaking, Robert."

He nodded, his blue eyes serious. "Of course. Jenny, I know that Meg is very young, but I love her. I'll take care of her." He sighed. "I wanted to talk to Sir George, but Meg assures me that he would have me thrown from the house."

Jenny smiled wryly. "She's right. Sir George intends Meg to marry a fortune—especially now that he's found he can't bend me to his will." She looked at him thoughtfully. "You weren't thinking of Gretna Green, I hope?"

Robert stiffened. "I would never consider taking Meg there."

"Well, don't poker-up about it," Jenny said mildly. But she was pleased by his response. It showed him to be a sensible man, not given to romantic flights of fancy. Coming to a decision, Jenny said, "I'll help you. I don't know how as yet, but I'll help you."

Meg flew to embrace her. "Oh, Jenny—thank you! I knew we could depend on you."

Jenny hugged her stepsister. "Don't become overexcited, Meg. I may be unable to help at all. But, I promise to do what I can."

Robert stepped forward with a smile. "That's all we can ask. Thank you, Jenny."

Jenny gave them both a warning look. "You may have to be patient. Meg cannot be married without Sir George's permission—and obtaining *that* will take some doing. Also, I have other matters that must be attended to." She watched as the young couple exchanged intense looks. "I'll leave you alone to say good-bye. Meg, if you aren't outside in ten minutes, I'll come in after you." With that, she quietly left the room.

As the two young ladies rode toward home, Meg kept up a constant flow of chatter about Robert. Jenny listened for the first five minutes and then began to lose patience with her stepsister's raptures.

Ruthlessly, she cut her off in midsentence. "Meg, why don't you ride on home? I have something I must do."

Meg smiled absently, caught up in her dreams. "All right, Jenny."

Jenny watched her ride away, then turned her horse toward the woods. She had a restless urge to check the hollow tree where she had told Spencer to leave messages. It had only been a few days since she had seen him, of course, but she had a feeling he may have learned of the missing dispatches by now. She had to get them back to the War Office some way, and giving them to Spencer seemed the best solution. He, at least, was no traitor.

Jenny wasn't sure why she was so positive about Spencer's loyalty to England. She simply was. However, her trust in his loyalty had little to do with her trust in him as a man.

Nearly an hour later, Jenny was reading a message from Spencer. It was a short note, stating simply that he needed to see her. She frowned slightly as she considered the note.

Spencer had probably learned of the missing dispatches. Or perhaps he merely wanted to see her again. Jenny was not being vain when she considered that possibility; the duke had seemed very curious about her when she had returned his jewels to him. It was possible that he would send for her in order to learn as much as he could about her.

Jenny thought of the dispatches, and carefully weighed the risks of taking them to Spencer. The risk of taking them herself was great; Jason had been right in saying that would be a sure way of getting herself hanged.

Yet, she had no choice. She slowly tore the message into tiny bits. She would take the dispatches to Spencer.

It was nearly midnight. Spencer sat at the desk in his study, looking over the deeds to some property he had just purchased. He had no expectation of receiving a visit from the Cat; he had left a message for her only that morning.

He heard no sound; there was no warning of her coming. One moment he was alone in the study, the next he felt a presence in the room. He slowly turned his head to see her standing silently inside the open window.

"Good evening, Your Grace."

He rose slowly to his feet, smiling. "Good evening. I didn't expect you to come quite so soon—I left the message only this morning."

She smiled easily. "You wanted to see me, I believe?"

"Yes." He moved carefully around to sit on the corner of his desk. "There are some important dispatches missing from the War Office. I thought you should know about it."

Jenny pulled a bundle from beneath her cloak and tossed it to him. Silently, she awaited his reaction.

He perused the documents for a few moments, then looked up at her. "That was quick work." There was a speculative gleam in his eyes.

She smiled wryly. "I suppose you may be forgiven for what you are thinking, Your Grace, though I find it hard to do so. No, I did not take the dispatches. A friend of mine—a highwayman—took them from a coach bound for the Channel. He gave them to me. I have no idea who removed them from the War Office. You may believe that if you choose."

He inclined his head gravely. "If you say that you did not take them, then of course I believe you."

"Why 'of course'?"

He placed the dispatches on the desk and studied her thoughtfully. "I trust you," he replied calmly.

She shook her head with a faint smile. "To trust a thief? You're a strange man, Your Grace."

"We have been over that before. I do not believe you are a thief."

"Then you are a poor judge of character," she responded coolly.

"I think not."

She stirred impatiently. "Shall we agree to differ on that point? I am only concerned that the dispatches are returned to the proper authorities. I assume that you will see to that?"

He rose, smiling. "Of course. But that wasn't the only reason I wanted to see you."

"Wasn't it?"

"No. I'd like to become better acquainted with you. I've been thinking of you—almost constantly—ever since we first met. There are several things about you which puzzle me."

As he spoke, he moved closer to her and Jenny, caught up in what he was saying, was unaware until too late what his intentions were. Instinctively, she reached for the pistol in her belt, only to find her wrists caught in his strong hands. With a calm smile, he gazed down at her enraged eyes. "I am most curious to discover whether or not there is a woman beneath that mask."

Jenny smiled thinly. "Brute force, Your Grace?"

"You must forgive my tactics, but they seemed the best—under the circumstances."

Jenny stared up at him, startled to discover how tall he was; the top of her head barely reached his shoulder. After a moment, she said quietly, "If you mean to remove my mask, I can do nothing to stop you. But if you do, I will hate you for the rest of my life."

The total lack of expression in her voice convinced him far more than any emotional outburst would have done. With a sigh, he murmured, "Yes, I suppose you would hate me—and that is the last thing I want. I won't try to remove your mask."

"Thank you." She smiled slightly. "And could you also release my hands?"

"So that you can shoot me?" His smile was wry.

"You said that you trusted me," she reminded him.

"So I did—until I gave you reason to shoot me."

"Very well. I give you my word that I will not shoot you." But the duke was no longer attending. He was staring at her, and something in his eyes gave his thoughts away.

Jenny felt the first stirring of panic. "Your Grace, you wouldn't—" She began to struggle, fighting desperately to free herself from him.

Spencer controlled her struggles easily. He looked down at her, a flame burning deep in his eyes. "There is more than one way to discover if there is a real, warm-blooded woman beneath that mask.

"Let me go, damn you!"

He pulled her against him suddenly, pinning her arms between their bodies. "I'm afraid that I can't do that. I must know, you see . . ."

Jenny stared up at him as his head slowly lowered to hers. Her fear left her the moment his lips touched hers. Suddenly, there wasn't anything to be afraid of.

Jenny had never been kissed before, but she was a woman and her response was instinctive. Her arms slipped around his neck, and she returned his kiss with an ardor she didn't know she possessed. For her, the world vanished. No thoughts of danger entered her head; she didn't worry about her identity being discovered. All that mattered were his arms around her and his lips moving possessively over her own.

Spencer had wondered if there was a real woman beneath the mask; he had asked himself if any woman could do the things that this one did. He had his answer now. No matter what had driven her to her strange career, she was quite definitely a woman.

He fought to keep a tight rein on his passion; he had no desire to frighten her away before he could learn her identity.

With obvious reluctance, he slowly drew away from her and gazed down at her upturned face. Her face was bemused, her eyes dazed with passion. His voice husky, Spencer murmured, "So—you are a woman, after all."

Jenny stared up at him, the dazed look slowly fading from her eyes. Her arms slid from around his neck and she stepped back, shaking her head in an unbelieving manner. "You—you don't play fair, Your Grace. I didn't realize how ruthless you could be." Her voice was low and haunted.

"I didn't mean to—"

"Oh, yes, you did. How did it feel, Your Grace, kissing the Cat?" There was as much hurt as anger in her voice— though she was unaware of it.

"It wasn't like that." He stepped toward her, his eyes grave.

"Wasn't it? Forgive me if I find that hard to believe. I hope you're satisfied, Your Grace. When they lead me to the gallows, you can tell all of your friends that you kissed the Cat." Her laughter rang out harshly in the still room.

"No." His voice was low and taut, his face strained. "I kissed you because I couldn't help myself—because I am attracted to you. It had nothing to do with your being the Cat."

"Didn't it?" She moved quickly to the window, and then

gazed back at him, cold mockery in her eyes. "A woman in a mask quite piques the curiosity, Your Grace. It was nothing more than that." She slipped out the window and disappeared into the night.

Spencer stood and stared after her. "You're wrong," he murmured. "It was much more than that."

# Chapter Seven

Jenny wearily pulled herself out of bed early the next morning. She had slept very little during the few hours she had been in bed, her mind filled with her visit to the duke's house. Over and over, she had considered his actions, finally coming to the conclusion that he never would have kissed her had she not been the Cat.

It was useless to remind herself that she never would have met him either if she had not been the Cat. She was interested only in his reason for kissing her. He had kissed her because she was the Cat; because his curiosity had been piqued by a strange woman in a black mask. It was a lowering reflection.

Jenny sighed and, fighting off her depression, began to dress for the day. She was braiding her hair when she heard a sudden commotion outside her bedroom door. Leaving the waist-length braid hanging over one shoulder, Jenny quickly went to find the source of the commotion.

Meg, with tears streaming down her cheeks, fell into

Jenny's arms the moment the door was opened. "Oh, Jenny, Mama says I can never see Robert again!"

Lady Ross, one step behind her, said sternly, "Jenny, Meg tells me that you were aware of this disgraceful situation. It was very improper of you not to have come to me. I am surprised at you. That any daughter of mine could condone anything so improper."

Jenny felt a headache coming on. Making no attempt to halt Meg's sobs, she said to her mother, "Mama, they love each other. It would be heartless to forbid them to see each other. I know I should have told you, but I was hoping to find some way of gaining Sir George's permission for them to marry."

"Marry! Jenny, Meg is little more than a child. And I have no very high opinion of a man who would meet a girl of Meg's age in so clandestine a fashion. This Robert is obviously a cad with no proper feelings at all. I will not allow it."

"On the contrary, Mama, Robert is every inch the gentleman. He is strongly averse to seeing Meg in such a manner, but what more can he do? Sir George would have him thrown from the house."

"Because he is penniless. I will not allow Meg to throw herself away by marrying a man who has not even the means to support her."

Deciding that the time for tact was long past, Jenny said brutally, "Then you will be condemning her to a loveless marriage. Would you like to see her sold to the highest bidder? You know very well that Sir George intends to do so. Just as he tried to force me to marry that horrible Lord Stoven."

Lady Ross said firmly, "Meg is too young to marry anyone at present. She is barely out of the schoolroom. And she will not be forced to marry anyone against her will. I will not allow it."

Continuing to employ brutal tactics, Jenny said, "Mama, you have never stood up to Sir George. He intends to line his pockets with marriage settlements, and now that I have refused to comply, he will be twice as determined to marry Meg to a fortune. How do you mean to stop him?"

Lady Ross felt a sharp pain somewhere inside her as she saw the scorn in her daughter's eyes. She realized then the damage she had done by bowing meekly to Sir George's autocratic demands. She had destroyed any respect that her daughter may have felt for her.

Meg lifted tearstained eyes from Jenny's shoulder and stared pleadingly at her stepmother. "Mama, I love Robert. I want to spend the rest of my life with him. I don't care that he hasn't got any money."

A plan began to weave itself through Lady Ross's mind, and she said rather sharply, "Don't be foolish, Meg. Without the comforts that money can provide, this love of yours would be destroyed within a year."

Quietly, Jenny said, "Money isn't everything, Mama. And I can give Meg a sizable dowry; that will help them quite a lot."

Slowly, Lady Ross said, "You won't come into your fortune for another year, Jenny."

"Yes." Jenny gave her mother a meaningful look, and then smiled at her stepsister. Gently, she said, "You will wait a year, won't you, Meg?"

Her eyes wide, Meg whispered, "But it's such a long time."

"I know, honey. But the wait will accomplish several things. It will give you the chance to grow up a little; it will give Robert a chance to make sure that he can provide for you; and it will prove to Mama that you are serious about Robert."

"But—a whole year." Meg's tears started up afresh. "I don't know if I can bear it!"

Jenny patted her back comfortingly and stared rather wryly at her mother. "It *is* a little much to expect her to kick her heels for a year. She needs something to occupy her mind."

"Yes," Lady Ross murmured softly. The plan in her mind had now flowered to completion. "Come with me." She turned abruptly and led the way toward the stairs.

The two girls followed as Lady Ross led the way, completely puzzled. It soon became apparent that her destination was Sir George's study.

Meg immediately panicked. Her eyes wide with terror, she gasped, "Mama, no! Oh, please don't tell Papa about Robert!"

Inexorably, Lady Ross said, "Come along."

Jenny, sensing that her mother had some set purpose in mind, hushed Meg and, with an arm around her for support, led her into the study.

Sir George looked up as the ladies entered, his brow dark with irritation. "What's all this? You know I hate to be disturbed. A pretty thing it is when a man can't even find peace in his own home."

Perfectly calm, Lady Ross informed him that she had caught Meg returning from a clandestine meeting with a young man unknown to any of the family except for Jenny. Since he was Meg's father, it was imperative that he be put in possession of the facts.

Sir George ranted. He raved. He said a great many things that were largely unintelligible to his listeners—and a good thing, too. They would have curled their hair.

Jenny, wincing from some of the descriptive epithets of her character (for Sir George was still enraged about Lord Stoven), wondered if the servants were being well entertained. His voice was no doubt audible in the village.

Ten minutes later, he was still going strong. He worked off his rage toward Jenny in fine style, tearing her character to shreds and depressing any pretentions she may have had toward being a human being of any consequence at all.

Jenny bore the abuse stoically, her face expressionless and her eyes veiled. Automatically, she patted Meg from time to time as the younger girl, convinced that she was next, sobbed pathetically into her shoulder. In a detached manner, she wondered if his rage would bring on a fit.

Having dispensed with Jenny to his satisfaction, Sir George finally began slashing verbally at Meg. He used words and phrases that would have shocked even the most depraved of women, and a spark of anger showed in Jenny's eyes.

Interrupting him in mid-insult, Jenny said coldly, "That is quite enough. Meg is completely innocent; it was your cruelty that drove her to meet Robert on the sly. You have no cause to say such horrible things about your own daughter."

"You hold your tongue, miss! I'll say what I like about her, and I say that she has the morals of a cat. I'll have no bastards in this house."

Jenny gasped in outrage, while Meg sobbed even harder. "How dare you." She immediately fired up in defense of her stepsister. "Meg is completely innocent of men. She would never do anything to disgrace her good name."

Sir George contented himself with uttering a derisive, "Ha!"

Furiously, Jenny said, "Meg must have gotten her virtues from her mother; they certainly did not come from you. You're an insensitive brute."

"I am the head of this house, and I'll not stand for this disrespect."

"You have to *earn* respect."

"That's enough!" Sir George's roar rattled the windowpanes. "Upstairs, the both of you. You're to be locked in your rooms until I say differently. You will learn to respect me." He glared at them. "And you will marry whomever I say."

"No." It was Lady Ross, her quiet voice cutting through every other sound.

Meg abruptly stopped crying and lifted astonished eyes to her stepmother. Jenny's eyes were no less astonished.

The room was filled with a quivering silence. All eyes turned to Lady Ross. She stood, frail shoulders squared and face determined, in a confrontation with her husband that she had avoided for six years.

Sir George appeared totally stunned by the unlooked-for interruption. "What did you say?" he sputtered.

She turned cool eyes to her husband. "I said that neither Meg nor Jenny will be locked in her room. And they will not be forced to marry against their will. It is one thing to forbid what is obviously an unsuitable match, quite another to force a girl to marry a man she abhors."

"I'm the head of this family!" Sir George bellowed. "I make the decisions."

Lady Ross glanced at the quiet figures of Meg and Jenny. "Jenny, you and Meg wait for me upstairs."

"Yes, Mama." Jenny immediately began shepherding her stepsister toward the door, feeling a new respect for her mother.

As soon as the door closed behind them, Sir George began his tirade. "What the hell is going on here? What do you mean by encouraging those girls to disobey me? I run this house and I'll thank you to remember it."

"I will thank *you* to remember," Lady Ross replied calmly, "that while you may or may not be the head of this family—depending, I suppose, on your point of view—I control the purse strings. The girls will go to London."

Sir George went beet-red with fury. "I am your husband! You will obey me!" he thundered.

"No," she said very quietly. "I will not obey you—not this time. My obedience to you in the past has all but lost me my daughter's respect." She gave her head a tiny shake, as if to throw off unwelcome thoughts. "In any event, Jenny and Meg are young women now and cannot be treated as children. They will go to my old friend, Lady Beddington, who is Jenny's godmother, and will make their come out this year."

"I forbid it."

"I am afraid you have no choice in the matter, George. You have several rather large outstanding gambling debts. Unless you agree to send the girls to London, those debts will not be paid. And since you sold your own estate and spent the proceeds long ago, you will find yourself at something of a stand."

For the first time in their marriage, Sir George felt oddly unsure of himself. There was an expression in his wife's eyes that he had never seen before—strongly resembling the glint of determination that he had seen in Jenny's eyes on more than one occasion. He had no doubt that she meant exactly what she said. And she was right—he had no choice.

Lady Ross entered Jenny's bedroom to find the girls waiting tensely. "Meg, Jenny, start packing—but only enough for two or three weeks. You will both need completely new wardrobes for your come out."

"Mama—" Meg burst into tears. "Please don't make me go. If you would only meet Robert . . ."

Lady Ross touched her cheek gently. "Meg, I'll make you a promise. Go to London with Jenny, go to all the parties and balls, laugh and dance and flirt with the young men. And when you come home in the summer, if you are still of the same mind, I will meet this Robert and we will see what can be worked out."

"But, Mama—"

"Meg. You will experience the pleasure of your come out only once in your lifetime. Enjoy it while you can—before you become tied to a home and family."

Jenny, who had been thinking hard, stepped forward then. "Let me talk to her, Mama." She smiled warmly at her mother.

Lady Ross smiled in return and quietly left the room. Jenny found a handkerchief and firmly dried Meg's tears. "Meg, listen to me. Where does Robert live?"

Meg's sobs died away and she stared at Jenny through suddenly hope-filled eyes. "In London!"

"Exactly. And the two of you will be able to see each other in a perfectly respectable fashion."

Meg threw her arms around her stepsister. "Oh, Jenny, isn't it wonderful? We'll dance together and go riding and—" She broke off with a gasp. "Good heavens—I must go and pack!" She raced from the room.

Jenny sighed rather wearily and turned to her own packing. She felt no compunction in raising Meg's hopes; if it was humanly possible, she meant to see the young couple wed within a year.

She straightened from her work and frowned slightly. She would send Robert a note and ask him not to make any attempt to see Meg for a few weeks at least. It would do no harm for Meg to meet other young gentlemen.

Thoughts of her own fate rose to haunt her. It was the height of folly for her even to consider living in London. One wrong word or gesture, and she would be completely undone. She would hang as an example to anyone foolish enough to commit the offense of highway robbery.

And what of Spencer? He knew her better than any of her victims. What if he recognized her? Could she trust him not to betray her?

For the first time in her life, Jenny declared a pox on all unanswerable questions.

# Chapter Eight

The following days were filled with preparations for the journey to London. A letter was sent off immediately to Lady Beddington, and her reply quietly gratified Lady Ross. Yes, indeed, she would be delighted to have Meg and Jenny stay with her for the Season.

Maids spent a great deal of time packing and unpacking trunks; Meg was constantly misplacing something or other, and would instantly search every trunk for the lost article—meaning that the disordered trunks had to be packed all over again.

Jenny managed, without Meg's knowledge, to have a quiet meeting with Robert. He was understandably reluctant to agree with her request that he not try to see Meg for a while, but finally gave in. He would remain in Kent for a few weeks.

That worry out of the way, Jenny also managed to send word to John and Jason that she would be out of touch for a while. She fully intended to continue in her search for her father's murderer, but she wanted time to settle in town first. It would give her a chance to sample public opinion. She was completely aware that, for the most part, there was a great deal of quiet championship for the Cat. The polite world was all agog to know who the mystery woman was—and why she had taken to robbery.

But public opinion could turn against her in an instant, and she wanted to be aware when and if that happened. Not that the tide of public opinion influenced her overmuch; she would simply have to be more cautious.

Jenny stared out the coach window at the passing scenery and felt a flicker of excitement as she thought of finally reaching London. She had ridden through London, of course, but only to return jewelry to its rightful owners. On those occasions, she had always been solely concerned with avoiding the watch. There had certainly been no opportunity for sightseeing.

Now, she was going to spend the next few months living in London. Unless, of course, someone realized that she was the Cat. In that event, she would not have to worry about anything—except what she wanted written on her headstone.

Jenny shook away that depressing thought, and began to dispassionately consider the reason behind her sudden urge to see London. It had never seemed so important before. She was not in the habit of deceiving herself, and she was fully, though reluctantly, aware that the foremost reason for her interest was the Duke of Spencer.

He was intruding on her thoughts far too often for her peace of mind, and Jenny was at a loss to know how to deal with such a situation. It was beyond her experience. Her traitorous mind conjured up a mental image of the duke at little or no provocation, causing her to lapse into sudden silences. Even her mother had noticed, and had worriedly inquired if she was feeling all right. Jenny had brushed away her mother's concern.

It was not quite so easy to brush away her own concern. Jenny had discovered that she had a very stubborn mind. It did no good at all to tell herself firmly that the duke would have nothing to do with a thief. The heart was not a logical organ. And neither, apparently, was a dream-fogged mind.

Jenny's worries were temporarily laid to rest upon the coach's arrival in London. Meg exclaimed excitedly over the traffic and the fine-looking gentlemen, and if Jenny searched the crowd rather intently for a tall, handsome gentleman, Meg was blessedly unaware of it.

The coach drew up before a fine-looking residence on Berkeley Square, and the double doors were immediately opened by a dignified butler with a forbidding aspect.

The butler (who informed them regally that his name was Somers) led them to the drawing room and announced their names. Before he could complete the introduction, both girls were engulfed in affectionate hugs from a middle-aged matron with a rather stout figure and mischievous blue eyes. She drew back far enough to smile happily at the girls, and then nodded a dismissal at the patiently waiting butler. "Oh, go away, do, Somers. I know very well who they are." Without waiting to see if the butler obeyed, she immediately launched on a nonstop dialogue to her guests about the parties and balls they would be attending, the handsome young gentlemen they would be meeting, the sad state of the king's health, the war with Bonaparte, and a terribly insipid ball she had attended the night before. She jumped from one topic to another in a bewildering manner that was calculated to totally confuse even the most astute of listeners.

Jenny and Meg listened rather blankly, and followed meekly when Lady Beddington led them upstairs, saying that they would no doubt wish to rest after their long journey.

"Just as if," Meg later confided to Jenny, "we had come from India instead of Kent."

The two girls were sitting on the bed in Jenny's room while their maids unpacked the trunks. Their chattering hostess had left them to rest, but since they were both country girls accustomed to plenty of exercise, they preferred to talk.

Meg laughed softly, saying, "I like Lady Beddington. She seems so cheerful."

Jenny laughed in response. "At least we won't have to worry about holding up our end of the conversation—not while she's present, at any rate."

"Jenny," said Meg, changing the subject abruptly, "promise me that you won't tell Lady Beddington that Mama has forbidden me to see Robert."

Jenny smiled at her stepsister. "I won't tell her, Meg. But you must remember what Mama said. Try to enjoy yourself here. It isn't such a long time until summer, you know."

"All right, Jenny," Meg replied doubtfully, "but it won't be easy to enjoy myself until I can see Robert again. It won't be easy at all."

However much Meg may have doubted her ability to enjoy herself in London, Lady Beddington saw to it that she had little time to do anything *but* enjoy herself. After innumerable shopping trips, dress fittings, and dancing lessons, the girls were ready to make their curtsies to polite society. They had been in London slightly above a week.

At their first party, the girls were immediately swamped with young men desirous of becoming better acquainted, and matrons had only good things to say about their manners and general deportment.

Overnight, Jenny became known as the Dark Incomparable, and Meg became so accustomed to hearing herself
described as an angel that she decided London was a very
nice place after all.

And when it became known that Jenny was an heiress,
her circle of admirers widened even more. She was slightly
amused by the fortune hunters, and did nothing at all to
discourage them. She preferred to treat all her admirers im-
partially, secure in the belief that she was well able to take
care of herself.

Within a very few days, however, Jenny found that she
was growing slightly jaded with all the attention she had
been receiving. She was cynically aware of the fact that at
least part of her suitors were interested in her fortune rather
than herself, and their flowery compliments soon began to
pall.

She was also aware of a restless urge to continue her
search for her father's killer. Jenny had spent many uneasy
nights wondering fatalistically when someone would recognize her as the Cat. She had finally persuaded herself to believe that the best place to hide a tree was in the forest; who
would look for the Cat in the midst of London society?

Thoughts of the Cat, however, were far from her mind
on the night that she first visited Almacks. She was slightly
disappointed at the bareness of the rooms, and the refresh-
ments were rather meager, but fashionable society had
turned out in full force, and Jenny was cheered to see the
ladies and gentlemen decked out in silks, satins, and jewels
of every kind.

She had little opportunity to study the crowd, however,
as she was swept off first by one young man, and then another.

Lord Rivenhall was the first; his bloodshot eyes gleamed
down at her with a mixture of avarice and desire. To Jenny's
discerning eye, the young lord revealed all the traits of the

experienced gambler and one, moreover, whose pockets were seriously to let. He was obviously after her fortune. With that fact painfully apparent, she was still able to laugh and flirt lightly with him; she was in no danger of losing her heart.

After Rivenhall, Jenny stopped trying to remember the name of every gentleman who swept her across the floor. She could see that Meg, dancing on the other side of the room, was enjoying herself; that was all that mattered.

Two hours later, Jenny whirled in the arms of yet another town buck and felt certain that her face would crack if she smiled at one more inane remark. It wasn't that she was not enjoying herself—quite the contrary, in fact. Observing the antics of polite society was causing her to enjoy herself immensely.

The simpering ladies and gallant gentlemen appeared to be the very souls of propriety, but Jenny had noticed several incidents that did not quite fit the general air of respectability.

Lady Darlington, for instance, slipping discreetly from the rooms, to be followed a few moments later by Lord Templeton. Lord Darlington did not appear to notice. Neither did Lady Templeton.

Then there was the infamous Viscount Salcombe, who had to be escorted (discreetly, of course) from the rooms after having pugnaciously challenged at least three other gentlemen to duels. (They refused. No one in his right mind would accept a challenge from Salcombe, who was accounted the best shot in England and hot-tempered into the bargain.)

No—society in itself was quite fascinating. If only the young gentlemen of London had something to speak of aside from empty compliments and useless platitudes. Jenny smiled up at her partner in response to another compliment (something about how her eyes were like yellow diamonds), and decided that she would like nothing better than to hold a quiet conversation with a sensible man.

The dance finally ended, and Jenny managed to stifle what would have been an audible sigh of relief. As soon as her partner led her off the floor, she was immediately surrounded by a group of eager and amorous young men.

Jenny pasted a smile on her face and listened rather wearily as the young men bantered back and forth between themselves about who was to have the next dance with her. As she attempted to stifle another sigh, her eyes met those of a gentleman standing some feet away.

The gentleman's cool gray eyes were amused, and Jenny realized that he had read her thoughts with uncanny accuracy. Her rather strained smile became completely natural, and her golden eyes gleamed with amusement. Immediately, the gentleman began to make his way toward her.

The group around Jenny fell strangely silent when the gentleman approached, and she wondered why. He was neatly dressed, and there was an air of dignity about him, but he did not look very important. He looked like a gentleman— nothing more. Or so she thought.

The gentleman stopped before her. In a quiet, cultured voice, he said, "Miss Courtenay, if you will allow me to present myself?"

Intrigued, Jenny nodded.

"George Brummell, ma'am, at your service."

Jenny extended her hand, lifting an eyebrow as she did so. "Beau Brummell?" There was a thread of amusement in her voice.

He bowed low over her hand, a responsive twinkle in his intelligent eyes. "Beau Brummell."

Gravely, Jenny said, "Mr. Brummell, I cannot tell you how delighted I am to meet you."

"Indeed? Why 'delighted,' Miss Courtenay?"

"Because," she replied solemnly, "any man who has the

power to hold all of London society beneath his very
thumb commands my greatest admiration."

The Beau began to chuckle. "Miss Courtenay—how
long have you been in London?"

Jenny smiled demurely. "Long enough."

"I can see that." He gestured toward a small bench.
"Shall we sit down?"

Jenny nodded and sank down gracefully on the bench,
amused to see that all of her eager swains had melted away.

Brummell sat down beside her. "If you will allow me to
say so, Miss Courtenay, it appears that you—not I—have
all of London society, if not beneath your thumb, then certainly at your feet."

She smiled easily. "Ah, but *my* fame is fleeting. There
will always be another pretty face—or fat pocketbook—to
come along and stir the town's interest. But there will never
be another Brummell."

The Beau inclined his head slightly at the tribute. "I
never contradict a lady," he responded smoothly.

Jenny, perfectly aware that they were the cynosure of all
eyes, asked gravely, "Are you being so obliging as to bring
me into fashion, Mr. Brummell?"

With equal gravity, the Beau replied, "I believe that to
be an unnecessary exercise, Miss Courtenay. Did I not remark that you had all of London at your feet?"

She laughed, and they began to talk as if they had
known one another for years. The watching eyes of the *ton*
were pleased or irritated, depending on their various atti-
tudes (and whether or not they had daughters of marriageable age), to see that Jennifer Courtenay had apparently
captured another heart.

Brummell could have disabused them of that particular
notion had he cared one jot what they thought. But since he
did not, he had no intention of explaining that his interest
in Jennifer Courtenay stemmed from the intelligence he

had seen in her eyes. He was utterly weary of simpering misses, and found Jenny's entertaining manners a refreshing change.

Something else about Jenny attracted the Beau's interest. There were shadows behind the laughter in her eyes, and Brummell sensed that this beautiful young lady had a great deal more than parties and suitors on her mind. He meant to discover her secret.

Jenny was never afterwards able to recall exactly what Brummell said. She only caught a phrase. But it was enough. Giving a slight start of surprise, she said, "I beg your pardon?"

"The Cat." Brummell gave her a thoughtful look. "She's a female footpad. Surely you've heard of her?"

Jenny had recovered her composure. "Oh—yes, of course. I believe I have heard something about her since I came to London."

"London has been talking of nothing else for more than a year. I am surprised you have only just heard of her."

She managed a faint smile. "Well, Mr. Brummell, I *have* had other things to think about, you know. Parties, gowns, the theater—the sort of things every girl thinks of when she begins her first Season."

Brummell smiled in response, and the conversation passed to other subjects. But the Beau wondered.

# Chapter Nine

After her first visit to Almacks, Jenny felt confident that she would be able to deal successfully with any further references to the Cat. The first such occurrence was, after all, surely the most difficult. She congratulated herself for having dealt rather well with the situation, and devoutly trusted that she would not be shaken quite so badly the next time it occurred.

Unfortunately, her trust was slightly misplaced. It was the night of Lady Jersey's party, and had Jenny but known what would happen, she would have pleaded a headache—or the pox—*anything* to avoid attending what she afterward described to herself as "that perfectly *dreadful* party."

From the first moment of being greeted at the door by Lady Jersey, Jenny heard of nothing but the Cat. "Miss Courtenay—have you heard the latest? They are saying at the War Office that the Cat is not a thief after all. Only fancy—she is actually trying to catch traitors."

Jenny blinked. "Indeed, my lady? I had not heard."

"Well, you shall hear of nothing else tonight," the lady promised merrily. "The entire *ton* is all agog with the news."

To her considerable dismay, Jenny soon found that Lady Jersey had spoken no less than the truth. Lord Rivenhall, who was the first to ask for a dance, was also the first to broach the subject. "I say, Miss Courtenay, have you heard about the female footpad? Apparently she's more than just a common thief; the War Office says that she's trying to find traitors. Why do you think she's doing that?"

"I cannot imagine," Jenny responded rather hollowly. "Perhaps she simply dislikes the thought of anyone being traitorous to England."

Rivenhall who, as his friends often reminded him, had a mind fit for cards and little else, subjected the matter to profound thought. "That could be it," he conceded. "But it seems a dashed silly way to go about the thing. I mean— why does she rob coaches?"

"I am sure I cannot say," Jenny responded.

The gambit failed. Rivenhall's intellect was not powerful, but it was tenacious. The movements of the dance drew them apart just then, but as soon as they were facing one another again, he immediately resumed his examination of the Cat's possible motivations. "Perhaps she knows of a particular traitor and is holding up coaches in hopes of finding him. Do you think that's it, Miss Courtenay?"

Despairingly, Jenny wondered why Rivenhall's wayward mind had latched onto the one possible explanation which was closer to the truth than anything else she had heard. In an effort to pry his mind away from a topic that was making her acutely uncomfortable, Jenny said reprovingly, "My lord, if you continue to go on about this—person, I shall begin to think that you have lost your heart to her."

Perceiving that he had offended his fair companion, and realizing that he would whistle a fortune down the wind if he wasn't careful, Rivenhall made haste to change the subject.

For the next ten minutes, Jenny was treated to a description of his estates which (though not overly large, of course) would be quite splendid if only a little money could be spent on them. Rivenhall then went on to explain why he could not, at the moment, spare the money. His excuses, though most entertaining, were highly improbable and contained less than an ounce of truth.

As soon as the dance had ended, Jenny hinted rather broadly that she was thirsty, and Rivenhall had the happy notion of procuring her a glass of lemonade.

Watching him stride through the crowded room, Jenny felt a sudden desire to develop a headache and go home. But that would never do. For one thing, Lady Jersey was one patroness it was wise not to offend. For another, she was also extremely difficult to deceive.

Jenny sighed and turned to find herself face-to-face with Lady Catherine. The lady's kindly blue eyes twinkled with amusement. "I suppose you've heard about the Cat, Miss Courtenay?"

Jenny resisted the urge to sigh. "Why, yes, my lady."

"I suppose everyone has by now. Well, all I can say is that the poor thing *must* have a reason for what she does—and if her reason is to search for traitors, I can only applaud her spirit. And she must have spirit, you know. Why, it would take a great deal of spirit just to climb up on that whacking great brute she rides, and never mind the rest.

"You—you've seen her, my lady?"

"Oh, no, but my husband was held up by her a while back, you know, and he told me all about it."

"Indeed?" Jenny hoped desperately that she did not look as startled as she felt, and tried to remember when she had held up Lord Amber's coach.

"Yes, indeed! He said that she was very polite and didn't threaten him at all. She asked him very nicely if he would mind very much handing over his purse and jewelry, then thanked him, wished him good evening, and rode off. She rode a great black stallion with strange red eyes."

"How—how terrible for him," Jenny responded weakly.

"Oh, not really," Lady Catherine said comfortably. "It was very exciting for Henry. Poor thing—he doesn't get much excitement these days, you know. And he was very pleased when she returned his jewelry a few days later." She smiled easily at Jenny, spotted an acquaintance across the room, and sailed off.

Jenny decided to find a nice quiet corner in which to hide until this wretched party was over. She was foiled in her desire, however, by Lord Buckham, who planted himself directly in her chosen path of retreat. "Miss Courtenay, have you heard about the Cat?"

Staring at his round, rather florid face and protuberant gray eyes, Jenny had an absurd desire to stand in the middle of the room and loudly announce that she was the Cat— just to shock them all into silence. She ruthlessly suppressed the urge. "Yes, my lord—I have heard."

"Shocking thing! Very shocking! I must say it's the outside of enough to have thieves doing the job that fine, upstanding citizens should take care of. It just won't do— won't do at all."

Amused in spite of herself, Jenny said, "You do not feel, sir, that a thief should be doing Bow Street's job? But what matters *who* does the job as long as it *is* done?"

The little man's face grew even more red. "Well, of course it matters, Miss Courtenay. It matters very much. That's why we pay taxes, after all. And they're trying to turn this thief into some kind of heroine. All they can talk about—morning, noon, and night. Why, if they can only discover who she is, I daresay they'll pin a medal on her."

Intensely curious about his somewhat obscure references to "they," Jenny said soothingly, "I am sure they would not dare, my lord."

"Oh, wouldn't they just!" he exclaimed bitterly. "It's exactly the sort of thing they *would* do."

"I beg your pardon, my lord—but just who are 'they'?"

"The *ton*, girl, the *ton*! M'wife and all those other females. It's a shame, that's what it is! A shame!" He favored her with a brief nod and strode across the room to find a new audience for his views.

Jenny fixed her eyes on an unoccupied corner of the room, and firmly resolved that *nothing* was going to stop her from reaching it. She reckoned without Mrs. Abercrombe-Finch.

Mrs. Abercrombe-Finch was heartily disliked throughout the *ton* because of her sharp tongue, and only tolerated because of her husband's money.

Jenny had already been exposed to the sharp side of Mrs. Abercrombe-Finch's tongue—several times, in fact. Mrs. Abercrombe-Finch had disliked Jenny on sight. Jenny was a very beautiful young woman, and Mrs. Abercrombe-Finch had a daughter of marriageable age, a daughter who was too tall, too thin, and sallow-faced into the bargain. Mrs. Abercrombe-Finch did not like competition—especially when the competition looked like Jenny.

Mrs. Abercrombe-Finch stepped into Jenny's path and looked her up and down in an insulting way that stiffened Jenny's spine. "I suppose you've heard what that brazen hussy has done now?"

Jenny noticed that Mrs. Abercrombe-Finch did not deign to address her by name. "If you are speaking of the Cat, ma'am, yes, I have heard."

Mrs. Abercrombe-Finch looked down her beak of a nose at Jenny—who was a good head shorter than she was. "I suppose you'd like to see the Cat get a medal, too?"

"Since I have little say in the matter, ma'am, and even less interest," said Jenny with exaggerated politeness, "I doubt that my opinion could possibly concern you." She bowed slightly to the affronted matron, and continued serenely on her way.

Her unoccupied corner was now occupied. Jenny sighed and glanced around for another one. She finally discovered a small seat half-hidden behind a potted plant, and sank down on it with a feeling of relief. Now perhaps Providence would favor her, and she could manage to survive the remainder of the evening without doing anything foolish. Perhaps.

Rivenhall was back with her lemonade. "I say, Miss Courtenay—I've looked all over for you. Thought for a moment you'd gone. Gave me a nasty turn." He presented her lemonade with a flourish which spilt half of it on the floor.

Jenny accepted the sticky glass with a strained smile, and wondered rather wildly if she would be able to survive the evening.

"Did you hear? They're going to give the Cat a medal."

In the middle of taking a sip from her sticky glass, Jenny choked and began to cough.

Rivenhall, his bloodshot eyes full of concern, produced a crumpled handkerchief and began to fan her with more enthusiasm than skill. "I say, Miss Courtenay—are you all right?"

Jenny dried her watering eyes with her own handkerchief, then gave Lord Rivenhall what he privately considered to be a very odd look, carefully cleared her throat, and said quietly, "I am perfectly all right, my lord. The lemonade simply—er—went down the wrong way."

Rivenhall sat down gingerly beside her. "Well, if you're sure," he said doubtfully. "I could fetch Lady Beddington."

"Quite unnecessary, I assure you." She fixed him with a limpid smile. "It's only a nervous disorder, you know. Common in my family, I'm afraid. Of course, we *do* hope that I won't end like poor Uncle John."

"Uncle John?" Rivenhall moved a discreet inch or so away from her.

"Well, yes. He had to be confined in a room at the top of the house with an attendant to make sure he didn't hurt himself." She sighed sadly. "Sure a pity."

Rivenhall rose carefully to his feet. "Miss Courtenay—uh—if you will excuse me? I—er—I promised the next dance to—er—Miss Abercrombe-Finch."

Gravely, she responded, "Of course, my lord."

Rivenhall quickly made his escape. Jenny tried to take herself sternly to task for having made up such an absurd farrago of nonsense, but since there was a bubble of near-hysterical laughter trying to escape from her throat, she was not very successful.

Jenny was enjoying a few precious moments of rumination when her thoughts were fortunately interrupted by the appearance of Mr. Brummell. Jenny was fatalistically certain of his first words. She held her breath in suspense.

"Good evening, Miss Courtenay. I suppose you have heard the latest about the Cat?"

Jenny slowly released her pent-up breath. She gave Mr. Brummell an injured look. "Mr. Brummell, I *did* hope that you, at least, would have something intelligent to say tonight."

The Beau looked startled, and then amused. "Why, thank, you," he responded gravely.

Jenny's cheeks pinked, and she cast Brummell an apologetic look. "I beg your pardon," she murmured. "I think I shall scream if I hear another word about the Cat."

"Never," Brummell said solemnly, "apologize for what you say or do."

She managed a faint smile. "Are you trying to turn me into an Original, Mr. Brummell?"

"I do not have to try," the Beau replied. "You *are* an Original—refreshingly so, if I may add."

Jenny blushed again and found, to her annoyance, that she had lost command of her tongue. Before she could regain it, Brummell spoke again.

"And now, Miss Courtenay, would you mind very much telling me why you appear to be as nervous as a cat?"

She gave him a resigned look, and wondered if he could possibly know how singularly apt his comment was. "I am not nervous, Mr. Brummell—you see before you a young woman on the verge of an hysterical fit. And please do not ask why. If I tried to explain, they really *would* have to lock me away like poor Uncle John."

"I beg your pardon?" Brummell looked rather blank.

Beginning to feel more herself, Jenny smiled mischievously. "That's what I told Lord Rivenhall," she confided. "He could not get away from me fast enough. By tomorrow morning, all of London will think I'm mad." She looked thoughtful. "And I'm not sure that they wouldn't be far wrong."

Brummell began to laugh softly. "I wondered what put the poor fellow into such a stew. He looked positively relieved to be dancing with Miss Abercrombe-Finch."

"What I would like to know," Jenny commented darkly, "is why no one has yet murdered the man."

"Did you feel inclined to murder him, Miss Courtenay?"

"Inclined! I tell you honestly, Mr. Brummell, if the man had not left when he did, I would probably have strangled him with my bare hands."

Brummell's keen gray eyes were amused. "Nevertheless, Miss Courtenay, I do not believe that Rivenhall was the sole cause of your tension."

More sure of herself now, Jenny nodded. "You are entirely correct," she said cordially. "There are at least three other people here tonight who contributed to my tension."

"And they are—?"

"Lady Catherine, who said that it was very exciting for

poor Henry to be held up by the Cat; Lord Buckham, who said that it was the outside of enough to have thieves searching for traitors and what was he paying taxes for?; and Mrs. Abercrombe-Finch, who looked down her nose at me and said that she supposed I wanted the Cat to receive a medal, too."

"And do you?"

"Want the Cat to get a medal?" Jenny tried to look blank, and hoped to heaven that she was actress enough to carry it off. "I know nothing about it."

Brummell's thoughtful stare made her slightly uneasy. Her suspicions proved to be unfounded, however, when he spoke. "I have a close friend whom you really should meet. You two would have a great deal in common."

"Indeed?"

"Yes. He—"

"Are you being a matchmaker, Mr. Brummell?"

The Beau appeared injured. "Miss Courtenay! How you could even think such a thing—"

"Quite easily, I assure you."

"Miss Courtenay," Brummell said severely, "it is very impolite of you to interrupt."

"Oh, I *do* beg your pardon. Pay no attention to me, Mr. Brummell; I have had a very long and trying day. Please—go on with what you were saying."

"Thank you. Where was I?"

"You have a friend who would have a great deal in common with me. Poor soul."

Ignoring her murmured comment, Brummell said politely, "Thank you. As I was saying, you really should meet my friend. You have exactly the same sort of humor he has."

"I am glad that *someone* has humor like mine."

Ignoring this quite unnecessary comment, Brummell went on. "You may have already met him."

"I can recall meeting no one even remotely like myself. Who is he?"

"The Duke of Spencer."

Jenny felt the room begin to spin gently around her. *Hounded,* she thought. *I will be hounded to my grave. How I ever thought I could get away with this—*

"Miss Courtenay? Are you feeling all right? You look dreadfully pale."

"No, Mr. Brummell," she replied with admirable restraint, "I am not all right. In fact—I think that I had better go home. If you would be so very obliging as to tell one of the footmen to call a cab for me? I have no desire to worry Lady Beddington."

"Nonsense. I'll escort you home myself."

Meekly, Jenny allowed Mr. Brummell to lead her from the room.

# Chapter Ten

Mr. Brummell, when he chose to exert himself, was easily the most charming man in London, and he proved this by soliciting Lady Jersey's kindness on Miss Courtenay's behalf.

"Well, of course, Miss Courtenay. You do look rather pale, my dear. Allow Mr. Brummell to escort you home, and I shall see that Lady Beddington is not worried."

Jenny smiled weakly and followed the Beau out to his carriage. Once safely ensconced within—and away from that dreadful party—she realized unhappily that she had allowed her panic to force her into an unwise retreat. Mr. Brummell would be sure to wonder why she had been suddenly taken ill—especially since she had been joking with him only a few minutes before.

Hoping to forestall the inevitable questions, Jenny said swiftly, "Mr. Brummell, I cannot thank you enough for your concern. It must have been the heat or—or something."

Her voice broke slightly as Brummell directed an extremely mocking look at her. "Unworthy of you, Miss Courtenay," he said softly. "We both know that you were not overcome by the heat; I thought the room was rather cool, myself. Nor are you physically ill—unless it is with nervous tension. You did, however, become deathly pale when I mentioned the Duke of Spencer." His glinting smile flashed in the carriage. "I wonder why?"

"Oh, that." Try as she would, Jenny could not contrive an explanation—other than the truth—to account for her reaction to Spencer's name.

Fortunately for her, Brummell's mind was apparently not on the Cat at all. "Yes, Miss Courtenay—*that*. Can it be that you have met Spencer?"

His words gave Jenny the germ of an idea, but she needed time to formulate it more thoroughly in her mind. "Well—I wouldn't exactly say that we had *met* . . ."

"Then what exactly would you say?"

"We—clashed." Jenny tried to pull the tangled threads of her story together. "I have a dreadful temper, you know, and he—"

"Also has a temper," Brummell supplied helpfully.

Since Spencer had shown no sign of a temper in her presence and had behaved with perfect calm (except for the one regrettable lapse when he had kissed her), Jenny had no way of knowing that the duke did, in fact, have a temper, and she was grateful for Brummell's statement.

She smiled at the Beau. "Yes, it wasn't very important, but we had a—somewhat violent—difference of opinion, and I stormed off in a temper."

"I see." If Brummell thought her story a thin one—considering her deathly pallor at the mention of the duke's name—he did not say so.

"You can see my position, sir. Spencer is a very important man, and if I offended him . . ."

In an odd voice, Brummell responded, "I shouldn't have thought that you would care for that, Miss Courtenay."

Jenny realized her mistake immediately. She had stepped out of character, and Brummell was far too astute to miss such a lapse.

Coolly, she said, "In the normal way, I would *not* care for Spencer's opinion. Lady Beddington *would*, however, and I have no wish to upset my godmother."

This appeared to satisfy Brummell, who nodded and remarked, "Perfectly understandable."

"So you see, sir," she teased, "your attempts at matchmaking were defeated at the outset. I doubt that the duke will wish to have anything to do with me."

"Oh, I don't know about that. Nick never disliked anyone merely because of a quarrel. If I know him, he probably liked your spirit."

Jenny, who had a very good idea of the duke's opinion of her, merely shook her head ruefully and lapsed into silence. Her thoughts were on Spencer, and she wondered tiredly if he would come up to her at the next soiree and announce loudly that she was the Cat. She had been surprised, though relieved, to have avoided him for as long as she had. At least, she *told* herself that she was relieved. If the truth were known, she was more than a little disappointed. Where had the man *been* for the past two weeks?

Brummell unconsciously picked up her train of thought. "I wonder where Nick is?" he murmured absently. "I haven't seen him in several days. He's had something on his mind for the past few weeks, and has been spending a great deal of time at the War Office."

"Perhaps he's searching for traitors," Jenny remarked, and immediately wished she had kept silent.

"Like the Cat?" Brummell frowned thoughtfully. "You could be right, but I have never heard him mention it." He stiffened suddenly, and Jenny had the unwelcome impression that he had been struck with a thought. "When I first noticed that he had something on his mind," Brummell said slowly, "I also noticed that he had begun asking questions about the Cat."

"Indeed?" Jenny silently cursed the Beau's mental abilities; they were far too acute for her peace of mind.

"Yes. He was coming to every *ton* party and searching the faces of all the young ladies as if he were looking for some particular feature. I wonder . . ."

Jenny knew that she was courting disaster, that she should encourage him to drop the subject, but she had to know what he was thinking. "You wonder, sir?"

"I wonder if Nick knows more about the Cat than the rest of us do," Brummell said thoughtfully.

"Could he?" Jenny knew that she would have to tread very carefully. If she wasn't careful, Brummell would begin to connect her reaction to Spencer's name with the duke's apparent search for the Cat.

"If he had been held up by the Cat, and had become interested in her," Brummell answered, "he certainly could. He would leave no stone unturned to find out as much as he could about her."

"You think that happened? That he was interested?"

"It is possible. From all accounts, the Cat seems to be ladylike in voice and manner. Nick could have taken a fancy to her." After a moment, he went on slowly, "I wonder if Nick believes that the Cat takes off her mask and dons a ballgown? Lord, wouldn't London be in an uproar if that were the case?"

The amusement in his voice did nothing for Jenny's peace of mind.

Noticing her silence, Brummell tried to read her expression. He was unsuccessful; the carriage was too dim. "Miss Courtenay? Are you perfectly all right?"

Jenny was thankful for the darkness of the carriage.

When she could command her voice, she murmured, "I beg your pardon, sir, but I feel rather faint. I cannot imagine what has come over me. I do not, in general, faint at the least provocation."

"That I can well believe."

Brummell's remark was perfectly innocent, but to Jenny's overworked imagination it seemed to have a decidedly sinister tone. If Brummell, of all people, should suspect—

The Beau reached to lower a window. "Perhaps some fresh air will help. I do believe," he continued in a demure tone intended to cheer her, "that you require rest, Miss Courtenay."

She uttered a somewhat shaken laugh. "You could be right, Mr. Brummell." A sudden thought occurred to her. "Mr. Brummell—I have just realized that by tomorrow morning all of the *ton* will know that you escorted me home. That will never do, sir! They will be expecting an announcement, and I shall be horribly pitied when you do not come up to scratch."

As he began to chuckle, she went on sternly, "And do not tell me that you make a habit of escorting young ladies home; you have not that reputation."

He inclined his upper body in a half-bow. "Since you are so brutally honest, Miss Courtenay, I shall be frank and say that I do not care one jot for what people may say. I may not wish to marry you, but I *do* enjoy your company very much, and I mean to make the most of it before some young buck snatches you away and teaches you to be a lady." He shook his head sorrowfully. "It would ruin you."

Jenny gave a gasp and burst out laughing. When she could control her voice, she said in mock offense, "Mr. Brummell! Are you saying that I am *not* a lady?"

He appeared to consider the matter. "I would not go so far as to say *that*—however, you are decidedly unlike any other lady of my acquaintance."

The carriage drew up at Lady Beddington's town house just then, and Jenny silently congratulated herself on having survived an extremely difficult evening. Now, if she could only reach the door without betraying her secret. . . .

Brummell escorted her from the carriage to the door of Lady Beddington's house. Halfway up the steps, he said suddenly, "I think that Nick knows who the Cat is."

Jenny stumbled, and would have fallen without the Beau's firm grip on her elbow. She murmured some excuse and wondered what, in God's name, she had done to offend the Fates that they should torment her so.

Brummell looked concerned. "Miss Courtenay, I do hope you are feeling more the thing tomorrow."

"I—am sure that I shall, Mr. Brummell."

"Good night, Miss Courtenay." He bowed.

"Good night, Mr. Brummell—and thank you." She smiled at him, opened the door, and went inside. As soon as she had closed the door behind her, Jenny leaned back against it and wondered if she were going mad. In a detached manner, she considered the possibility. It wouldn't surprise her a bit if she ended her days in Bedlam.

After a moment's thought, she felt slightly cheered, however. Brummell, at least, had not guessed her secret. She smiled rather wearily to herself and headed toward the stairs—and a well-earned rest.

Brummell directed his coachman to take him to his rooms, climbed inside the carriage, and began to laugh softly. He felt no sense of compunction at having taken shameless advantage of Miss Courtenay's nervous tension. The truth was that he had not enjoyed himself so much in years.

There were those among the *ton* who claimed, not without reason, that Beau Brummell's sense of humor was more malicious than mischievous. He was famous—or infamous—for creating situations which became vilely uncomfortable for all involved, and then leaving his victims to shift for themselves. Needless to say, he had made many enemies.

However, such was his power that even his enemies dared not raise their voices against him. By the mere lift of an expressive eyebrow, he could forever blight the hopes of any aspirant to society. He was a close friend of the Regent, and since it was commonly believed that the old king could not last much longer, many people maintained that Brummell would soon become the power behind the throne.

There was, however, a side to the Beau that very few members of the *ton* had ever seen. To those he cared about, he was a good and loyal friend, who could be counted on not to make mischief when the case was serious.

Brummell had liked Jennifer Courtenay from the first moment he saw her, and he had neither the desire, nor the intention of disclosing his suspicions to society. He was well aware that the disclosure—even if he were wrong—would brand her as an outcast.

His plans for her were somewhat involved, but he had no desire to ruin her. In fact, he had every intention of helping her in whatever way he could. For one thing, he was certain that she and Spencer would be perfect for one another. But he had no intention of poking his finger into that particular pie. Spencer was well able to handle his own love life.

He could, however, make Jenny's social appearances a little less trying. If he professed himself bored with the subject of the Cat, society would quickly follow his lead. Jenny would not be forced to endure another night like this one.

That, at least, he could do for her. Brummell frowned slightly as he realized that he would have to dance attendance on the Regent for the next day or two. He felt irritated as he realized also that he would most probably be absent when Jenny and Spencer first met.

Well, it could not be helped. He had no wish to offend the Prince; he might possibly need the royal goodwill at a later date. If Jennifer Courtenay *was* the Cat, her name would have to be cleared sooner or later.

He could be wrong, of course, but he did not think so. He was an excellent judge of people. Besides, there was no other logical reason to account for her extreme tension this evening, nor her deathly pallor at the mention of Spencer's name. She certainly did not want to meet Spencer.

Brummell wondered about that. He had an odd feeling that the duke was probably the only one of the Cat's victims who stood a good chance of being able to identify her without her mask.

Perhaps Spencer *had* taken a fancy to the Cat. The Duke of Spencer in love with a female footpad . . .

Brummell smiled to himself in unholy amusement. The next few weeks should be quite interesting—to say the least.

# Chapter Eleven

Spencer had just resigned himself to an evening of boredom when, looking up from the dowager who had claimed his attention, he glanced across the room and saw the most beautiful girl he had ever seen in his life.

She was dressed all in gold, with golden ribbons threaded through her raven hair. She was smiling up at her dancing partner, and even from across the room, Spencer was struck by the brilliance of her eyes.

He felt a touch on his arm and turned to find the dowager regarding him with an indulgent smile. "I see you have noticed my goddaughter, Your Grace. A lovely girl, is she not?"

"Yes," Spencer replied with a faint smile. "Yes, she is very lovely. I do not believe I have met her."

The dowager lowered her voice significantly. "Poor little thing. That nasty stepfather of hers has been keeping her in the country all these years, but her mother managed to send her to me two weeks ago. I'd be delighted to present you, Your Grace."

Spencer inclined his head and followed the dowager across the room. The dance had ended and, as they drew nearer to the girl, Spencer realized what his first impression had been—she was lovely.

Jenny heard Lady Beddington call her name, and turned to see her godmother bearing down on her—with the Duke of Spencer at her side. Jenny's habitual calm served her well; she was able to smile easily.

Lady Beddington returned the smile, an imp of mischief in her bright blue eyes. "Jenny, I would like to present the Duke of Spencer. Your Grace, my goddaughter, Jennifer Courtenay."

Jenny extended her hand to the duke, curtsying as she did so. "How do you do, Your Grace?"

The duke bowed low over her hand. "Miss Courtenay, I am delighted to meet you." The music began, and he continued with a smile, "May I have this dance?"

Jenny responded just as her godmother had taught her. With laughter in her golden eyes, she said, "If you please, sir."

Spencer led her out onto the floor, feeling oddly lightheaded. As he took her into his arms for the waltz, he felt certain that he had met her before. Giving in to impulse, he said, "Miss Courtenay—have we met before?"

Jenny fought down a rising panic and concentrated on keeping her voice light and careless as she replied, "Why, no, Your Grace—I am certain that we have never met. I have only been in London for a week or so." She gazed up into his eyes and felt absurdly startled to find them smiling down at her. *My, but he was big.*

"I hesitate to contradict a lady," he responded, "but, I feel certain that we have met before."

Jenny called all her acting talents into play. With a brilliant smile, she said, "Perhaps you saw me riding in the park one morning."

Giving in gracefully, Spencer replied, "Perhaps I did. Do you enjoy riding? I believe that Lady Beddington mentioned you are accustomed to living in the country."

Jenny felt some of her tension ease. "Why, yes, I am used to riding every day, though I must admit that it seems a trifle tame to be obliged to hold my mount to a gentle canter."

Spencer smiled sympathetically. "I feel the same way, I assure you. It is especially trying when one's mount has not been out of the stables in several days."

Jenny laughed. "Indeed it is. Do you hunt, Your Grace?"

He nodded. "My estate is in the heart of some of the best hunting country in England." With a smile, he continued, "My mother used to complain that I spent more time on my hunters than I did with my books."

"My mother used to say the same thing." She smiled up at him. "I always liked horses better than people. Mama was in despair when I began to go out hunting with Papa. She insisted that ladies did not know how to handle guns."

Spencer felt an odd little tingle somewhere near the back of his mind. He dismissed the feeling, telling himself that it was nothing. "I would venture to say, then, that you were something of a tomboy."

"How astute of you."

Again, the duke was conscious of that odd feeling. Her comment seemed to echo in his mind, as if he had heard it before. Then he remembered.

Jenny felt her hand nearly crushed suddenly, and looked up at him in protest. Her words died in her throat as she saw his eyes. They were strangely dazed, as though he had suddenly realized something.

"Your Grace." He looked down at her as though he were seeing someone else. "My hand—you're hurting my hand."

He blinked and immediately loosened his grip. "I beg your pardon, Miss Courtenay," he murmured.

Jenny had the uneasy suspicion that he had been thinking of her—or the Cat. She wanted to divert his thoughts, but found herself totally unable to say anything at all. She could only stare up at him, her heart pounding in her breast.

Spencer gazed down at her pale face and, seeing the fear in her golden eyes, knew that he had to reassure her—she knew that he had guessed her identity.

With a strangely gentle smile, he said softly, "I told you once that I would not betray you; I meant that. Your secret is safe with me."

"Secret?" Jenny refused to admit defeat. "Why, Your Grace, whatever can you mean? I—I have no secrets."

He continued to smile. In a meditative tone of voice, he said, "I remember meeting a certain young lady one dark night. She was a woman of fire and spirit, and possessed great courage. I admired that woman very much. I never thought that I would hear her play the fool."

His words had the desired effect. Jenny's eyes flashed with anger. Without considering her words, she said, "And you haven't heard it yet. I may be many things, Your Grace, but I am not a fool." She stopped, appalled by what she had said.

He was grinning openly, his eyes bright with laughter. "No, but you certainly have a temper," he said quietly.

In a low voice she asked, "How did you know?"

"That first night you came to my house you made quite an impression on me. I remember everything you said to me. When I asked you what you were searching for, you said that it was 'astute' of me to have guessed that you were searching for a particular article of jewelry. When you used the same words just now, I suddenly realized that you were the Cat."

"Hush!" She glanced around nervously. "Are you so

anxious for me to hang that you mean to expose me here—now?"

"I don't mean to expose you at all," he replied quietly. "I told you that before."

"Forgive me if I find that hard to believe." Her voice was dry. "There's quite a price on my head."

He shook his head sadly. "You still don't trust me, do you?"

She shot him an irritated look. "Well, what an absurd question! Of course I don't trust you! I don't enjoy having my life in the hands of a stranger."

"There is a remedy for that, you know."

She looked suspicious. "Oh? And what is that?"

He smiled. "You can become better acquainted with me, and then I won't be a stranger any longer. Does that not sound logical?"

"You're asking a woman about logic?" Her smile was wry.

"When the woman is you, yes I am. Well? Do you think you could bear to spend some time with me?"

Jenny began to understand how a cornered fox must feel. The duke was an excellent hunter. But she had a strange feeling that she would enjoy any time she could spend with the duke. "I might—possibly—be able to bear it," she responded with a faint smile. "Provided, of course, that you don't intend to talk about how I spend my spare time."

He smiled at her. "I promise. Now—how would you like to come riding with me tomorrow?"

Throwing her fate to the winds, Jenny smiled back at him. "I would love to, Your Grace."

The dance ended just then, and Spencer led her to a secluded corner of the ballroom, where they sat down on a small bench. Spencer smiled and said, "We can begin to get to know one another now—unless, of course, you are in dire need of a glass of lemonade."

Jenny smiled reprovingly. "That was not very gallant of you. You made it sound as though I would be committing a crime if I admitted to thirst."

He laughed. "Yes, but if you are thirsty, then I will have to go and fetch you a drink, and when I return, some buck will have taken my place."

Amusement gleamed in her golden eyes. "In that case, you may rest at ease; I am not in the least thirsty."

"Good. Now, tell me about yourself."

"There isn't much to tell. My home is in Kent—near the village of Maidenstone. I was an only child until my mother remarried six years ago."

"And your father?"

"He died eight years ago."

"I'm sorry. That must have been hard on you."

For a moment, her eyes were clouded. "Yes," she murmured. "Yes, it was." The haunted look faded away. "But that was a long time ago. As I said, my mother remarried."

She went on to tell him something of her life at Courtenay Manor and, encouraged by his obvious interest, lost all track of time.

The two were so engrossed in one another that they failed to notice that nearly every eye in the room was focused on them. Matrons who had tried every possible way of attaching their daughters to the highly eligible Duke of Spencer felt their bosoms swell with indignation as they watched Jennifer Courtenay capture His Grace's attention with no trouble at all. They wondered what it was about her that had captivated the duke so thoroughly. It wasn't beauty; the duke had met many a beauty in the past ten years. He had no need of her fortune, which was, if all accounts were true, quite large. What was so special about her?

Jenny suddenly noticed the attention they had attracted. With a slight flush staining her cheeks, she fell silent.

"Miss Courtenay?" Spencer frowned. "Is something wrong?"

She nodded slightly toward the crowded ballroom. "You may be accustomed to being the center of attention, but I am not," she answered wryly.

He followed her gaze and swore beneath his breath. "All the privacy of a goldfish. Perhaps if we ignore them, they will go away."

She smiled and rose to her feet. "I think not. In any case, I should return to my godmother. She will be wondering about me."

Spencer smiled ruefully as he got to his feet. "I'm afraid I chose a rather bad time for us to get to know one another. We shall do better tomorrow."

As they began to make their way across the room, Jenny said, "A gentle canter, Your Grace?"

He laughed softly. "Convention dictates, I'm afraid."

There was a challenge in her smile. "Shall we challenge convention?"

He looked down at her, amusement in his eyes. "Why not?"

"Good." She nodded, her eyes bright with mischief. "I have a gray that I've been anxious to try out. He's a little on the wild side, and I've hesitated to ride him in the park—for fear that he would disgrace me. But with the Duke of Spencer at my side, I need no longer fear any loss of credit."

"And what if my credit isn't good enough to carry you off?"

"I have no fear of that." Her smile was demure. "A duke may do as he chooses—and no one will say him nay."

He chuckled, amused by her casual use of his consequence. "Do you care so much for your reputation?" He wasn't surprised at her answer.

"Not at all," she replied coolly. "But while I am living in my godmother's house, I must contrive not to disgrace her. I owe her a great deal."

They came up to Lady Beddington just then, and the duke smiled at the dowager and then bowed to Jenny. "At what time shall I call for you, Miss Courtenay?"

"Two o'clock?"

"Two o'clock it is." He smiled again, nodded to Lady Beddington, and then moved away.

"Jenny?" Lady Beddington's plump, cheerful face was avid with curiosity.

Jenny smiled at her godmother. "We're going riding tomorrow."

"Well!" The dowager wore a triumphant expression. "I've never seen him so taken with any of the young ladies. You mark my words, Jenny. You'll be a duchess before the season is over."

Jenny smiled wryly as she watched her godmother preen herself. She was under no illusions as to the reason for Spencer's interest. He knew she was the Cat, and he was curious—nothing more.

She watched beneath her lashes as he led Lady Jersey onto the floor, and knew a flicker of regret that he was only interested in her because of her strange career.

Lady Jersey smiled archly up at Spencer. "I see you've discovered the new beauty, Nick. Tell me, what do you think of her?"

He smiled easily. "She's very beautiful."

"The man has eyes in his head," she marveled. "That wasn't what I meant—and well you know it."

"I just met the girl, Sally. I don't know what I think of her yet."

There was a gleam of mischief in her eyes. "She's quite out of the common way, you know. Intelligent as well as beautiful. But I daresay you wouldn't let a little thing like that stand in your way."

"Stop trying to marry me off, Sally," he responded imperturbably.

"Well, someone has to! You're—what?—thirty two, thirty-three?"

"Thirty-two."

"Practically in your dotage. Your poor mother would like to see her grandchildren before she dies—she told me so the other day."

"My mother," he said calmly, "is as healthy as a horse. She isn't likely to 'depart this mortal coil' for some time yet."

Lady Jersey shook her head sadly. "Well, at any rate, if you mean to try for Jennifer Courtenay, you'd better hurry and get your bid in. In addition to her beauty, she's also very wealthy. Half the bucks in town are after her. Including Rivenhall."

Spencer frowned. "Planning on lining his pockets?"

"You can hardly blame him. The poor man's been one jump ahead of his creditors for years."

"If he wouldn't spend his nights at cards," Spencer responded unsympathetically, "he wouldn't be so pressed for money. All the Rivenhalls are gamblers."

Lady Jersey shrugged. "He may not have to worry much longer. Miss Courtenay seems to favor him. If she's looking for a title, she may settle for an earl. The family is good—he can trace his lineage back to the Conquerer."

Spencer smiled mockingly. "Half of England can trace its lineage back to the Conquerer."

Lady Jersey smiled reluctantly. "True." The dance ended and, as he led her back to her place, she said, "In any case, Miss Courtenay may not feel that she is good enough for a duke. Her father committed suicide, you know."

He looked surprised. "I didn't know, but I should like to know what that has to do with her."

Lady Jersey resumed her seat and smiled up at him. "As far as I'm concerned—nothing. But the girl may be sensitive. Many girls would."

"That's nonsense."

"Perhaps." She tilted her head to one side inquisitively. "Mean to try your hand, Nick?"

His frown disappeared. "Don't try matchmaking me, Sally. I can handle my own affairs."

The lady smiled as she watched him move away. These confirmed bachelors, she thought. Sometimes it was necessary to stir their interest a bit.

Spencer made no attempt to talk to Jenny again. He had given the gossips of London enough to talk about by singling her out for his attention. He was anxious to spend more time with her, but he had no intention of allowing half of London to observe his courtship.

With that in mind, he danced with several other ladies, and even flirted a bit with some of the older ones. He was far too astute a bachelor to give any of the younger ladies cause to think he had serious intentions toward them.

The party began to break up around two A.M., and Spencer watched Jenny leave with a feeling of anticipation. Tomorrow he would begin to unravel the mystery of Jennifer Courtenay.

# Chapter Twelve

Spencer called for Jenny promptly at two o'clock the next afternoon. He was admitted to Lady Beddington's house by a stern-faced butler, and stepped inside just as Jenny came down the stairs.

Her riding habit was black velvet, trimmed with gold braid, and a gold scarf trailed from her hat. She looked beautiful.

Forgetting the servant's presence, Spencer said impulsively, "How lovely you are."

Jenny halted, confused, and then slowly descended the rest of the stairs. With a shy smile, she extended her hand. "Good afternoon, Your Grace—and thank you for the compliment."

He bowed low over her hand. "My pleasure, Miss Courtenay. Shall we go?"

She smiled and nodded, making no attempt to withdraw her hand from his grasp.

The butler showed them out, his stern face having soft-

ened at the duke's loverlike greeting. He sighed nostalgi-
cally as he watched them ride away.

The duke kept a watchful eye on Jenny's horse for the
first few minutes. He was a beautiful horse with a great deal
of spirit, and not really suited for a lady. But Jenny obviously knew horses well, and had no trouble controlling his
playful attempts to unseat her.

Spencer smiled at her. "I should have known you were
an excellent horsewoman after seeing you on that black
stallion of yours."

She gave him a warning look. "You promised."

"So I did." He inclined his head slightly. "And I mean to
keep that promise. But you must forgive a slip of the tongue
now and then."

"A slip of the tongue," she responded dryly, "could put
a noose round my neck."

He started to speak, then apparently thought better of it.
"Blast that promise!"

"I'm holding you to it."

"Then, for heaven's sake—don't talk about hanging."

Jenny laughed. "Very well. What shall we talk about?"

"You."

"Oh, no. We talked about me last night—today it's your
turn."

He grinned ruefully. "What would you like to know?"

"You were in Spain with Wellesley, weren't you?"

He nodded. "For a year or so. I was wounded at Ciudad
Rodrigo and sent home. My mother insisted that I stay—
since I am the last of the Wares."

"She was right."

"Perhaps." He shrugged. "But I'd like to go back."

Jenny shook her head slowly. "I hate war."

He studied her intently. "Why? I mean aside from the
fact that it's a bloody, unpleasant business."

"Because," she replied quietly, "war turns men into traitors."

"You're too intelligent to believe that," he said gently. "Traitors are born, not made. War simply brings their innate tendencies to light."

"Perhaps you're right." She sighed and tried to throw off her feeling of depression. "It's too beautiful a day to talk of war and traitors." She smiled at him. "I thought we were going to challenge convention."

"So we were." He grinned at her. "Shall we startle all of London by galloping through the park?"

By way of answering him, she pointed her whip at a stand of trees at the other end of the park. "Race you!" she cried and was off.

Pedestrians were treated to a startling sight as two horses came thundering through the park. First came a magnificent young woman on a gray and, just behind her, the Duke of Spencer on his chestnut.

Jenny arrived at the stand of trees first, and pulled her horse to a stop. With a breathless laugh, she said, "There! I won!"

The duke laughed. "I demand a rematch; you caught me by surprise."

"Nonsense!" She smiled brilliantly. "You just won't admit to defeat, that's all."

"Well of course not. We dukes never admit to defeat, you know." There was a teasing glint in his eyes.

She laughed. "Ah—the truth will out. You depend on your consequence to pull you through."

"*Blast* my consequence!" He burst out laughing. "Miss Courtenay—no, that will never do. May I call you Jenny?"

"Please do." She smiled at him.

"Jenny, I assure you that dukes are no different from anyone else."

"Of course not. It's natural for people to be referred to as 'Your Grace.'"

"Which reminds me—" He smiled at her, his eyes serious. "Please call me Nick."

She nodded. "If you wish."

"I do."

"Very well then—Nick." She nodded toward the carriageway. "Lady Jersey has been trying to attract your attention for the past five minutes. Don't you think perhaps you'd better go over and talk to her? Or aren't dukes obliged to be polite?"

"Jenny! Will you please stop throwing my title in my face."

She smiled mischievously. "But, Nick, it's such fun to see your expression when I do."

He sighed. "Let us go over and talk to Lady Jersey."

When the couple approached Lady Jersey's barouche, she was greatly encouraged to see that they appeared to be on excellent terms. In fact, the duke had a definite gleam in his eye, and Miss Courtenay seemed highly amused.

With a laugh in her voice, Lady Jersey said, "Galloping in the park. Really, Nick, you should know better. And at your age, too."

"Rules were made to be broken, Sally."

Lady Jersey laughed and turned to smile at Jenny. "Miss Courtenay—I wanted to make sure you are planning to attend my little party this evening."

Jenny smiled and nodded. "I am looking forward to it, my lady."

"Good." She lifted an eyebrow at Spencer. "Nick, are you coming?"

He bowed. "If I may."

"You may. I'll see both of you tonight, then. And no more galloping." She signaled her coachman, and the carriage moved on.

Jenny watched as Lady Jersey's barouche moved sedately along the carriageway, and then smiled at the duke. "After that scold, we dare not gallop again. Shall we content ourselves with a gentle canter?"

Spencer chuckled. "After my crushing defeat, I would not have dared to gallop even without the scold. Let us, by all means, canter."

The two horses broke into an easy canter, and Spencer barely had time to note that Jenny's expression was suspiciously demure before she was off again. The gray went from an easy canter to a dead run in nothing flat, and the duke was hard-pressed to keep pace.

By the time he did catch up, the gray was walking calmly, and Jenny wore an expression of angelic innocence.

With all the air of one making a great discovery, Spencer said, "I have just learned an important lesson."

"Indeed? And what might that be?"

"I have learned never to tell you *not* to do something."

Jenny began to laugh. "No, have you really? Well, I expect that it does you good to learn something occasionally."

"I have also learned," he went on rather quizzically, "that you appear to favor Rivenhall."

She looked startled. "Wherever did you hear that?"

"A little bird whispered in my ear."

"I wonder why the bird thought you would be interested?" Before he could respond, she went on rather dryly, "I have never been overly fond of fortune hunters."

His mind relieved of one care at least, the duke immediately latched on to her murmured question. "What makes you think that I would *not* be interested?"

With an unconsciously wistful expression, Jenny answered, "You are interested in the novelty of a lady thief—nothing more."

Spencer at once set out to prove to her that he was interested only in the young lady in his company—and he succeeded very well. So well, in fact, that word flew round London within the hour that the elusive Duke of Spencer had tumbled head over heels in love.

Jenny, weary of the secrecy and tensions of the past year, gave herself up to the pleasure of the duke's company. The future would take care of itself; for the present, she was happy.

At least two pairs of watching eyes in the park that day were singularly uninterested in the romance, however. Those eyes belonged to two men who were rather shabbily dressed and sported bright red waistcoats. They had kept Jenny and the duke under close observation, and now stood with their heads together.

The taller of the two, who had a ruddy face and penetrating blue eyes, nodded toward the opposite side of the park—and Jenny. "That's 'er all right," he pronounced in a grating voice.

The shorter man grunted something which was apparently intelligible to his companion.

Impatiently, the taller responded, "Well, she fits the description. Small, with black hair an' queer yaller eyes."

The second man grunted again.

"I *know* it don't make sense. I ask you, Sam—why would a pretty little thing like 'er take to thievin'? It ain't like she needs the money. From all accounts, she's got plenty o' brass."

The next grunt contained a questioning note.

"Well, I don't like it anymore than you do, Sam. But it's our dooty to ask 'er some questions. The orders come from the Chief Magistrate, y'know." He went on in a confiding tone. "I don't mind tellin' you, Sam—I ain't got much likin' for this assignment. It's a bad thing to go accusin' a member of the Quality. 'Specially when that Quality is a lady."

He gave his head a shake and gazed toward the riders. "An' would you look who she's ridin' with. The Duke of Spencer. Now wouldn't it be a pretty kettle o' fish if *he* got up in the boughs over the whole thing. You an' me could find ourselves on the first ship bound for the colonies."

Another grunt from Sam.

"No, o' course it weren't him informed against her. It were her own Pa. Now that just goes to show, don't it? 'Er own Pa! I tell you, Sam, the Quality is queer as Dick's hatband—ever' one of 'em."

Another grunt.

"Why does 'e think she's the Cat? Said 'e saw 'er sneakin' out 'er window late at night dressed like a man. 'Course *that* don't prove nothin'. She coulda been sneakin' out to meet 'er sweetheart—an' Lord knows it 'ud be easier to climb down a tree in breeches 'stead o' skirts."

The next grunt was more of a growl.

"No, we ain't got any proof. Whoever the Cat is, she don't keep that black stallion of 'ers in Lunnon. If we could just find that damned 'orse. There ain't another 'orse like that in England."

Another grunt.

"Well, o' course it's important. That 'orse could point the way to the Cat sure as I'm standing in' here. And there ain't even a *smell* of a black 'orse in Lady Beddington's stables. 'Sides the carriage 'orses, there's just three of 'em—Miss Courtenay's two, the little mare an' that gray she's ridin' now, an' Miss Ross' bay."

He sighed gustily. "An' when you ask somebody if they seen a black stallion, they look at you like you just growed a extra head. You know, Sam, sometimes I get the feelin' the Quality don't want us to catch the Cat. It don't seem to bother 'em at all that she stealin' their brass."

A rather impatient grunt.

"All right, all right. You don't have to get snippy. We'll talk to 'er—but we'll wait 'til the duke takes 'er 'ome. We don't need 'im around when we question Miss Courtenay."

Sam grunted.

# Chapter Thirteen

Jenny stood in the hallway, slowly removing her gloves. Her face was expressionless, her golden eyes thoughtful. She was thinking of the past hour, and as she remembered the duke's teasing, her lips curved in a smile. It was some time before she became aware of the butler's presence by her side.

Hastily wiping the smile from her face, Jenny turned to the servant. "What is it, Somers?"

Somers inclined his head slightly. "You have a visitor, Miss Jenny. He called while you were out and, upon hearing that you had gone riding, elected to wait here until your return."

Jenny tilted her head thoughtfully to one side as she studied the butler. To anyone unacquainted with the ways of servants, Somers's voice would have seemed perfectly expressionless. Jenny knew better. It was obvious that the butler's dignity had been sorely tried by the persistence of the "visitor."

Jenny smiled faintly. "He refused to leave his card?"

Somers stared expressionlessly into space. "I suggested that he do so, Miss Jenny, but he appeared determined to remain here."

She sighed. "Lord Stoven."

The butler nodded. "In the Green Room, miss."

Jenny lifted a wry eyebrow and said, "Pray inform Lord Stoven that I will be with him as soon as I have changed."

Somers nodded. "Of course, Miss Jenny."

She made her way to her room, a crease of irritation between her brows. Damn the man! Could he not take no for an answer? She was not looking forward to this interview. She changed quickly, scorning the assistance of her maid. Minutes later, she was quietly entering the Green Room.

Stoven was standing by the window. He turned quickly when he heard the door open. Immediately, he moved toward Jenny, his hand outstretched. "My dear Jenny—how lovely you look today."

Jenny allowed him to take her hand, but her voice was cool and formal when she said, "Lord Stoven. How good of you to pay us a visit." She suppressed a shudder as his cold lips touched her hand. As soon as she could, she withdrew it from his grasp and moved to seat herself on the settee. "Please, sit down."

He took a seat close beside Jenny. She swore silently for not having had the forethought to sit in the chair by the window. It was too late now. The earl's small eyes were roving over her, a hungry expression in their depths. His hand reached for hers.

Jenny tried to evade him, but was a fraction of a second too slow. His sweaty hand closed over hers. She attempted to pull away from his grasp, but there was an unexpected amount of strength in his pudgy grip. "My lord," she said coldly, "will you please have the goodness to unhand me immediately."

Stoven smiled slyly. "Now, love, we both know why you came to London. You wanted to get away from Sir George. I understand that—I know that you had to get away from him. So as soon as I could, I followed you here."

Jenny's eyes glittered with fury. "Sir! I have not given you permission to address me in such terms, nor have I ever given you reason to suppose that your suit would prosper." She jerked her hand away and rose to her feet.

Stoven rose also, his face darkening with anger. "Don't be a fool, Jenny! The matter was settled between your stepfather and myself long ago. We will be married in the summer."

She drew herself up, her face hardening. "I will never marry you," she said flatly.

The earl's face twisted in a soundless snarl. Before Jenny could move, he caught both of her wrists in a painfully tight grip. A leering smile made his face even uglier than usual. "You'll marry me, pet—even if I have to force you into it."

"Why?" Jenny's voice was calm, in spite of the fact that her stomach was twisting itself into knots. "You certainly don't need the money."

"Because I love you." The leering smile remained. "And because you are a very desirable young woman. I want you, Jenny. And I intend to have you."

She shook her head. "You won't ever possess me, my lord."

The earl's eyes contained an evil glint. "Don't count on it, pet!" Without warning, he jerked her hard against his body, holding her wrists pinned at the small of her back. "I could take you here—now. You'd have to marry me then."

Jenny felt sick to her stomach. Goose bumps of fear rose over her body. But, during the past year, she had learned to depend on her own resourcefulness whenever danger threatened.

In a coldly mocking voice she said, "Your threats mean

nothing to me, sir." At the same instant, her right heel came down sharply on the earl's toe, and her left knee jerked up with deadly accuracy.

They were standing so close together that Stoven had no way to protect himself. He doubled over, groaning in agony, and Jenny was free. She quickly moved to the fireplace and stood with one hand on the bellrope. Her voice still cold, she said, "A friend of mine taught me that trick. He said that it would come in handy if I were ever to be attacked." She smiled. "He was right."

By this time, Stoven had collapsed in a groaning heap on the settee. "You little bitch! You've killed me!" His voice was hoarse and full of pain.

"Hardly." There was no trace of sympathy or remorse in her voice. "I merely gave you—I hope—something to think about. I trust that you will remember this interview should you ever decide to lay a hand on me again."

Pale and shaking, Stoven managed to get to his feet. His small eyes were filled with rage. "You'll pay for this!"

"I think not." Jenny pulled the bellrope. "You will leave this house immediately. You will not return. Should you ever decide to try your luck with me again, you will find yourself in far worse case than you are now."

A sneer twisted Stoven's face. "You won't catch me off guard twice, I promise you. Next time I'll be ready for you."

Jenny smiled gently. "If there is a next time—which I strongly doubt—your heir will be thanking the Fates for his good fortune. Because you will be very dead."

The earl stiffened and managed to go a shade more pale. "You couldn't kill a man."

"Of course not. But there are men available who will do almost anything—for a price. I suggest you remember that, my lord."

Before Stoven could respond, the door opened and Somers stepped inside. His alert eyes flicked over the earl's pained expression and mussed clothing, but he made no comment, merely looking inquiringly at Jenny.

She nodded toward the earl. "Show Lord Stoven out, Somers."

The butler nodded. "If your lordship will follow me?"

The earl cast a fulminating glare at Jenny's calm face, and stomped angrily from the room.

Jenny watched the door close behind them, then lifted a shaking hand to her face. She suddenly became aware that she had made a dangerous enemy for herself. Stoven wanted her. Jenny had a sick feeling that the earl would do almost anything to possess her.

She moved slowly to the settee, and sank down on it, trying to slow the frightened pounding of her heart. The look in Stoven's eyes terrified her. She had seen desire in men's eyes before—but nothing like the all-consuming hunger that glowed in the earl's eyes whenever he looked at her.

Jenny sat very still on the settee and gazed sightlessly into the cold fireplace. The only thing she could do was to stay out of Stoven's way. It wouldn't be easy, since he was likely to attend the same social affairs that she did.

Jenny frowned slightly. It would cause comment if she refused to stand up with him in public, but she had no intention of talking to him—much less dancing with him.

She was still frowning when the door opened to admit the butler. He waited until Jenny looked up before asking quietly, "If Lord Stoven should call again, Miss Jenny?"

Jenny stared at the servant's expressionless eyes for a long moment before saying quietly, "I am not at home to Lord Stoven, Somers. No matter what the reason for calling, I am not at home."

The butler nodded in understanding, started to withdraw from the room, and then paused. His keen eyes were fixed on Jenny's face. "Miss, are you all right?"

She smiled in answer to the worried query. "I'm fine, Somers. I can take care of myself."

"I had that impression, Miss Jenny. If you will allow me to say so, you appear well able to deal with any—problems." Before she could respond, he went on quietly, "There is a gentleman to see you, miss. A Mr. Robert Collins."

Jenny frowned slightly. Irritably she wondered why trouble always came in bunches, and why Robert had ignored her advice by coming to London. "Send him in, Somers."

She was standing by the window when the door opened to admit Robert Collins. She gazed wryly at his sheepish expression. "Robert, you know I am terribly fond of you and it's always delightful to see you, but what are you doing here?"

He grinned. "I just stopped by on my way to Scotland, Jenny."

"Scotland? Why on earth are you going to Scotland?"

"I'm not planning an elopement with Meg, so you can stop looking at me like that! By the way—whatever happened to 'Hello' and 'How are you'?"

"Hello, how are you, and why on earth are you going to Scotland?"

Robert chuckled at her exasperated tone. "I've been called back to the ancestral home. My uncle has died and left me everything—isn't that wonderful?"

Jenny stared at him. "Yes. That is—I hardly think your uncle would feel that it's wonderful."

He chuckled again. "You're wrong there. My uncle was nearly ninety, had a bad case of the gout, and hated every living creature. He was probably glad to go."

Jenny sat down and gestured toward a nearby chair. "Sit down, Robert, and tell me why your uncle left you everything."

Robert sank into the chair and grinned, his blue eyes alight with laughter. "The letter didn't explain, but I think he made me his heir because I didn't care a bit more about him than he did about me. At least that's what one of my aunts told me years ago."

Jenny blinked. "Well, it certainly seems strange."

"It wouldn't—if you knew my uncle." He sobered abruptly. "Don't you see, Jenny? At least now Meg's husband won't be penniless. I don't know exactly how much the estate is worth, but my uncle was thought to be well off. I'll be able to support Meg, if not in luxury, then at least in comfort."

She smiled gently. "I'm very happy for you, Robert. I know how worried you were about your ability to support Meg, and I'm delighted that things have worked out so well for you."

Robert held up a cautioning finger. "We'd better wait until I've seen the estate. The old man may have left me nothing more than a rickety house and a few suits of tattered clothes."

Jenny chuckled. "How long do you expect to be in Scotland?"

He shrugged. "I really don't know; I've never had to settle an estate before. A month—perhaps longer. As soon as I know, I'll send word to you and Meg." He shot her a penetrating look from beneath his brows. Of course, you may have a different address by then."

She looked startled. "The Season has only just begun, Robert; we are fixed in London for quite some time. How would I have a different address?" For one dreadful moment, she thought that he had discovered her identity as the Cat, and was trying to hint that she would soon be residing in prison. But his next words showed her how far off the mark she was.

"I thought perhaps you might be thinking of getting married yourself," he responded casually.

Jenny frowned. "Whatever gave you that idea?"

"Isn't that the sole reason for young ladies to come to London? To find husbands?"

"You know very well why I came to London. Because Mama found out about you and Meg."

He grinned. "Perhaps. So who was the dashing blade I saw you riding in the park with a couple of hours ago?"

"Oh. That—that was the Duke of Spencer."

Robert lifted an eyebrow as a slight flush rose to her face. "A duke? I can see that you've been very busy since coming to London. Are you quite certain that you're not planning to change your address?" His voice was teasing, but Jenny refused to rise to the bait.

Calmly, she replied, "Quite certain. The duke is merely an acquaintance. We met at a party last night. He has no special interest in me—or I in him."

Hard on the heels of her statement, the door opened and Somers announced, most inopportunely, "The Duke of Spencer."

# Chapter Fourteen

Spencer entered the room to see a young blond gentleman struggling to rise to his feet while being consumed by an alarming fit of laughter. He turned pained eyes to Jenny, only to find that she was similarly afflicted. In a resigned voice, he said, "I suppose I should understand why my entrance would cause such hilarity, but I confess the reason is beyond me."

Jenny gave a gasp and tried to still her laughter. "Oh, Nick. I'm sorry." Her eyes dancing with amusement, she managed to say, "Nick, allow me to present Robert Collins—Robert, the Duke of Spencer."

The two men shook hands, and Jenny gestured for them both to be seated. Feeling a need to explain Robert's presence, she told Spencer, "Robert is unofficially engaged to my stepsister."

"Indeed?" Spencer smiled easily at the younger man. "Do you plan to be married soon?"

Robert flicked a glance at Jenny and replied, "I've just

come into some property in Scotland. Meg and I may be able to set a date once I see how I stand."

Jenny smiled at the duke. "I didn't expect to see you again today, Nick."

Spencer smiled at her. "I found your whip in the park," he said, "and thought I'd bring it by."

Jenny dared not look at Robert; after her statement that she and the duke were totally uninterested in one another, to have him come calling with such a flimsy excuse was almost more than her sense of the ridiculous could stand. It was flattering, of course, but highly amusing all the same.

She got to her feet rather hastily and went to pull the bell. Turning back to the two men, who had stood when she did, she smiled at Robert and said, "I'm sure you would like to say good-bye to Meg."

The young man's eyes lit up and he grinned happily. "I certainly would."

The door opened to admit Somers, and Jenny said, "Show Mr. Collins to the Blue Saloon, Somers, and then tell Miss Meg that she has a visitor."

Robert bowed to Spencer and then shook Jenny's hand with a great deal of enthusiasm before preceding the butler from the room.

Spencer waited until Jenny sat down before seating himself and asking quizzically, "Am I never to know why my entrance provoked such laughter?"

Jenny flushed slightly. "It was nothing—really."

"*Something* amused the two of you."

"Robert was just—telling me a funny story, that was all."

Taking pity on her obvious discomfort, Spencer merely nodded and changed the subject. "I gather from Collins's air of gratitude that you are supporting the young lovers?"

"Yes. Meg's father isn't the most even-tempered of men. When he becomes angry, which is quite often, he roars like a bear. Poor Meg cannot tolerate loud voices and arguments;

I honestly believe that a marriage to Robert—even though she is very young—would be the best thing for her."

"How does your mother feel about it?"

Jenny smiled ruefully. "Mama says that Meg is too young. That's why she sent us to London—so that Meg could grow up a little."

"And possibly make a more eligible match?"

"I'm sure she hoped that would be the case. Unfortunately for Mama, Meg believes that the sun rises and sets on Robert. She isn't likely to form another attachment."

Without warning, the duke asked, "Jenny, are you quite well?"

Silently cursing his uncanny perception, Jenny said lightly, "Yes, of course I'm well. Why shouldn't I be?"

"You look pale." He frowned, then asked abruptly, "Was it Stoven?"

Caught off guard, Jenny exclaimed, "Good heavens! How did you know about him?"

Spencer smiled grimly. "He arrived in London this morning; at White's, I overheard him boasting that you were going to marry him."

Jenny's voice was wry. "I must admit he had some justification for saying that. He and my stepfather made an agreement months ago. Stoven and I were supposed to be married this summer. I, of course, was not consulted."

"The man's old enough to be your father. What was your stepfather thinking of?"

"Settlements," she replied flatly. "But I refuse to be sold to the highest bidder. Within the year I will be twenty-one and my own mistress. Sir George can go hang if he thinks that I will marry anyone while I remain beneath his guardianship."

Ignoring the unladylike aspects of this statement, the duke assumed a judicious expression and said, "What a leveler!"

Jenny looked startled. If he meant what she *thought* he meant—

In a mournful voice, he went on, "Here I was dreaming of a wedding in June and a honeymoon in the country, and now you tell me I'll have to wait a year. Really, Jenny, you could have warned me before I lost my heart."

The light note in his voice convinced Jenny that he was only flirting with her—though it didn't seem at all like him. Entering into the spirit of the discussion, she lifted an eyebrow and spoke disdainfully. "What makes you so certain I would even consider marrying you?"

He dropped his head into his hands. "I knew it! You were only playing fast and loose with my affections. Jenny—how could you?"

"Don't take on so," Jenny advised him kindly. "It isn't you personally—my husband will have to be as rich as Croesus. I have a fancy to live on the moon, you see."

"The moon?" Spencer wore a doubtful expression. "I suppose it could be arranged but—Jenny, are you quite sure? It's awfully far from town."

She gave a gasp and tried to steady her voice. "Oh, yes. It—it must be the moon. I will settle for nothing less."

He appeared to be considering the matter carefully. In a voice of doom, he finally spoke. "And I suppose you want a star or two thrown in for good measure?"

"Certainly. As a matter of fact, I have decided to have a summer home built on a nearby star. It would be so romantic," she said soulfully.

The duke sighed. "Are there any other requirements for your future husband?"

"Well—" She looked thoughtful. "Of course he would have to be a very patient man—I'm not at all easy to live with—and he would have to shower me with gifts. Diamonds and emeralds. And take me on trips all over the world."

Again, the duke appeared doubtful. "There's the war, you know," he said apologetically.

"Oh, the war won't last forever."

"Yes, but while the war is continuing, it isn't wise to do extensive traveling. Couldn't we wait a year or so?" There was a pleading note in his voice.

"Certainly not. My husband will be brave enough to—to fight his way through *anything*."

The duke sighed.

Jenny smiled encouragingly. "No need to fret. There are plenty of other women in the world."

"Not in *my* world," he responded sadly. "In my world there is only one—a golden-eyed, raven-haired beauty with an odd liking for robbery."

Jenny rose hastily to her feet and wandered aimlessly toward the fireplace. His voice had been just a shade too serious for her peace of mind. Deliberately, she changed the subject and began to talk about Lady Jersey's party.

Spencer, a cautious hunter, allowed his quarry to slip from his grasp. There would be another time—he would see to that.

The two Runners stared rather warily at the imposing portals of Lady Beddington's house on Berkeley Square. The shorter of the two men grunted and nudged his companion.

The taller man frowned. "No we can't come back another time. What's wrong with you, Sam? We got our orders. Somebody thinks that Jennifer Courtenay is the Cat, and we got to check it out."

Another grunt.

"I don't care how you feel about it. An' don't tell me again that it don't make sense, because we've been all over that. If she *is* the Cat, she's bound to have a reason—maybe the tradesmen are dunnin' her for something. All I know is we have a dooty—we got to ask her some questions."

A questioning grunt.

"I told you before, Sam—no, we ain't got no proof. 'Less she confesses, we ain't got a hope in hell of convictin' her."

A querulous grunt.

The taller man heaved an exasperated sigh. "Sam! I *told* you why we got to question her. 'Cause it's our dooty to, that's why! Now stop askin' stupid questions an' come with me."

He managed to take two steps before his agitated companion grabbed his arm and grunted insistently.

"*All right*, Sam—I'll do the talkin'. You just stand quiet-like an' you an' me might just brush through this thing with both our skins."

Resolutely, the Runners trod up the steps and applied the knocker vigorously. The door was opened by a stone-faced butler who looked at them with chilling indifference. "Yes?"

The taller man held out a rather grimy card. "We come to see Miss Jennifer Courtenay."

The butler accepted the card reluctantly and stared at it for a moment. Lifting cold eyes to the Runners, he said, "Miss Courtenay is entertaining a guest at the moment. It would be more convenient if you came back another time."

But the Runners were not to be fobbed off. "Now look here, you!" the taller one exclaimed. "You go an' tell Miss Courtenay that we've come to talk to her, and don't dilly-dally around. Step lively, now—we ain't got all day."

With offended dignity, the butler allowed the men to step inside. He closed the door behind them and told them to wait there while he went to inform Miss Courtenay.

Leaving the Runners standing uneasily in the hall, Somers went to the door of the Green Room and knocked softly.

Hearing an acknowledgment from inside, he entered to find Jenny and the duke standing before the fireplace.

Somers came forward apologetically. "I beg your pardon, Miss Jenny, but there are two—callers to see you."

Immediately recognizing the butler's way of announcing inferior persons, Jenny asked, "Who are they, Somers?"

Wordlessly, the butler held out the grimy card. Jenny stared at the card for a long moment before saying quietly, "Show them in."

Spencer waited until the butler left the room. "Jenny? Who is it?" he asked concerned.

She flipped the card into the cold fireplace, and replied in a colorless voice, "A Mr. Simmons—from Bow Street."

When Simmons and his partner entered the room, both were appalled to see the Duke of Spencer lift his quizzing glass to stare at them.

The hideously magnified eye and the unwavering stare reduced both men to a state of speechlessness. Simmons had the uncomfortable feeling that just so would the duke stare at a fly that had found its way into his soup.

Simmons was not a very brave man, and he withered noticeably under the duke's cold eye. He desperately wished he had heeded his companion's request that they come back another time. Even his superiors at Bow Street would understand his reluctance to question Miss Courtenay with the duke standing by.

His worst fears had been realized. The duke would not take kindly to having Miss Courtenay accused of being a thief. Simmons had seen the way the duke looked at her when they had been riding a few hours ago. No man would like the idea that his lady love might end her days on the gallows.

But there was no alternative but to continue. The duke showed no signs of leaving the room. In fact, he gave every impression of having just taken root—like an oak tree, strong and immovable.

Simmons's attention was drawn away from the duke when the slender young woman with strange golden eyes spoke.

"You wanted to see me, I believe?" she asked.

Simmons struggled with himself and finally found his tongue. It had already occurred to him many times that this young lady simply did not look the part of a thief. Nor did she act like one. She seemed remarkably calm for someone who was receiving a visit from two Runners. But Simmons was grimly determined to do his duty. "Yes, ma'am." He glanced rather nervously at the duke. "I think maybe—if you don't mind—that we should talk alone."

The duke dropped his quizzing glass. "Miss Courtenay may not mind, officer, but I assure you that I do."

Desperately, the Runner said, "It would be better, Your Grace, if we—"

"Better for whom, officer? For Miss Courtenay or for yourselves?"

Making a last effort, Simmons said, "Really, Your Grace, we need to talk to her, and she'd maybe like it better if it was just between us."

"It will be between us, officer—the four of us."

Simmons looking pleadingly at the lady. "Miss Courtenay?"

She smiled calmly. "The four of us."

Goaded beyond endurance, Simmons snapped, "Very well—Miss Courtenay, we would like to ask you a few questions. We have reason to believe that you are the Cat."

# Chapter Fifteen

Spencer's voice was cold. "How dare you intrude into a private home, hurling accusations at innocent young women."

The two Runners shifted uneasily. Simmons, his ruddy face deepening in color, spoke hoarsely. "No offense meant, Your Grace, but the young lady here fits the description of the Cat."

"And what is that?"

Simmons cleared his throat and began to recite as if by rote. "A small, slender woman with black hair and golden eyes—strange golden eyes."

From the corner of his eye, Spencer saw Jenny stiffen, but she remained silent. "That isn't much to go on, Simmons."

"Happen it's not, Your Grace, but I'm sure the young lady wouldn't mind answerin' a few questions."

Before Spencer could respond, Jenny spoke coolly. "Of course not, officer. I have nothing to hide."

Simmons nodded and pulled a small black notebook from inside his coat. Muttering to himself, he flipped through the pages until he found what he was looking for. Directing a piercing look at Jenny's calm face, he asked, "Can you handle a gun, miss?"

Jenny smiled faintly, her wild golden eyes unreadable. "As a matter of fact, officer, I can. My father taught me when I was a child."

"Are you a good horsewoman?"

She lifted an eyebrow in faint surprise. "Of course."

"Now, miss," Simmons turned the page of his notebook and shot another penetrating look at her, "do you own a black stallion?"

She folded her arms and continued to smile. "I feel sure that—as conscientious as you are—you have already searched the stables. Tell me, did you find a black stallion?"

The Runner's eyes grew cold; he disliked the feeling that the young lady was toying with him. "No, ma'am, we found no stallion."

"Then I suggest, officer, that I do not own one."

He continued to stare coldly into her wild eyes. "Tell me, miss," he said deliberately, "why is it that you often ride out late at night—alone and dressed like a man?"

Jenny's face remained expressionless. "I have trouble sleeping," she replied softly. "And as for my attire—if you were a woman, officer, you would know the answer to that. Breeches are far more comfortable than petticoats."

"This has gone far enough," Spencer said coldly. "You have only speculation on which to base your accusations. You have no proof—nothing that would stand up in court. And let me remind you, gentlemen, that even if you caught the Cat red-handed, you would be hard-put to raise support against her. The Cat has won the respect and admiration of many influential people. She has also assisted the War Office in its fight against traitors."

The Runner's voice was every bit as cold as the duke's. "Happen that's so, Your Grace—but even a heroine would hang for murder."

Spencer stiffened, his eyes locked with the Runner's. "Have a care what you say, officer," he said gently. "This lady has promised to become my wife." He heard Jenny catch her breath in surprise, but continued to stare at the Runner.

After a long moment, Simmons angrily stuffed his notebook back into his pocket. He was well aware of Spencer's influence at Bow Street. He crammed his hat on his head and said coldly, "I'll be watching." A moment later, the Runners were gone.

Jenny went silently to the window and watched the two men stride away. She turned to face the duke, a faint frown on her face. "Black hair," she murmured.

Spencer, who had been expecting a different comment, looked startled. "I beg your pardon?"

"He said that the Cat had black hair."

"You do."

"Yes," she said impatiently, "but how did he know that? The Cat wears a black hood and mask—her hair is never seen."

"Perhaps someone mistook the hood for your hair."

Jenny began to pace restlessly. "No, no, I don't think so. Someone informed against me—someone who has a strong suspicion that I am the Cat."

"Or someone who knows," Spencer responded slowly.

Jenny stopped pacing to stare at the duke. "Only four people know who the Cat really is. Three of them I would trust with my life."

"And the fourth?"

"The fourth is you."

"You still don't trust me." He shook his head slowly. "Why, Jenny? Why don't you trust me?"

She turned her back abruptly, staring into the fireplace. "I don't know you. Why should I put my life in the hands of a stranger?"

"But I am not a stranger. Didn't you hear what I said to the Runner?"

"Of course I heard. I am much obliged to you for what you said. It frightened them away—at least for the moment."

Spencer wanted nothing more than to take her into his arms and tell her how much he loved her. But he knew that, for the moment at least, he must force himself to be patient. He must proceed carefully or she would withdraw from him as an animal retreats to its shell. Casually he said, "I meant it, you know. I *do* want you to be my wife."

"You don't know what you're saying."

"That is a very unflattering response to a proposal of marriage," he said lightly.

"*Will* you be serious," she snapped, her nerves on edge.

"I am serious, Jenny," he said gently. "The first time we met, I fell in love with a pair of wild, restless eyes. I didn't even know who you were—but I knew that I loved you. Now I do know who you are—and I love you even more."

"Stop it!" she cried, turning suddenly to face him. She was as pale as death, her eyes even wilder than before. "You *can't* love me. I'm a thief. I've spent the past year of my life riding all over the country dressed like a man and shooting at people. I can outride, outshoot, and outthink most men. Is that who you want for your duchess? Is that who you want to take home to your family?"

He stepped forward, one hand outstretched. "I want *you*, Jenny. Your past isn't important except that it shaped you into the woman you are today. I've fallen in love with that woman. I love your courage, your spirit; I love your intelligence and your ability to remain cool and calm in the face of incredible danger."

"You heard what the Runner said. He said I could hang for murder. Do you want to spend the rest of your life with a murderess? Do you want to be forced to flee the country because of me?"

"Jenny." His face was tense, his voice strained. "Foolish girl. My happiness doesn't rest on this miserable little island. It rests on a stubborn, determined chit of a girl with the beauty of a queen and the courage of a Viking."

The wild eyes went grave suddenly. "I—I can't. I'm not fit to be any man's wife. Least of all—least of all yours."

He stepped closer, his gray eyes gentle. "If it's only that you don't love me—I can teach you. I *can*, Jenny."

She managed a faint smile. "I don't think I'm capable of love—not any longer. Too much has happened."

He came to stand before her. "Perhaps you have forgotten, but I have not. There was a night, weeks ago, when I held a woman in my arms—a warm, responsive woman. That woman was capable of love. Have you changed so much in a few short weeks?"

She turned her back to him, afraid of what he might see in her face. "That night was a mistake. It should never have happened."

"But it *did* happen."

"It—it was only lust."

Spencer's face went grim suddenly. "There is one way to find out."

Jenny turned in time to see the purpose in his expression as he reached for her. Another face rose in her imagination, and she flinched away from him, panic in her face.

He froze, and a spark of pure rage in his eyes. "It was Stoven, wasn't it? He put this fear into you."

"I—you just startled me."

"Did he hurt you, Jenny?"

Jenny fought down panic as he gently put his hands

on her shoulders. Breathlessly, she replied, "No. He didn't hurt me."

Slowly, the duke drew her into his arms, resting his cheek against her hair. "I love you, Jenny. I would never do anything to hurt you."

For a long moment, she remained stiff. Then, slowly, the rigidity flowed from her body and her arms slipped shyly around his waist. "Oh, Nick." Her voice was husky. "I don't want to love you—please don't make me love you."

Spencer held her tightly. "You can't fight love, kitten."

She raised tear-bright eyes to his. "My father always called me that—kitten."

"Because you're so like a kitten." He smiled. "Biting and scratching one moment, purring the next."

Slowly he lowered his head until his lips found hers. The kiss, gentle at first, deepened as he felt her response.

Passion flared in both of them, racing through their bodies like molten fire. Jenny felt no fear in Spencer's arms, only the need to be closer, to be part of him. His lips left hers to blaze a trail down her neck, lingering in the hollow of her shoulder. She caught her breath as his hand found the softness of her breast, which seemed to swell at his touch. His lips returned to hers, and she felt shattered as the kiss deepened beyond anything she had ever imagined. If he had not been holding her tightly, she would have collapsed in a heap at his feet.

But a moment later, he abruptly pulled away and turned his back to her. She swayed slightly, and watched him with eyes still dazed with passion.

Slowly, he turned to her, his face pale. "Jenny," he said hoarsely, "I love you—and I need you. I want you to be my wife."

Jenny tried to calm her racing heart. "The—the problems—" she faltered.

"The problems can be resolved."

She stared at him, her mind filled with the vision of him always by her side. For the first time, she admitted to herself that she loved him. She hadn't meant to fall in love with him, but she had. Suddenly, she was tired of fighting against it.

He took her hand and raised it to his lips, looking anxiously at her still face. "Jenny?"

Slowly, her lovely smile appeared. Her eyes were soft, bemused. "I love you," she whispered. "And I want to marry you with all my heart."

He hugged her fiercely. "Thank God," he said unsteadily. "I'll speak to your stepfather, and we can be married as soon as possible." He smiled down at her. "The Cat will disappear, and everyone will think she has fled the country."

Jenny abruptly pulled away from him, and his smile faded as he saw the torment in her face. "Jenny? What is it?"

"Nick, I—I can't stop yet. It isn't finished."

A frown drew his brows together. "What do you mean? Of course you'll stop. The Cat must disappear, Jenny— there's no other way."

"But not yet."

"Jenny, you don't seem to understand—you'll be my wife. You won't have time to ride all over the country." Ignoring the gathering storm on her face, he added, "I won't allow it. The danger is too great. Jenny, you've done enough; I don't want my wife to end up on the gallows."

"Stop it." Her voice shook with rage. "Nick, will you listen to yourself? Do you hear what you're saying? You're condemning to death everything in me that you professed to love not ten minutes ago. You can't change what I am—I won't let you. The Cat will not disappear, because her job isn't finished—not yet."

He stared at her grimly, the tenderness of moments ago forgotten. "I won't allow it."

Suddenly, her face went deathly pale. "You don't have any say in the matter, Nick," she said quietly.

"I do. You'll be my wife—"

"No. I will not be your wife. If you cannot accept me as I am, there will be no marriage."

"Jenny, for God's sake—"

"I mean it, Nick."

He saw the determination on her face, and realized that she could not be swayed. "So be it, then." A moment later, he was gone, the door closing behind him with a thundering crash.

Jenny stood stiffly, her eyes fixed on the door, but he did not return. She was still there, unmoving, when Meg came in a few moments later.

"Jenny? I saw the duke ride away; his face was so angry! What happened? Jenny?" Meg suddenly fell silent as she looked intently at her stepsister's face. It was the face of a stranger—pale and still. Her normally wild golden eyes were utterly without life.

When she spoke, her voice was as dead as her eyes. "Why, Meg? Why can't life be as simple as one of your fairy stories? Why must it be so complicated?"

"Jenny?"

"What have I done, Meg? Dear God—what have I done?"

Meg flew to embrace her, sensing a loss she didn't understand. "It's all right, Jenny. Everything will be all right."

Feeling an overpowering need to be alone, Jenny gently disentangled herself from Meg's arms and said in a low voice, "I need to be alone for a while, my dear. I need to think."

She produced a rather twisted smile for Meg, then slowly left the room, heading for the library. That would be a good place to sort out her thoughts.

# Chapter Sixteen

Jenny sat alone in the silent library and wondered wearily how much longer she could go on. For the first time in her life she felt totally alone. As a child, she had felt that her father was near and that he stood, silently supportive, at his daughter's side. That comforting presence had been gone for many years now.

Now Jenny was frightened. Since her father's death, she had scorned the idea that she would ever need to depend on someone other than herself, but now she felt a desperate need to share her burdens.

She was tired of playing games with her life. She was tired of distrusting everyone she met, of guarding her every word and gesture. She was tired of pointing guns at people, and breaking laws she had been raised to obey. But most of all, she was tired of being alone.

And she had just rejected the man she loved. Why had she not told him the truth? Why had she not confided in him? She could find no answer within herself. Pride, perhaps, had prevented her. Or perhaps simply a stubborn desire to be accepted and understood without the need to explain her motives.

Whatever her reasons, she had effectively shut the duke out of her life. He would not chance another rejection.

Jenny sighed and dropped her head into her hands. Her question to Meg had come straight from her heart. Why *did* life have to be so complicated? If this were a fairy story, she could be certain of a happy ending, no matter how painful the interval might become. But this was reality, and reality did not supply happiness on a silver platter. Reality required that happiness be earned.

Which happiness was she to earn? The happiness of avenging her father's murder? Or the happiness of loving the man of her dreams and being loved by him? Which did she most desire?

Jenny felt a leaden sensation somewhere deep within her. The choice had been made long ago. She could do no less than honor that choice. She would avenge her father's murder—or die.

Having made her decision, Jenny felt at peace. She would finish what she had begun.

She became aware of a presence in the room. Looking up, she saw that Somers waited for her to acknowledge him. "Yes, Somers?"

"Sir George Ross to see you, Miss Jenny." The butler's face was expressionless. "In the Blue Room."

Jenny's limbs, which had been weakened by fear and loneliness a short time before, now stiffened with determination. She nodded. "Thank you, Somers."

The young lady who faced Sir George a few moments later was as calm and collected as he had ever seen her. "Sir George. How good of you to pay us a visit." Her voice was touched with irony.

Sir George bowed mockingly, appearing for once none

the worse for drink. "You are in excellent looks today, my dear stepdaughter. I sincerely hope that no ill fortune has befallen you since last I saw you. You have not, for instance, received disturbing news from Bow Street, I hope?"

Jenny stiffened slightly, her golden eyes darkening as she considered her stepfather's triumphant expression. Softly, she said, "Yes, of course. It would have to be you. You informed against me."

He bowed again, a bland smile on his face. "I did. May I dare hope that you have been exposed for what you are? Does the hangman know your name, my dear Jenny?" His voice was full of satisfied certainty.

Jenny smiled very gently and moved a step closer to him. "I am afraid not," she replied.

His smile faded. "What do you mean? What are you talking about?" he asked hoarsely.

"The Runners did come. However, I answered all their questions satisfactorily, in addition to which I was also vouched for by a very influential man."

"Who? Who was the man?" The hoarseness had not left his voice.

Nor had the smile left Jenny's face. "The Duke of Spencer. He was here when the Runners came and defended me quite admirably."

Violent rage flashed in Sir George's small eyes. "Spencer? Perhaps His Grace would like to know just how true the accusation is." His smile was not pleasant. "I've heard the rumors, Jenny. The talk of London is that His Grace seems quite taken with you. I wonder if his feelings would change if he were told the truth."

Jenny wandered to the settee and sank down gracefully. Her voice was casually unconcerned when she replied, "You may tell him what you choose. I assure you the duke knows all there is to know about me." She forgave herself the lie.

Sir George frowned. "He knows you're the Cat? I find that hard to believe."

Jenny lifted one eyebrow, a faintly puzzled look on her face. "The Cat? I'm sure I haven't the vaguest idea what you mean."

He smiled tightly. "I didn't expect you to admit it, Jenny. Nevertheless, we both know the truth. I've known for months. You think I didn't see you sneaking out of your bedroom window late at night?"

"I have always preferred to ride at night. Ask my mother."

"And the horse? Have you always hidden him?" Sir George asked sarcastically.

"Only since my mother married you," she replied calmly. "The horse is valuable, and I had no desire to see you sell him."

Sir George flushed angrily. "A pretty opinion you have of me," he said shortly.

Jenny looked at him steadily. "Any man who would to go Bow Street and accuse his own stepdaughter of being a notorious thief couldn't be considered a gentleman, now could he?"

"Only if the accusation were untrue. But it isn't, is it, Jenny?"

She had no intention of helping him put a noose round her neck. "Don't be ridiculous. What possible reason would I have for becoming a thief?"

He folded his arms and stared at her grimly. "That has me baffled. You certainly don't need the money, so it must be the excitement."

She sighed wearily. "This isn't getting us anywhere, Sir George. I have all the excitement I can handle at the moment."

"Trying to catch a duke?" he asked nastily.

Jenny stared at him for a moment before saying deliberately, "That's right. If you want to dispose of me, you're going about it the wrong way. Leave me alone for the Season in London, and I can safely promise you won't be bothered by me again."

She watched her stepfather's changing expression with satisfaction. Visions of marriage settlements seemed to dance in his eyes. He fully intended to make some man pay through the nose to become Jenny's husband and, for once, she was grateful for his greed.

Slowly, he said, "So you mean to marry Spencer. You didn't want to be a countess, you wanted to be a duchess. That's why you rejected Stoven." He stared at her.

"Something like that." Jenny wasn't in the least disturbed that her stepfather thought her mercenary. Carefully playing her role, she went on irritably, "You nearly ruined my chances by sending the Runners here. If you don't want to endanger them further, you'll go back to Kent and let me handle my own affairs."

Sir George nodded. Having a mercenary mind himself, he was easily convinced of calculating motives in others. "I'll expect a visit from Spencer before the end of the Season, Jenny."

She rang for a servant to show him out, without responding to his statement. She knew in her heart that her stepfather would not receive a visit from the duke, but she had to keep Sir George away for at least the remainder of the Season. By that time, she hoped to have found her father's murderer. If not—she would deal with that when the time came.

Jenny watched as the butler showed Sir George out, then wearily climbed the stairs to her room. She was drained, exhausted from the strain of confronting her stepfather, and the tensions from what seemed like the longest day of her life. And the day was far from over. There was still Lady Jersey's party to be gotten through. Spencer would be there.

Jenny lay silently on her bed and fought a cowardly impulse to crawl beneath the covers and never come out again. One part of her wanted to see Spencer and resolve the misunderstanding between them. Another part realized that what had happened between them was far more serious than a simple disagreement.

In any case, she reminded herself, she had made her decision regarding Spencer. The search for her father's murderer would continue.

The burden for that search would rest on her shoulders alone—as it always had. That burden, carried for so long, was becoming unbearably heavy.

Jenny shook the thought away. She would go on; it was impossible to go back.

Jenny swung herself from the bed as her maid entered the room. Hours of reflection had done much to ease her troubled mind and stiffen her resolve.

She would attend Lady Jersey's party and no one—no one!—would suspect the ache in her heart. The Dark Incomparable would treat the *ton* to an evening they would not soon forget.

With an oddly feline smile, Jenny said to her maid, "The black evening gown, Mary, and the yellow diamonds."

The maid's face was shocked. "The *black* gown, miss?" Black was for mourning—or matrons.

Coolly, Jenny replied, "The black gown."

Mary slowly went to her mistress's wardrobe, wondering if Miss Jenny were losing her mind. It was against social dictates for a young, unmarried woman to wear black unless she was in mourning, although the black gown would have been totally unsuitable for such a somber time. Made of French silk, it was one breath away from being indecent.

An hour later, Jenny stood before the full-length mirror

in her room and stared at her reflection. The black gown was every bit as wicked as she had remembered. She turned, twitching away the graceful folds of the half-train, and stared at the side view the mirror presented. The gown lent her a grace and dignity she had not known she possessed.

The yellow diamonds caught the light as she turned, glowing against her white skin with a brilliance only surpassed by the radiance of her golden eyes.

Jenny smiled and slowly drew on the long black gloves. She was perfectly aware of the danger of appearing in such a gown, but she also knew that if anyone could carry it off, she could. There was no vanity in the thought; the hypocritical opinions of London society could always be influenced to pardon an outrageous heiress.

Outrageous heiress. If they only knew, she thought, if they only knew!

Lady Beddington twittered nervously all the way to Lady Jersey's. She had tried vainly to convince Jenny not to wear the black gown, but the determined glint in her young friend's eyes had defeated her. Now she envisioned terrible social ruin for them both, and wondered desperately what Lady Ross would have to say when her daughter was sent home in disgrace.

But Lady Beddington's fears proved groundless. Lady Jersey greeted them at the door, saying, "Why, Miss Courtenay, you look delightfully wicked! If only I had the coloring to wear black!" Her acceptance set the tone for the entire evening.

Jenny found herself besieged with admirers, and even the staid matrons with daughters of marriageable age were considered merely resentful when they remarked acidly that Miss Courtenay was obviously fast.

The official seal of approval was bestowed on Jenny when Mr. Brummell bowed low before her and requested a dance. The acid-tongued matrons subsided noticeably after that.

Brummell, performing the steps of the waltz with faultless grace, smiled down at Jenny. "Miss Courtenay, you are absolutely bewitching tonight. If I were not so averse to matrimony, I would be languishing at your feet."

Jenny laughed softly, not in the least deceived by his flattery. "You are too kind, sir. But it does seem a shame that I cannot ensnare you—it would be the coup of the Season."

The Beau's gray eyes were amused. "Ah, but to ensnare a duke is quite enough of a coup." He immediately regretted his statement, for the lady's beautiful golden eyes dulled, and her smile disappeared.

She recovered almost immediately, however, and with a note of forced gaiety in her voice, said lightly, "Once ensnared does not mean forever, sir."

"I see." Brummell was given credit for a great deal of perception by the members of the *ton*, and Jenny would have been considerably dismayed if she had known exactly how much the Beau did see. "Is there anything I can do to help?"

With a bright smile, Jenny replied quickly, "No—but thank you."

Quietly, Brummell said, "It seems a shame. Perhaps you are mistaken; lovers often quarrel, or so the poets say."

Jenny managed a shaky laugh. "The poets say a great many things that are not strictly true. In any case, it doesn't matter now. It's over."

"Is it?" Brummell smiled faintly. "Then why is Spencer standing in the doorway staring at you like a mooncalf?"

# Chapter Seventeen

Hours earlier, in the library of his town house, Spencer had paced restlessly back and forth. His anger had died, and with its death had come the realization that he had made a terrible mistake. He should have known better than to try and make Jenny's decisions for her. She was a strong-minded woman; she could be led, perhaps, but never driven.

The troubled duke sank down in a wing-backed chair by the fireplace and wondered wryly if it were true that God watched over little children and fools, never doubting for a moment what his proper category was. If so, perhaps he still had a chance with Jenny.

He found himself wondering, as he had wondered so often during the past weeks, what it was about Jenny that had tumbled him so abruptly into love. He knew, of course, that it was his duty to find himself a wife and set up his nursery. In fact, he had a strong desire to see his son step into his shoes one day—rather than the distant cousin who would presently inherit if he were to suffer an untimely demise.

But that had always seemed a remote and unlikely possibility. He had plenty of time. For the past ten years, he had sat back and watched beautiful young women make their curtsies to polite society. None had roused even the slightest bit of interest in him.

And then, on a moonlit night, he had gazed up at a pair of wild eyes glittering through a black mask, and felt as if someone had snatched the ground from beneath his feet. Those strange eyes had slipped in under his guard—and he was well and truly caught at last.

How ironic. The most eligible bachelor in England, the Duke of Spencer, had fallen helplessly, mindlessly in love with a nameless, faceless thief.

And then he had discovered that his love had a face, that she was everything he had ever desired in a woman, with a name as old and dignified as his own.

Not that it really mattered. He had not fallen in love with her name or her face. He had fallen in love with the spirit he had seen shining in her golden eyes. And he had just done his best to destroy that spirit.

Spencer leaned his head back against the chair and closed his eyes with a weary sigh. And so the man who was renowned throughout England for his savoir faire had made a thorough botch of his love affairs.

The room darkened until the only light came from the dying fire, and still the duke brooded silently. Some time later, he was disturbed by a soft cough from the doorway. He turned his head to see his valet, Cranston. "Yes, what is it?"

The valet's voice was as colorless as usual. "I beg pardon, Your Grace, but if you mean to attend Lady Jersey's ball, it is past time to dress."

"The ball?" Spencer's forehead creased with a slight

frown, and then abruptly smoothed. Of course. Jenny would be there.

Spencer considerably surprised his valet by dressing far more quickly than usual, and by berating Cranston impatiently for his slowness. The valet bore all this with remarkable patience; he had seen the signs weeks before. The duke was in love.


Spencer stood in the doorway of Lady Jersey's ballroom and scanned the crowded room intently. Had she come? And if she had come, would she even talk to him?

He was totally unaware of the interested and amused glances he was receiving, being unconscious of the eager light in his eyes.

At last he saw her. She was dancing with Brummell, and was utterly bewitching in her clinging black dress. Spencer caught his breath as the yellow diamonds at her throat blazed from the light of the chandelier.

Oblivious of the determined look on his own face, the duke began to make his way toward Jenny and her partner. He would not, by God, be fobbed off with some paltry excuse. One way or another, he meant to have a few words with his wayward love.

Jenny stared up at the Beau. "You—you mean he's here?"

The music stopped just then, and Brummell smiled down at Jenny. "He is indeed. As a matter of fact, he is headed this way—with a very determined look on his face. I believe he intends to ask you to dance."

Before Jenny could voice the protest rising in her throat, Spencer was bowing low before her. "Jenny, may I have this dance?"

Jenny stared at the man she loved for a moment before silently going into his arms for a waltz. She had intended to refuse, but the pleading look in his eyes had defeated her. Surely every woman had a right to dance one last time with the man she loved.

She fixed her eyes on the diamond pin in his cravat, refusing to look up even when he murmured her name.

"Jenny . . . ? Will you at least give me a chance to apologize?"

"It isn't important." Her response was barely above a whisper.

His hand tightened convulsively around hers. "How can you say that, Jenny? I love you—I want to marry you."

"You want a woman fit to be a duchess. A woman you can respect. Not I." Her voice was very sure.

Spencer cast an impatient look around at the other couples and fought to keep his voice low. "I respect *you*. Jenny, I didn't mean all those things I said."

"You meant them," she responded quietly. "Your wife must be above reproach. And a thief could hardly be considered above reproach, Your Grace."

The cool formality in her voice chilled him. He abruptly stopped dancing and with his hand firmly on her elbow, guided her forcefully into the hall. "Damn it," he muttered, "you *will* listen to me." He pulled her into an empty room off the hall, and swung around to meet her enraged eyes.

The ever-cool, ever-calm duke once again forgot common sense in the heat of the moment. Angrily, he said, "Jenny, don't be a fool. I want you to be my wife—the mother of my children! I don't give a damn if the world calls you a thief."

Outraged, Jenny shot back, "The world doesn't *know* I'm a thief. Unless you mean to shout it from the rooftops."

"I don't mean to shout it from the rooftops. For God's sake, will you stop twisting everything I say? I only meant that I don't care about the opinions of others."

Both were too engrossed in their argument to see

Brummell, a decided gleam in his eyes, silently close the door to prevent their raised voices from reaching the ballroom.

"Then you're a fool. You have to live in this world—or perhaps you think that dukes are above having to consider what others think of them."

"Stop throwing my title in my face."

"Stop hiding behind your title."

"Damn it, I'm not hiding behind anything."

"And stop swearing at me."

Unaware of the childish turn the argument had taken, the two continued to avoid the real issue.

"I'll swear at whomever I damn well please."

"You won't swear at me." Jenny angrily flounced from the room, leaving Spencer muttering to himself.

A moment later, Brummell entered and closed the door behind him. "You know," he remarked in a meditative voice, "if you two keep going the way you're going, you'll never patch things up."

Wearily, Spencer said, "You don't know the whole story, George."

The Beau folded his arms and regarded his old friend with considerable amusement. "You mean I don't know that the beautiful Miss Courtenay is none other than the notorious thief for whom the Runners have been searching high and low during the past year?"

Spencer was obviously startled. "How did you know that?"

"If I had not closed this door a few minutes ago, the whole of London would now know." He smiled. "I have not been so entertained in years!"

Rather grimly, the duke said, "I hope you don't mean to make mischief, George."

Brummell waved away the suggestion. "Of course not.

No need to fear, my friend. I have no intention of addling the eggs."

Spencer nodded. "Good. The gallows is not exactly a fitting place for a lady."

Very gently, the Beau remarked, "But a fitting place for a thief, wouldn't you say?"

Angrily, Spencer turned on his old friend. "She isn't a common thief. For God's sake, George—you've spoken to her—danced with her. You know she's a lady. She has a reason—she *must* have a reason—for what she does."

"Exactly." Brummell removed an enameled snuffbox from his pocket, flicked it open, and took a delicate pinch. "And what is her reason?"

His anger draining away, Spencer shook his head wearily. "I don't know. She hasn't told me."

"Have you asked?"

"Not—recently," the duke murmured.

"Perhaps you should."

Spencer stared at the Beau for a long moment. "Yes. Yes, perhaps I should." He smiled suddenly, his lips twisting wryly. "If I can get anywhere near her after tonight."

"That might indeed prove to be a trifle difficult. You were not very wise just now, my friend." The gentle reproof had the desired result; Spencer immediately assumed a very determined expression.

"Then I shall do better next time, George. I mean to marry Miss Jennifer Courtenay and I will not allow anyone—including her—to stand in my way."

Brummell watched him stride from the room. After a moment of thoughtful silence, he tapped the lid of his snuffbox with one slender finger and murmured to the empty room, "'Ware rabbit holes!"

The expression was a common one among huntsmen and the duke, had he been privileged to hear it, would have understood immediately that the Beau was conveying a gentle warning to watch for dangerous pitfalls directly in his path.

Spencer's determination to clear matters between himself and Jenny was not met with encouragement from that wayward lady. In fact, she avoided him quite successfully.

At social events, she was invariably surrounded by eager and amorous young gentlemen, who, heartened by Miss Courtenay's falling-out with Spencer, were anxious to capture her affections. They danced with her, rode with her, paid her lavish compliments and, however unaware they may have been of the fact, shielded her from Spencer's determined presence.

As the days passed, the duke grew more and more desperate. The nightly vista of his love in the company of other men was driving him to distraction, and added to that was fear for her safety; the Cat had held up at least three coaches in the past fortnight.

The letters he sent her were returned unopened, and whenever he called at Lady Beddington's, Miss Courtenay was "not at home." Worried over his inability to speak to Jenny and uneasy about the Cat's continued escapades, Spencer finally decided on a drastic means of gaining her attention.

And so it was that Spencer rode out of London early one cool spring morning. His destination was the hollow tree where Jenny had told him to leave messages. It was, he knew, a long shot; since he was aware of her identity, Jenny could very well assume that there was no further need to send messages in such a fashion. But the duke had a strong suspicion that her highwayman friend (she could hardly have allowed him to know who she was) also made use of the hollow tree. If that were indeed the case, perhaps it was not such a long shot after all.

In any event, he had run out of alternatives. His stubborn love obviously had no intention of allowing him to right himself in her eyes, and he was every bit as determined to do so—even if he had to deceive her in the attempt.

Spencer made his way to the hollow tree and dismounted. He stood for a moment, holding the note in his hand and weighing the consequences of what he was about to do. Then, with a smothered oath, he thrust the note into its hiding place. Mounting his horse, he rode back toward London before he could change his mind.

Jenny lifted a hand in farewell to John and watched as he rode off toward Maidenstone. When he had disappeared into the darkness, she turned her weary horse toward London. The mare had been able to rest while Jenny rode Bandit, but the journey from London earlier in the night had exhausted both her and the horse.

Aware of the mare's weariness, Jenny reluctantly allowed her to set her own pace—a slow trot. With a fresh horse, it was a good three-hour ride to town, with an exhausted horse, Jenny resigned herself to the knowledge that she would not reach town before dawn.

Grimly, she also admitted that she could not continue her nocturnal rides while living in London. Leaving town at dusk and returning at dawn was simply too risky.

There was also the matter of the Runners. Simmons and his apparently mute partner had been watching Lady Beddington's house every night, and Jenny was sensible enough to realize that she could not continue to come and go beneath their very noses. Sooner or later she would be caught returning from a ride, and that would be the end of her masquerade.

Automatically, her thoughts turned to Spencer. She had not seen him for almost two weeks, except in passing during her afternoon rides in the park and the parties they both attended. He had stopped trying to talk to her or dance with her; he had stopped calling at Lady Beddington's. Apparently he had decided to respect her wish that their relationship be ended.

The thought gave Jenny no satisfaction. If he had loved her as deeply as he had professed, would he have given up so easily? Of course not! So—he obviously did not love her very much. This conclusion brought another sharp pain to Jenny's heart.

In an effort to wipe away the thoughts that made her so unhappy, she made up her mind to forget about the duke, and concentrated instead on the question of whether or not Jason had had any luck in tracking down the traitor.

Jenny frowned slightly. If Jason *had* found out something, he might have left a message for her. He didn't often do so, preferring instead to have John send for her while he waited at the inn. But there was always a chance . . .

Nearly an hour later Jenny stopped her mare beside the hollow tree and dismounted. She reached inside the tree and brought forth a note. It was difficult to read in the faint light cast by a quarter moon, but she managed to make out the words. "I have found that which you seek. Spencer."

For a long time, Jenny stood in the moonlight, her mind in a whirl. Then, thrusting the note into the pocket of her cloak, she quickly mounted her horse and urged the tired animal toward London. As she rode, she planned her next move.

Her mind balked at the thought of asking Spencer to come to Lady Beddington's, and she could not go to visit him—God help her if *that* should get out! But the Cat, of course . . .

# Chapter Eighteen

Spencer paced restlessly around the library, casting an occasional worried glance at the open window. Why didn't she come? It had been nearly two weeks since he had left the message within the hollow tree.

Unbidden, the thought came that perhaps she was unable to come. Visions of her lying cold and dead on some deserted back road whirled about in his head, and he felt a chill trace its way down his spine. No. No, she was alive. He knew it. He *felt* it.

He pushed the fear from his mind. She was alive. Why, then, didn't she come? And when she *did* come, how would he explain his message?

He halted by the fireplace. *How indeed.* He was under no illusions as to the strength of her temper; she had warned him once against betraying her. She would be furious that he had lied to her.

He turned to the window and felt relief wash over him as

he saw her. She was standing silently inside the room, her face pale beneath the mask, her eyes cold. "Where is it?"

He stepped toward her and then halted as she stiffened. "Jenny, I must talk to you."

She ripped off the hooded mask. "Where is the talisman ring?"

He watched her carefully. "Whose ring is it, Jenny?"

The glitter in her eyes increased. "My father's, damn you. Where is it?"

Very quietly, he replied, "I do not know, Jenny."

She flinched as though he had struck her. "You lied to me." Her voice shook with rage. "You—you *bastard*. You left that message *knowing* I would come."

"Jenny, I had no choice. You wouldn't see me or talk to me. I couldn't just let you walk out of my life."

"If I remember correctly, it was you who walked out—not I."

"After you threw my proposal back in my face, what was I supposed to do?"

"You should never have made the proposal in the first place."

"Jenny, I *love* you. I wanted—want—you to be my wife." He started toward her, intent on taking her into his arms and showing her how much he needed her. She quickly eluded him, and suddenly he found himself staring down the barrel of her pistol.

There was a tense silence. Coldly, she said, "You swayed me once with your kisses—not again."

"I'm sorry." His voice was quiet. "That wasn't well done of me, was it?"

"No," she replied. "But then, I never expected you to play fair. You lied—so why not cheat as well?"

"I'm sorry," he repeated. "A desperate man will do almost anything—even lie and cheat—when he feels that the woman he loves is slipping away from him. I *do* love you, Jenny. I want to help you find your father's talisman ring."

"I don't *need* your help."

"You do, Jenny. For once in your life, why won't you admit that you need someone."

"I don't. I can take care of myself." She glared at him. "You don't know anything about it."

"No, I don't know anything about it—but I'd like to. I can help you, Jenny. And, no matter how much you deny it, you *do* need help. Let me help you—I love you."

"People in love don't try to change the person they love."

"I know that—now." His voice was so low she had to strain to hear it. "I wish I had cut my tongue out before I said what I did. You were right—I was wrong when I tried to make such an important decision for you." He smiled faintly, his eyes resting on her still face. "I won't try to do that again, Jenny. It's *your* decision—but I'd like to help you."

Jenny stared at him, some of the wildness leaving her eyes. "How do I know you're not lying?"

"I only lied to get you to come here. I promise that I'll never lie to you again." He took a step toward her.

Her fingers tightened on the pistol. "Don't come any closer. I mean it, Nick—I'll shoot if I have to."

He smiled gently. "Then I guess you'll just have to shoot me, because I intend to come much closer." He slowly reached out to take the pistol from her hand.

"Damn you," she whispered. "Why did I have to hold up your coach? Why did I have to fall in love with you?" A moment later, she was in his arms.

He held her tightly. "Oh, Jenny—I've missed you." Drawing back slightly, he smiled down at her. "As soon as this is over, you *will* marry me. I won't take no for an answer."

It was characteristic of Jenny that, having once

surrendered, she did so totally. Smiling up at him mistily, she said, "You won't *get* no for an answer. I would like very much to marry you."

"I was afraid I had destroyed forever what you felt for me. I never meant it to be so, Jenny. I only wanted to keep you from danger. I couldn't bear it if anything happened to you."

She looked grave. "Nick, I know that what I do is dangerous, but it's necessary."

"Why, Jenny? Why is your father's talisman ring so important?"

She slipped from his arms and moved across the room to stand before the fireplace. For a long moment, she stood silent, the flickering firelight outlining the contours of her slender body. "The ring is important because the man who holds it in his possession is the man who murdered my father." Her voice was low and haunted.

"I was told that your father committed suicide."

"That was the ruling of the Court of Inquiry. He was found in his study, shot through the temple—his pistol in his hand."

"Jenny," he hesitated, "how do you know that he *didn't* kill himself?"

"Because," she replied quietly, her voice filled with pain, "I was there. I saw a man kill my father, and then I saw him remove my father's ring and place it on his finger. It was very late—everyone was in bed. I had had a nightmare and left my bed to find Papa." She smiled sadly. "I always went to Papa when I was afraid." Her smile faded. "I saw the light beneath the study door and I opened it very quietly. My father had his back to the door. He was standing by the fire, the way he always did when he had something on his mind."

"Did you see the killer's face?"

"No. Just as I started to go inside, I saw a man creep up

behind Papa with a pistol in his hand. Before I could call out, the pistol went off, and Papa fell. The man knelt on the floor and put the gun in Papa's hand, and then he took the ring."

Gently, Spencer asked, "What happened?"

Her voice was weary. "He opened the window, climbed outside, and then closed it behind him. I was frozen—standing at the door—until I heard the servants stirring. I ran to hide in the closet beneath the stairs. One of the servants found me there hours later." She turned to face him, her eyes dark with pain. "I couldn't eat or sleep—I couldn't talk to anyone. I cried for days. The doctor said I was in shock."

Spencer gathered her into his arms and held her tightly. "So you couldn't tell anyone what you had seen."

"I *tried*, Nick." She burrowed closer to him. "Later—when I could think again. But no one would pay attention to a twelve-year-old child. Not even Mama."

"What about the ring? Didn't your mother notice that it was missing?"

Jenny shook her head. "A few weeks before he was killed, Papa had lost the ring during a hunt. He was very upset about it; the ring had been in the Courtenay family for generations. That day—the day he was killed—I found the ring while I was out riding. Just before I went to bed, I gave it to him. Mama never saw the ring."

Spencer tilted her face up and gently kissed her. "I'm sorry, kitten. I see now why it was so important for you to find the ring."

She gazed up at him, her lovely face serious. "I tried to think of some way to find the ring. And then I decided to become the Cat. As a thief, I could carefully examine the jewelry of every gentleman I came across."

"Are you certain that the killer is a gentleman?"

Jenny smiled faintly. "I am not very likely to forget

what I saw. The man is a gentleman—or at least he dresses like one."

Spencer shook his head ruefully. "Jenny, do you realize how many gentlemen there *are* in England? You could go on holding up men for years without finding the one you seek."

"I know." She drew away slightly. "But I have to keep searching, Nick, and I won't rest until I find that ring. Not until I find the man who killed my father." She hesitated, then continued slowly, "I—I know it was wrong of me—for whatever reason— to become a thief, but I could see no other way. I've always returned the jewelry and, as for the money, every cent of it is being kept in a safe place. I keep a list of how much is taken from each man, and I plan to return it all as soon as Papa's killer is found."

For a moment, she was silent, and then, very quietly, she said, "I never hurt anyone, Nick. The rumors and the speculation—none of them are true. I have never killed."

"And the man who rides with you?"

"John? He's as gentle as he is large. John has been like an uncle to me for as long as I can remember. He was Papa's head groom and then, when Mama remarried, John bought a little inn not far from the manor. He and his sister run it."

Spencer hesitated and then asked gravely, "What about Conover?"

Jenny's smile was wry. "I have a—friend. A highwayman. He knew I was searching for a traitor, and promised to help me. Shortly before I met you, he held up a coach—I assume it was Conover's—and the documents were in the gentleman's purse. When Jason realized what he had, he brought them to me. I returned them to the War Office. I never saw Conover."

"Did your friend kill Conover?"

"I don't know," she replied rather dryly. "To be perfectly honest, I didn't ask. There is an unwritten law among thieves—no awkward questions. Asking Jason if he killed Conover could easily be construed as an awkward question."

"True." He smiled faintly. "Do you think Jason could have killed Conover? Is he capable of killing?"

"Of course." She smiled tightly. "Any of us could kill under the right circumstances. But I don't think Jason killed Conover."

"Woman's intuition?" His voice was teasing.

"If you like." She smiled. "Whatever the reason, I don't think Jason killed him."

"You said Jason knew you were searching for a traitor. What makes you think your father's murderer is a traitor?"

"His journal—Papa's, I mean. In the week before he was killed, Papa wrote that he was on the trail of a traitor. My guess is that the traitor found out how close Papa was to discovering his identity, and killed him."

Spencer frowned slightly. "Could you be wrong about that? Could anyone else have had reason to kill your father?"

Jenny sighed softly. "I don't think so, Nick. Papa had no enemies."

Spencer began to pace restlessly around the room. "Is that the only clue you have to the identity of the killer—that he's a traitor?"

For a long moment, Jenny was silent. There was a frown of concentration on her face and her eyes were distracted.

Spencer stopped pacing long enough to direct a searching look at her. "Something?"

Jenny continued to frown. "Yes," she murmured. "Yes—there is something else. Something I've seen or heard. If only I could remember."

"Don't worry about it—I'm sure you'll remember sooner or later." He smiled at her. "In the meantime, we'll continue with what we have."

She smiled in return. "It's all we can do," she agreed. "I only hope that what we have is enough to find the killer."

# Chapter Nineteen

The Duke of Spencer strolled slowly along St. James, his mind occupied with the problems that stood between him and his marriage to Jennifer Courtenay. He had every intention of helping Jenny find the man who had killed her father; he also intended to find some way of turning the Cat into a heroine in the eyes of the world.

The latter, as far as he could see, would present something of a problem. The duke, no stranger to the hypocrisy of his society, was keenly aware of the rules governing the behavior of young ladies. Those rules did not bend easily and, even for someone of the duke's undoubted influence, it would be somewhat difficult to establish a young lady who had an unfortunate habit of riding about the country dressed like a man—not to mention robbing people.

But the duke had faith in his abilities. He also had a rather rueful belief in Jenny's ability to land on her feet. Between the two of them, the problems would be worked out eventually.

He nodded to an acquaintance, and then turned in the direction of White's. There was still the problem of locating Thomas Courtenay's murderer. The best place to begin *that* search would be with Richard Standen. Perhaps he would remember Courtenay's search for a spy.

Spencer stopped just inside the door of White's and blinked at Mr. Brummell. "Hello, George. It's a little early for you to be up and about, isn't it?"

The Beau gave his friend a reproachful look. "You must have lost an hour or so somewhere along the way, Nick—it's gone four o'clock."

"As late as that?" Spencer murmured. "I suppose I was woolgathering."

Brummell nodded wisely. "And how *is* Miss Courtenay, by the way?"

Spencer grinned. "We've patched things up."

"Have you indeed? Then tell me—before I expire from curiosity—why such an engaging young woman would enjoy her—er—peculiar pastime."

The duke glanced around and then nodded toward a vacant room. "In private, if you don't mind, George."

Brummell followed his friend into the room and waited until he closed the door behind them. "Well?"

"She doesn't enjoy it, George. She's searching for her father's talisman ring."

The Beau's keen gray eyes narrowed slightly. "Oh? The ring is important?"

"Very. It will point the way to Thomas Courtenay's killer."

"I was under the impression," the Beau remarked slowly, "that Courtenay committed suicide."

"No. Jenny saw him murdered. She also saw the killer take Courtenay's ring."

"Does the killer know that there was a witness to his crime?"

"No. Jenny didn't get a clear look at his face. But she

saw him take the ring. *That* is why she became the Cat—to search for that ring."

Brummell smiled faintly. "A courageous young woman. I assume she knows that there is a hangman's noose dangling above her head?"

"She knows." Spencer frowned slightly. "I may need your help, George. One way or another, I mean to clear her name."

"Happy to oblige. But tell me—is Bow Street suspicious of her?"

"Yes. Someone gave them a damn good description of the Cat. Two Runners came to Lady Beddington's and asked Jenny some awkward questions. I was able to frighten them off—but I have no doubt that they are watching every move she makes."

"Who informed against her?"

"I don't know. I think Jenny does, but it doesn't seem to worry her. I suppose she has already taken care of the informer."

"My dear friend, I do hope you don't mean she killed someone!"

"Of course not, George—she isn't a killer."

The Beau looked relieved. "Then how did she rid herself of the informer?"

"I haven't the faintest idea."

Moved to expostulate, the Beau said, "Nick, we cannot have an informer lurking about in the woodwork—even if Miss Courtenay *isn't* worried about him."

The duke sighed. "Knowing Jenny, I'm sure she found some devious way to dispose of him. I'll ask her; I'm going to Lady Beddington's later today."

"Do you mind if I tag along? I have a fancy to hear about the informer."

"I don't mind, of course. Just remember that she isn't aware you know she's the Cat."

Brummell smiled gently. "I also have a fancy to see her face when I tell her that."

Jenny looked up with a smile when Somers announced the duke and Mr. Brummell. She was alone in the drawing room, Lady Beddington and Meg having gone to rest for a soiree they were to attend that evening. Since Jenny had been expecting the duke, she had remained downstairs.

When greetings had been exchanged, and Mr. Brummell and the duke seated, the Beau immediately spoke. He could see that Jenny was anxious to know if the duke had discovered anything about a traitor, and wanted her to know that she could speak freely in his presence.

"Miss Courtenay, I feel perhaps I should tell you that I know all about the Cat."

"You what . . . ?" Jenny asked faintly.

"I know you are the Cat."

She cast a rather helpless look at Spencer. The duke smile ruefully. "He heard us arguing at Lady Jersey's ball."

"Oh." Jenny stared at Brummell. "I—I know what you must think of me, sir—"

"I think, Miss Courtenay, that you are a remarkable young woman. I know of no other who would have had the strength of will to search so long and so hard for a dangerous killer and traitor."

A soft flush rose to pinken her cheeks. Her eyes wide with surprise, she said, "I—I don't know what to say, Mr. Brummell."

"Say nothing, Miss Courtenay." The Beau smiled gently. "I only ask that you allow me to participate in this adventure of yours. To a small degree, that is."

Jenny smiled. "By all means, Mr. Brummell." She looked rueful. "But I cannot help but wonder exactly how many others are in possession of my 'secret.'"

"Mama knows."

All eyes turned to the doorway, where Meg stood. A slight blush covered her cheeks. She closed the door and slowly advanced into the room. Nodding rather shyly to the two gentlemen, she said apologetically, "I didn't mean to eavesdrop, Jenny."

Jenny waved her to a chair and said, "That's all right, Meg. But what did you mean about Mama?"

"She knows," Meg replied simply. "She's known all along."

"How do you know that?"

"Before we left Kent, Mama asked me to try to convince you to be careful. She said she had known from the start that you were the Cat, and that she was afraid for you."

"She never said a word," Jenny murmured.

Meg smiled. "She told me you were exactly like your father. That you possessed a sort of—fearless courage."

"Meg, why didn't you tell me that Mama knew?"

"You've been so worried, Jenny. I knew it would upset you, and you had enough on your mind."

Wryly, Jenny responded, "Then why tell me now?"

Meg looked surprised. "Well, because of the duke, of course."

Jenny shot a look at Spencer. "What do you mean by that?"

Meg blushed again. "Now that the two of you are reconciled, you won't be alone anymore, Jenny. The duke will take care of you—and you won't worry as much."

With an amused glance at the duke, Jenny said, "Well, I suppose that's *one* way to look at it."

"I thought of that myself," Spencer said gravely. "However, Miss Ross, your stepsister seems determined not to share her problems with me."

"Well, you know all about the Cat, and if *that* isn't a problem, I don't know what is," Jenny exclaimed.

"What about the informer?" asked the duke.

"Oh—that."

"Yes, *that*. Who informed against you, Jenny? And don't tell me you don't know, because I won't believe it. If you didn't know who it was, you would be moving heaven and earth to find out."

Jenny look uncomfortable. "I believe I told you once, Nick, that you think too much."

"Who is the informer, Jenny?"

Abruptly, Meg rose to her feet and headed for the door. "Go ahead and tell them, Jenny—I've already guessed." The door closed behind her.

Spencer looked rather grimly at Jenny. "Does that mean what I think it means?"

Jenny sighed wearily. "Sir George informed against me. He told me so himself."

Mr. Brummell, who had been silent until now, frowned and asked, "Your stepfather?"

"Yes. He wants to be free of me. He seemed quite delighted at the thought that I would hang."

Spencer looked furious. "When I get my hands on that man, he'll wish he'd never been born."

Jenny laughed softly. "Never mind. I've been handling Sir George for years—I managed to squash his threats."

"How?" It was Brummell, his gray eyes curious.

She grinned, her eyes alight with amusement. With a sidelong glance at the duke, she said demurely, "I played on his sense of greed. I told him that I was trying to catch a duke, and that he should go back to Kent and leave me alone. He was quite happy to do so—envisioning a substantial marriage settlement, I've no doubt."

"I'll be damned if he gets one cent," the duke declared roundly. "I'll see to it that your mother receives the settlement."

"Can you do that?" Jenny asked curiously.

"Yes," Spencer said flatly. "I can and will."

"Oh." Jenny looked at him thoughtfully. "If you can do that—perhaps you can help me with another of my problems."

"Which one?" asked the duke wryly.

"Do you think that you could persuade Sir George to consent to Meg's marriage to Robert?"

Spencer smiled. "It will be my pleasure. As soon as we've caught the killer, I'll post down to Kent and have a little—talk with him."

"Famous! Then that takes care of everything but the killer. Nick, did you find out anything at the War Office?"

"Not a thing. They are being very careful at the War Office these days with so many documents having been stolen and shifted around in the past months. I talked to Richard Standen, but he couldn't help me. He couldn't remember anyone who might have heard your father talk about a traitor."

Ruefully, Jenny said, "I suppose the Cat is their primary suspect."

"On the contrary," Spencer smiled at her, "the general feeling is that the Cat is searching for traitors. Half the War Office believes that the Cat should be given a medal for her services."

"And the other half?" Jenny asked.

He laughed. "The other half believes she should be made queen."

Jenny and the Beau joined Spencer in laughter. With a gasp, Jenny said, "I hope they don't offer me the job—I have enough problems as it is!" She looked faintly puzzled. "But how did they know I was searching for traitors?"

Calmly, the duke said, "I told them you were when I returned those dispatches."

She nodded. "I had forgotten all about those."

"Dispatches?" Brummell looked curious.

Jenny nodded again. "A highwayman friend of mine

took the dispatches from a coach that he held up. He gave them to me, and I gave them to Nick."

"A highwayman? What very strange friends you have, to be sure."

"Jason has been a very good friend to me," she responded firmly, "and I mean to see that he receives part of the credit for catching the killer—when we catch him, that is."

Spencer sighed. "You see what I'm letting myself in for, George? Highwayman!"

"At least she isn't dull," the Beau said in a consoling tone.

Jenny looked from one to the other. "Well, really!" she exclaimed.

Spencer's eyes laughed in a solemn face. "Why do I have the feeling that my life from this point on will become filled with missing dispatches, highwaymen, spies, troubled young lovers, infamous stepfathers, and Bow Street Runners?"

"I can't imagine," Jenny stared carefully into space, "how you could possibly think such a thing."

"The idea suggested itself when I saw two Runners hiding in the shrubbery when we came in."

Jenny fought to keep from laughing. "You mean Simmons and his talkative friend."

"The very same. Jenny, how have you been able to slip past them? The Cat has held up at least three coaches since they started watching the house."

Correcting him, Jenny said, "Five. And it hasn't been easy, believe me."

Brummell started to smile. "You mean to say that you have been coming and going beneath the noses of two Bow Street Runners?"

Jenny grinned. "Luckily for me, Simmons has caught a dreadful cold from—er—hiding in the shrubbery."

Brummell laughed. "Why is that lucky for you?"

"He sneezes occasionally, you know."

Brummell had to struggle to maintain his air of casual nonchalance. "I didn't realize how accurate my statement was," he finally managed to say. "You certainly are not dull."

Spencer had dropped his head into his hands. "She was born to be hanged," he said in a voice of despair.

He then raised his head and gave Jenny a thundering scold on the subject of foolish young women who behave in a manner quite unsuited to their stations in life.

Jenny listened to these strictures with an air of great interest, before saying reproachfully, "But, Nick, I've been very careful."

The duke sighed and rose to his feet. "Come along, George—if I remain here a moment longer, I shall be tempted to strangle her."

The two gentlemen took their leave, and Jenny enjoyed a quiet laugh.

Outside, the duke and Mr. Brummell passed the concealed Runners just in time to hear a muffled sneeze. With a wink at the Beau, Spencer said loudly, "You should take care of that cold, Simmons."

The bushes parted, and a startled face peered after the departing gentlemen.

# Chapter Twenty

Several days later, as Spencer drove his curricle toward Lady Beddington's house, he noticed a large man just stepping outside. There was a nagging familiarity about the man. He was dressed neatly, but more like a merchant or an innkeeper than a gentleman.

Spencer frowned and tried to peer round a coach that blocked his view. When the coach moved away, the man had disappeared. Spencer halted his curricle in front of the house and motioned for his tiger to go to the horses' heads. A moment later, he knocked on the door, still frowning.

The butler answered the knock, his forbidding face softening into something resembling a smile when he saw the duke. "Good afternoon, Your Grace."

"'Afternoon, Somers." His frown disappeared. "Is Miss Courtenay in?"

Somers stepped back to allow the duke to enter. "Yes, Your Grace; Miss Courtenay is in the Red Room." He made as if to lead the way, but the duke stopped him with a gesture.

"I know the way." He gave the butler a conspiratorial smile. "You don't need to announce me."

Somers returned the smile, an understanding gleam in his eyes. "Of course, Your Grace."

Spencer made his way to the Red Room and knocked softly on the door before entering. Jenny was standing at the window, her head bowed.

The duke looked searchingly at her still, silent figure. "Jenny?"

She started in surprise and turned to face him. "Nick. I—I didn't hear you come in." Her voice was strained, her eyes burning in an unnaturally pale face.

He quickly crossed the room to stand before her. "Jenny, what is it? What's wrong?"

She glazed down at her clasped hands. "John came to see me. He just left."

Spencer remembered the stranger he had seen, and suddenly realized why he had seemed familiar. "Yes, I saw him leave. What did he say, Jenny?"

"He brought me a message from Jason."

"The highwayman?"

"Yes." She raised her eyes to his, a queer blind look in them. "I told you—Jason has been trying to help me find Papa's killer. He's the one who took the dispatches I gave you."

"I remember." He nodded. "The dispatches from Wellesley."

"He's been trying to find that man again. I was hoping he's the man I'm searching for . . ." Her voice trailed off. After a moment, she continued quietly. "He found the man. Nick—it's Stoven."

"Stoven!" Spencer frowned. "Jenny, are you sure?"

"That he's a traitor? Yes. That he's my father's murderer? I don't know." She shook her head slowly. "But if he is—Nick, he *offered* for me. How could he do that if he killed my father? How could he look me in the face and swear that he loved me?"

Spencer smiled faintly. "Perhaps he did. You're very easy to love."

She managed a faint smile. "Nevertheless, I must know for certain." She stared out the window with a frown. "I'll have to hold up his coach."

Spencer did not seem at all pleased with her remark. "Jenny, if Stoven is a traitor, and if he is your father's killer, he's a very dangerous man. Is there no other way?"

She stared up at him, her face grave. "Nick, I must find out if he has the ring. He doesn't wear it, but I suspect that he carries it on him somewhere."

He sighed. "If you're determined to rob him, I intend to go along."

A flicker of amusement showed in her eyes. "Nick, you aren't a thief."

"Neither are you."

"Yes, but you're a *duke*."

He looked startled. "What has that to say to anything?"

"Dukes don't rob coaches."

"Jenny—" He shook his head with a laugh. "Nor, let me remind you, do ladies."

She responded gravely. "I never said that I was a lady."

He laughed again and drew her into his arms. "Lady or no, you are soon to be a duchess. Do duchesses rob coaches?"

She smiled up at him. "I have no idea. Shall we find that out for ourselves?"

"That sounds like a good idea." He lifted an eyebrow. "Though, for now, I believe I have a better one."

She looked innocent. "Oh? And what is that?"

He bent his head toward hers. Just before their lips met, he murmured, "Deeds—not words."

By dint of a few careless questions, Spencer managed to discover that Stoven planned a trip to his estate at the end of the week. The estate was outside London on a little-traveled road, and the earl, who had a penchant for night travel, planned to set out just after dark.

Jenny and the duke agreed that the time and place were right, and they made plans to hold up Stoven's coach on Friday night. Jenny sent word to John to have the black stallion—and Jason—standing by.

It remained only for them to while away the rest of the week, which they did in a very agreeable fashion. The *ton* grew accustomed to seeing the two of them together, either riding or driving about in the duke's curricle. They were observed walking in the park; they danced every dance together at Lady Catherine's ball; they were seen at the theater; and they graced Lady Jersey's masquerade by appearing as Cleopatra and Marc Antony. Jenny had toyed with the idea of appearing as the Cat, but her devoted duke had threatened dire consequences.

Society, never slow on the uptake, had gotten wind of their unofficial understanding, and they eagerly awaited word of a betrothal. They waited in vain. The couple had no intention of announcing their plans until a certain traitorous murderer had been brought to justice.

On Friday evening, Spencer and Jenny met outside a tawdry inn about a mile from Stoven's estate. The duke's first words upon entering the dilapidated structure were: "For God's sake, Jenny—this building looks as though it's about to fall on our heads!"

Jenny set her lantern down on a rickety table and grinned at him. "When in Rome . . ."

He stared at her. In a considering tone, he said, "If this is the type of place you've become accustomed to during the past year, I don't think I want to meet your highwayman friend. He's very likely a cutthroat."

She laughed. "Jason's a hard man, but I wouldn't call him a cutthroat. He's been a great deal of help to me, Nick, and I want you to meet him."

Spencer smiled ruefully. "I suppose you mean to invite him to the wedding."

"Oh, no." She grinned wryly. "He'd be most uncomfortable. But, I do hope he'll come to us any time he needs help." She stepped toward her love and gazed up at him with a coaxing smile. "Nick, do you think we could do something for him? So he could stop being a highwayman?"

Spencer stared down at her, bemused. After a moment, he shook his head slowly. "I don't know when you're more dangerous—when you're wearing that mask and holding a pistol, or when you're practicing your womanly wiles."

"Could we?" Jenny refused to be sidetracked.

"I suppose we could. Would he accept money?"

"Not from you or I." She smiled brilliantly. "But if we could arrange for a reward—for helping to capture a traitor—I'm sure he'd accept that."

Spencer nodded. "Very well. I'll see what I can do." Jenny threw her arms about him and was about to give him a strong indication of how grateful she was when she was interrupted by a loud cough from the doorway.

Jason stood on the threshold, having just arrived. "Don't mean to interrupt," he said uncomfortably, "but I brought the horse."

Jenny turned to face him. "Jason, I wondered where you were. You're late."

Keeping a wary eye on the duke, Jason responded irritably, "I wouldn't have made it here at all if that horse of yours would have had his way. That animal ought to be shot. Damn near took my arm off at least a dozen times."

Jenny frowned. "I told John to put a muzzle on him."

Jason nodded. "Aye—and so he did. Took that devil about half a mile to chew his way through it."

"I do apologize for my unmannerly beast, Jason." Jenny smiled at him and then indicated the duke. "This is Nick—the man I told you about."

The two men eyed each other for a moment, and then Spencer held out his hand. "Glad to meet you, Jason."

Jason grasped the outstretched hand and nodded briefly. "Same here. Leastways, I think it is. I don't take too kindly to strangers," he said bluntly, "but Jenny said as how you was a right one."

Spencer nodded in a dazed sort of way, and Jenny spoke up hurriedly. "I think we'd best go, Nick. It's getting late."

As they stepped outside, Spencer murmured, for her ears alone, "It's so reassuring to have my character approved of by a thief."

Jenny shot him a warning look, which was belied by the amusement in her eyes. They made their way toward the horses in silence.

Jenny's stallion was standing apart from the other horses, the leather muzzle hanging about his nose in tatters. As the three approached him, he was engaged in a spirited attempt to chew his way through the rope that held him to the tree.

Spencer made as if to reach out and touch the horse, but jumped back hurriedly when the animal lashed out with both forelegs.

"Take my advice," said Jason with a wry smile, "and don't go near him. He's a devil."

Jenny looked offended. "He is not. He just doesn't like men, that's all." She walked over to the stallion and began to stroke his glossy black neck.

The red glare faded from the creature's eyes. He hung his head like a bashful boy, gently nuzzling the girl's shoulder.

Spencer exchanged a wry glance with Jason. "He's obviously a one-woman horse. What's his name, Jenny?"

She grinned. "What else? Bandit."

The duke laughed. "I should have known."

Jason shifted slightly. "I'll brush off now, Jenny. You won't need my help tonight."

She turned to stare at him, surprised. "Jason, you must come with us."

He looked uncomfortable. "Why? The two of you can handle Stoven."

"Oh, but that's not the problem. If Stoven *is* the man I'm searching for, it will take both you *and* Nick to keep me from losing my temper and killing him."

Spencer nodded, following her lead. "It's a terrible thing, her temper—quite a spectacle," he said gravely.

"An eruption to rival Vesuvius," Jenny added with equal solemnity.

Jason stared suspiciously at their innocent faces, which were growing dimmer in the deepening twilight. "Why do I have the feeling that I'm being led down the garden path?" he grumbled.

Jenny laughed. "Get your horse, Jason."

"All right, then," he said irritably, "but I'm staying out of sight."

"Fine—just as long as you come."

Jenny watched as the two men went to get their horses, then turned to remove the tattered remains of the muzzle from Bandit's nose. The horse was calm and quiet now that she was with him. The wildness was gone from his eyes. He stood docilely while she climbed into the saddle, and then waited for her signal before moving forward.

The three riders were soon on their way. There was little

conversation during the ride. They were all aware of the gravity of what they were about to attempt.

A few moments later, they turned off the main road and onto a narrow road leading to Stoven's estate. Jason halted. "I'll stay here and signal when the coach passes me."

The other two nodded and continued down the road. They came to a wide place and pulled their horses off to the side. As they waited, they talked in low tones.

"I've wondered about something," remarked Spencer, "ever since you held me up."

"Oh?" Jenny smiled faintly. "What is it?"

"Why my horses stopped so suddenly and stood so calmly while you robbed me. They've never acted that way before or since."

She continued to smile. "Why do *you* think they acted that way?"

"I don't know." He grinned suddenly. "My coachman swore that you were a witch and that Bandit was your familiar."

Jenny smothered a laugh. "Nothing quite so fanciful, I'm afraid. Actually, I don't quite understand it myself. Bandit just seems to have that effect on other horses."

Before he could respond, they heard the hoot of an owl. Jenny tensed slightly, her head cocked to one side in a listening attitude. The call was repeated twice, and she quickly began to draw on her gloves. "That's Jason's signal."

Spencer donned the hooded mask that Jenny had brought for him and pulled a pistol from the pocket of his greatcoat. "Jenny, be careful."

Jenny smiled wryly. "I will. And you keep quiet—if you say anything, your voice will give you away in an instant."

"Very well." He watched as she drew on her own mask and pulled a pistol from the pocket of her cloak. The sounds of an approaching coach could now be heard, and

Jenny said softly, "If I know Jason, he'll be across the road—just in case." She nodded toward the road and murmured, "I'll go first. When the horses come to a stop, keep the coachman covered."

Spencer nodded and listened as the coach drew nearer. From the corner of his eye, he saw Jenny speak softly to the stallion and, though he couldn't hear her words, he saw the stallion's instant response. The animal gathered his powerful haunches beneath him and tensed in preparation for the leap which would take him into the road—and into the path of the oncoming coach.

There was a moment of taut silence, and then the great horse leaped into the road, his eyes glaring red. The coach horses immediately stopped. There was no threshing about; the horses showed no indication of fright. They simply stopped and stood quietly.

Spencer, leaving the woods just behind Jenny, immediately covered the terrified coachman with both his pistols. The man cowered in his seat, his eyes fixed on the duke's imposing figure.

Jenny moved her horse toward the door of the coach, her pistol out and ready. In a cold, mocking voice she said, "Step out of the coach, if you please, Lord Stoven—slowly."

The earl carefully climbed out of the coach, one trembling hand clutching his cane, his face pasty-white in the moonlight.

Jenny gestured casually with her pistol. "Your money and jewelry, if you please, my lord. And, my lord, don't try anything foolish. My silent friend has a very nervous trigger finger."

She watched him glance uneasily at the duke's still figure, and then tossed a leather pouch to land at his feet. He bent to pick up the bag and, straightening, slowly began to place his money and jewelry in it. When the pouch was filled, Jenny held out one black-gloved hand. Stoven tossed the bag to her.

Jenny placed the bag in the pocket of her cloak and then, on impulse, said coolly, "The cane."

Stoven clutched the cane with both hands. "No! It—it was given to me by my father."

"Was it indeed? Then I promise to take very good care of it. Hand it over."

The earl maintained his death grip on the cane. "It isn't very valuable—you have no need of it."

"It amuses me." There was an audible click as she drew back the hammer of her pistol. "Hand it over."

Stoven, fearing her wrath more than he feared the loss of the cane, quickly handed it to her. She twirled it casually and said, "Thank you, my lord—and a very pleasant evening to you." With these mocking words, she whirled her great horse and disappeared into the woods, her henchman at her heels.

Moments later, the three riders were reunited in the tumbledown inn. There was no conversation; the three were too tense for that. Jenny removed her mask and then turned up the lamp which she had left burning. She placed Stoven's cane on the table and quickly brought out the pouch and upended it. A few gold coins, two fobs, and a diamond stickpin rolled out onto the table. There was no ring.

Spencer picked up the cane and examined it carefully. "Stoven seemed strangely anxious to keep this," he murmured. He gave the cane a slight shake, and a muted rattle was heard. His eyes met Jenny's. He handed the cane across the table to her.

With steady hands, Jenny carefully twisted the cane until the silver head came off. There was a soft thump as a ring rolled out and fell onto the table. It was a dull gold ring with strange symbols carved into it. A talisman ring.

## Chapter Twenty-one

The room was deathly silent. Jenny slowly drew a long breath. In a shockingly normal voice, she said, "Well—I guess I have my answer. Stoven killed my father."

"Jenny—" Nick hesitated. "Stoven could have been given the ring by someone else."

"And then hidden it in his cane?" Jenny shook her head. "No, I don't think so. Besides, I've known, for a long time, I think, that it was Stoven."

Spencer looked startled. "What do you mean? Why were you so certain?"

Jenny sighed; she looked very tired. "I saw something the night my father was killed. It was an impression, I suppose. Later, I couldn't remember what it was; I only knew that I had seen something that could point to the killer's identity. It haunted me for years. Then, when Jason sent word that it had been Stoven's coach he had held up, everything began to come together in my mind."

Spencer and Jason exchanged puzzled looks. "What was it, lass?" Jason asked. "What did you see?"

"Something I've seen a dozen times in the past year—seen, but never really noticed. The killer had a peculiar scar beneath his right ear—a scar shaped like a horseshoe."

Quietly, Spencer said, "Like Stoven's."

Jenny nodded. "Like Stoven's. Finding the ring only confirmed my suspicions. Stoven killed my father."

Spencer sighed and rested a hip against the rickety table. "The problem is, how do we force him to admit it? He wouldn't be convicted on the evidence we have. We must find some way of making him confess."

Jason folded his arms across his chest and regarded the other two wryly. "Sounds like a tall order to me. His lordship ain't likely to admit to killin'. 'Specially in front of witnesses."

Jenny shrugged irritably. "Then we'll just have to scare the hell out of him."

"Jennifer!"

Jenny grinned at the duke's mock look of outrage, and then turned sad eyes to the highwayman. "He only calls me Jennifer when he's angry with me."

Jason chuckled. "Happen he don't like to hear you swearing like a sailor."

"Is that what I was doing?" she asked innocently. "Nick, do you object to my language?"

Dryly, Spencer replied, "Yes, but I know better than to try and stop you."

Jenny chuckled. "As fascinating as this conversation is, gentlemen, it is hardly to the point. Stoven must be exposed as a traitor and a murderer. Now, how can we do it?"

Jason lifted a questioning brow. "We?"

In a grave voice, Jenny responded, "I'm very grateful for everything you've done to help me, Jason. If you want to duck out now, I'll understand completely."

Jason frowned. "What are you saying, lass? Are you telling me you don't want my help anymore?"

"Oh, no—that isn't it at all. Three heads are always better than two, and if you want to help us plan Stoven's capture, I'll be very grateful. Of course, it won't increase the reward, but if you want to help—"

"Reward?" Jason looked startled. "Who said anything about a reward?"

Spencer picked up his cue. In a casual voice he said, "There is always a reward for anyone who helps to capture a traitor." He shrugged slightly and, picking up the talisman ring, began to study it intently. "You deserve the reward."

"Me?" He looked suspiciously at Jenny, only to find her apparently absorbed in thought. "Jenny?" He had to repeat her name, rather impatiently, before he gained her attention.

She blinked at him. "What is it, Jason? Have you thought of a plan?"

He glared at her. "Damn a plan! I'll accept a fair share of a reward, but I won't take the whole thing."

Jenny looked faintly puzzled. "But, Jason—I don't need any money. I've got more than I can handle now."

The highwayman stared at her, and then turned his gaze to Spencer. "What about you?"

The duke shrugged. "I don't need the money either. Besides, you're the one who pointed the way to Stoven."

Jason's eyes narrowed in sudden suspicion. Abruptly, he said, "There's something bloody familiar about you. I can't put my finger on it—but I know I've seen you somewhere."

Spencer, who had been endeavoring since first setting his eyes on the highwayman to keep his face away from any direct light, continued to study the talisman ring in his hand. "Indeed." His tone was not encouraging.

Jason was undaunted. "Where? Where have I seen you?"

Jenny looked from one to the other, having by this time

given up all pretense of being deep in thought. She folded her arms and waited, curious to hear Spencer's response.

The duke sighed and dropped the ring onto the table. Wryly, he said, "Cast your mind back about a year. It was last April—on the Great North Road."

Jason gave a start of surprise. "I remember. I held up your coach." He frowned suddenly. "That is—I *tried* to hold up your coach."

Jenny looked intrigued. "What happened?"

The highwayman gave an irritated snort and seemed disinclined to answer.

"Nick?"

Spencer rubbed his nose reflectively. "I—er—I'm rather afraid I took a shot at him."

Jenny's eyes widened. "You—" She hurriedly brought her voice under control—it had a tendency to shake with suppressed amusement. "Did you hit him?"

"You shall have to ask him."

"Jason?"

The highwayman avoided her eyes. "He winged me." He glared at Spencer. "No wonder you looked so bloody familiar. And there was a crest on that coach—you're a damned nobleman, aren't you?"

The highwayman's accusing question tickled Spencer's sense of humor. "I am very sorry," he said apologetically, "but I'm afraid I am a duke."

Jason looked thunderstruck. After a moment of silence, he turned reproachful eyes to Jenny. "Lass, you know how I feel about noblemen. You might have warned me."

"I'm sorry, Jason." Jenny fought to keep amusement out of her voice. "If I had told you that Nick was a duke, you wouldn't have come here. And I wanted the two of you to meet."

Jason was not impressed. "It's bad enough having to

associate with a lady," he said severely, "without throwing a duke into the pot."

"Jason." Jenny was deeply wounded. "I never knew that you felt like that. Why, I thought you were my friend."

The highwayman looked irritated. "Now don't go gettin' female on me. You know I'm your friend, but don't, for God's sake, go spreading the word around. If some of my friends found out that I was holding up coaches with a lady and a duke, I'd be laughed out of England."

The duke chuckled. "Don't worry, Jason. We promise not to tell a soul."

"Jason," Jenny smiled and said, "I wanted you two to meet because you've both been very important to me. You helped me find Papa's killer, and Nick—" She turned glowing eyes to the duke. "When all this is over, Nick and I are going to be married."

"Is that so?" Jason looked from one to the other. "I thought maybe that might be it." He shrugged slightly. "Well, if that's the case, I guess it won't hurt me to associate with a duke—temporarily, that is."

"Thank you, Jason." Impulsively, Jenny hugged the highwayman and kissed him on the cheek.

"Watch it, lass," Jason said gruffly. "I don't want this fancy duke of yours to take another shot at me—he had pretty good luck the first time."

Nick extended a hand to Jason. "I wouldn't think of it."

The two men shook hands solemnly, and then Jason said, "Well, have you come up with any ideas about how we're going to put a noose around Stoven's neck—I mean, aside from hauling him out and hanging him ourselves? Getting a confession from him in front of witnesses ain't going to be easy."

Spencer frowned slightly. "I think Jenny had the best idea," he said slowly. "We'll have to scare a confession out of him."

"How?" Jenny frowned.

Spencer picked up the talisman ring and slowly restored it to its hiding place within the cane. "I think I have an idea how we can accomplish that." He turned his gaze to his love. "Jenny, tomorrow night you'll return Stoven's jewels to him. You'll also return the cane—with the ring inside."

Jason grunted. "You do have a plan, don't you?"

"Yes. If my plan works—and I think it will—Stoven will make his confession in the presence of the cream of London society." He turned briskly to the other two. "Now, this is what we'll have to do . . ."

Jenny crept silently through the dark garden until she reached a window leaning into the library of Stoven's town house. Carefully, she peeked into the window. The room was empty. A freshly built fire and lighted lamps indicated that the master of the house was expected. Jenny knew that he was, in fact, on his way home at this very minute. She carefully tried the window, letting out a silent sigh of relief when it sprung open beneath her touch. A moment later, she was in the room.

Without a wasted motion, Jenny quickly crossed to the desk and placed a small leather pouch in its center. She left the cane there also. Seconds later, the room was again empty of life.

Jenny waited outside the window. A short time later, she was joined by Spencer, who had been waiting by the corner of the house, watching for Stoven's arrival.

"He's here. Did you have any trouble?"

Jenny shook her head. "No. The window was unlocked. I only hope he doesn't become suspicious when he finds that the ring is still in the cane."

The duke reached for her hand and squeezed it reassuringly. "I doubt he will. He'll probably think you overlooked it as a possible hiding place."

"I hope you're right." The two of them stared through the window, watching as Stoven entered the room. He noticed the pouch and cane immediately. Ignoring the pouch, he snatched up the cane and twisted the head. A relieved expression spread over his face when the ring rolled out in his hand.

Jenny and Spencer watched as the earl held the ring, staring thoughtfully into the fire. After a moment, he replaced the ring in its hiding place. Only then did he open the leather pouch and study its contents. Satisfied that his property had been returned to him, he dropped the pouch into his pocket, picked up the cane and, twirling it jauntily, left the room.

Jenny found herself suddenly in the duke's arms, and realized that she was trembling. "He put the ring back in the cane. Oh, Nick—I was so afraid he'd hide it somewhere else," she murmured against his broad chest.

Spencer chuckled softly. "Well, he didn't. So we can begin step two of our plan tomorrow." He began to lead her toward the mews, where their horses waited.

Jenny shivered slightly. "You mean the War Office—and Bow Street?"

The duke stopped and gazed down at her. "Jenny, don't be frightened. You know I wouldn't ask you to reveal the Cat's identity if I thought you would be harmed in any way."

She smiled up at him. "I know that, Nick. It just seems strange, after the secrecy of the past year, to think about going up to someone and announcing flatly that I'm the Cat."

Spencer grinned at her. "By the time we've rung down the curtain on Monday night, you'll not only be forgiven for being the Cat—you'll be called a heroine."

Jenny looked dubious. "If you say so."

"Allow me to know my peers. Believe me, love, society will be enchanted by your story, and totally in sympathy with your strange career."

"What are you going to tell them?" She frowned.

He grinned again. "Your story. The plain and simple truth." He led her through the back gate and into the mews.

Jenny prepared to mount her horse, smiling faintly. "All right. But I'll be prepared to run like the devil if it doesn't work."

The duke watched her swing onto her horse before following suit. "If it doesn't work, love," he said with a tender smile, "we shall find ourselves a new world, you and I."

"Nick." She glared at him in mock anger. "Don't *say* things like that. At least not until we're married—then I can do something about it."

His shout of laughter followed her as she spurred her horse toward home.

# Chapter Twenty-two

Jenny crept silently down the stairs early the next morning, hoping to reach the front door before any of the servants saw her. It would be difficult to explain why she was up and about so early, and to not explain would only give rise to the sort of gossip that could ruin her reputation. What possible reason could she have for leaving the house dressed in her shabbiest morning dress and wearing a hat with a heavy veil? It was just the sort of thing to make the servants wonder.

She was halfway to the door when Somers suddenly popped out of the sitting room. The butler's surprise was momentary; he immediately assumed his normal lack of expression. "Shall I send for the carriage, Miss Jenny?"

"Er—no thank you, Somers." Jenny hesitated. "I have an important errand this morning which I would rather not disclose to Lady Beddington. I trust that I can count on you not to betray me?"

Somers bowed. "I believe I have already expressed my belief in your ability to take care of yourself, Miss Jenny." He permitted himself a smile. "I shall not betray you."

Jenny smiled back. "Thank you. And if you ever find yourself needing a job, Somers, I do hope that you will come to me."

The butler opened the front door for her before replying. With a slight bow, and a decided twinkle in his eye, he murmured, "To you—and the duke, Miss Jenny?"

Jenny paused just inside the threshold and gave the man a rueful look. "You don't miss much, do you, Somers?"

"If I may take the liberty of saying so, miss, a blind man would have difficulty in missing what has been obvious for some time."

Jenny chuckled softly and passed from the house, hearing the door close behind her. She made her way swiftly down the street toward the corner, where a hackney cab waited. Fashionable society was sleeping peacefully behind closed doors; the streets were silent except for the sounds of servants stirring and merchants moving busily toward their shops.

When Jenny reached the cab, the door was flung open and Spencer descended to the pavement. He smiled, swept his greatcoat aside in a graceful bow, and murmured, "Your carriage, milady."

She laughed, and accepted his assistance to enter the cab. Spencer climbed in after her, and the cab moved off down the street.

The duke reached for her hand. "You aren't nervous, are you, Jenny?"

"Why would I be nervous? Just because I am going to present myself at both the War Office and Bow Street as the Cat—who is known as a notorious thief. *That's* no reason to be nervous, is it?" She smiled rather weakly.

"No reason at all. You'll be forgiven immediately, once your story is known. Trust me."

"Of course I trust you. But are you sure you know what you're doing?"

Spencer chuckled. "Very sure. I found out who to talk to at the War Office—Lord Carrington. If he approves, you will have nothing to fear from the War Office. I must say, he was very intrigued when I spoke with him yesterday. He didn't even object to having to be at the Office at such an ungodly hour."

"I sincerely hope he has had his breakfast. I have never yet known a man who was the least bit reasonable when his stomach was empty."

The duke grinned. "You are the delight of my life. I never know what you're going to say next."

Carrington was a tall man of about the duke's age. His features were alarmingly satanic; his dark brows sloped upward toward his temples, and the almond-shaped eyes were a brilliant green. His face was darkly tanned; he bore the manner and appearance of a man who had traveled much in foreign lands.

Those strange brows shot up when Jenny lifted her veil. "But—it's Miss Courtenay, is it not?"

"Yes, my lord." Jenny glanced at Spencer and received a reassuring smile. Very steadily, her eyes met Carrington's puzzled ones. "I am also the Cat."

The green eyes widened. "Well, I'll be damned," he said softly. After a moment of silence, a smiled appeared and his eyes began to twinkle. "Won't London be in an uproar!"

His amusement did much to dispel Jenny's uneasiness. "May I tell you my story, sir?"

"By all means, Miss Courtenay, by all means."

She told him the whole story, beginning with her father's murder and ending with the discovery that Stoven was the man she had been searching for. Spencer then stepped in to reveal his idea of how to force a confession from Stoven.

There was a long silence in the room. Carrington frowned thoughtfully. "I do not believe the War Office will choose to press charges against the Cat, Miss Courtenay." He smiled suddenly. "In fact, we will publicly applaud the capture of a traitor—and the woman who brought him to justice."

Jenny's relief was too great for words. "Thank you, my lord," she murmured.

Carrington said seriously, "I cannot speak for Bow Street, of course, or the Regent. Either one could make trouble for you."

Spencer smiled wryly. "Brummell promised to use his influence with the Regent."

"Indeed? Then I shouldn't worry if I were you, Miss Courtenay. With Brummell in your corner, I would say that you have nothing to fear." He stood up and extended his hand to Jenny. "I would like to shake the hand of a very remarkable young woman."

Jenny rose and gave him her hand. "Thank you very much, my lord. You have been most kind."

"Nonsense, Miss Courtenay. My friends will tell you that I am never kind. We *will* be grateful if you can force a confession from Stoven. One less traitor will help England a great deal."

He then shook hands with Spencer and escorted them both to the door. "Good luck with Bow Street," he said at the door. "And with your grand finale!"


Brummell was waiting for them on the pavement, a faint frown on his face. He was absently twirling an ivory-headed cane, and held a sheaf of papers in his other hand.

His frown cleared as soon as he saw them. "Tell me the worst. Will the War Office prosecute?"

Spencer appeared faintly surprised to see the Beau up and about so early in the morning, but he answered easily, "No. Carrington said that the Office will back Jenny—especially if we manage to force a confession from Stoven."

"Splendid!" He bowed gracefully to Jenny. "Would you mind very much, Miss Courtenay, if I accompanied you to Bow Street? I have a fancy to meet these Runners of yours."

"They aren't *my* Runners, Mr. Brummell. And of course I don't mind," She eyed the papers he carried uneasily. They bore the royal seal.

Brummell made no mention of the papers until he was sitting across from them, and the cab was moving toward Bow Street. With a slight flourish, he handed the packet to Jenny. "A Royal Pardon," he said lazily, "for one Jennifer Courtenay—alias the Cat."

Jenny carefully broke the seal and examined the documents, while Spencer smiled at Brummell. "Thank you, George," he said quietly.

"Think nothing of it, my friend," the Beau replied lightly. "I am only too happy to help."

Jenny lifted shining eyes from the documents. Her voice husky, she said, "I don't know how to repay you, Mr. Brummell. I don't even know how to thank you."

With unwonted gentleness, Brummell responded, "Please don't try, Miss Courtenay. Spencer will tell you that I never do anything unless I wish to. Believe me—it was my pleasure."

Jenny's lovely smile swept across her face and Brummell, after studying it with the eye of a connoisseur, said very seriously to Spencer, "You will have to lock her up, Nick."

Having no idea how her smile affected men, Jenny looked startled. Nick merely nodded. "I knew that the first time I saw her," he said wryly.

Baffled, she stared from one to the other. "What *are* you talking about?" she asked blankly.

Spencer chuckled softly. "Your beautiful smile, love," he said. "It's dangerous."

Jenny pinkened and fixed her eyes on the documents she held. The two men watched in amusement as she tried vainly to think of some response. Deciding to ignore his remark, she made a determined effort to change the subject. "How did you persuade the Prince to pardon me, sir?"

The keen gray eyes twinkled. "Very easily, I assure you, Miss Courtenay. The problem was to keep him silent until you could make a public disclosure. However," he smiled modestly and said, "I was able to persuade him."

Jenny laughed. "Carrington was right," she remarked. "With you in my corner, I shouldn't have worried."

Brummell sobered. "I am afraid I have no influence at Bow Street. If they choose to prosecute, there is nothing I can do about it."

Calmly, Spencer said, "I, however, do have some influence at Bow Street. Lord Bradford was a good friend of my father's."

Brummell looked startled. "Lord, is he still around?"

"Very much so. He's been the guiding spirit behind Bow Street for years. He will meet us at the office, along with Simmons." He grinned at Jenny. "And his talkative friend."

"Oh, dear," Jenny murmured. "Simmons will not like the way I've been slipping past him lately."

"He may not like it," Brummell said philosophically, "but there is little he can do about it. He must follow the orders of his superiors, after all."

"What if his *superiors* don't like it?"

Spencer reached for her hand and grasped it strongly. "You worry too much, Jenny. Bradford will not choose to prosecute—I'll see to that."

"Either way, it will soon be over," Jenny responded. Her

voice was quiet, absent almost. "I will no longer be forced
to guard every word I say, to look at each man and think
that he might be the one who killed my father. I will no
longer tense when someone mentions the Cat, or see a
hangman's noose above my head when I look into a mirror.
Either way, it will soon be over." She shrugged.

The two men were silent for a long moment, realizing,
perhaps for the first time, what Jenny had been going
through for the past year, and even before—as a child,
growing up in the shadow of her father's murder, knowing
that only she could expose a killer.

"I'm sorry, Jenny," Spencer said quietly.

She looked at the sober faces of the two men, and
smiled suddenly. "So am I. I had no intention of making
you two gentlemen so melancholic. Believe me—I would
not have missed a single day of the past year." Her golden
eyes began to twinkle. "I have met some *very* interesting
people."

Brummell, following her lead, laughed softly. "Present
company included, I assume?"

"Present company—especially."

The cab halted just then, and they realized that they had
arrived at Bow Street. The two men climbed out, and offered assistance to Jenny. She replaced her veil, stepped
carefully out of the cab, and stood on the pavement with a
rather determined look on her lovely face.

Spencer and Brummell silently offered their arms, and
Jenny felt pleasantly reassured as the three entered the
building. Once inside, a sour-faced man in a red waistcoat
curtly requested that they follow him, and led the way to
one of the offices.

A grizzled-haired man with a dashing mustache rose
from behind a massive desk as they were ushered into the
room. He nodded cordially at Spencer, bestowed a faintly

surprised glance on Brummell, and then turned his eyes to Jenny. When the sour-faced man had left the room, she lifted the veil, and felt uneasy upon perceiving that Bradford was not particularly surprised.

He gestured for them to be seated, sank down behind the desk, and then fixed steely blue eyes on Jenny's face. Spencer and Brummell were silent; both had the feeling that Jenny would prefer to handle this confrontation alone.

They were quite right. Subtle threats and innuendos unnerved her, but she was perfectly capable of dealing with a direct threat. With a tiny smile, she remarked, "You are not surprised to see me."

Bradford's lined face was expressionless. "No."

Jenny nodded. "Of course—you would not be. You did set two of your Runners to watch me."

"I did. Reluctantly."

"Why reluctantly?"

Bradford leaned back in his chair, folded his hands over his ample stomach, and continued his unwavering stare. "I have little faith in Sir George Ross's accusations."

"And yet you took action in spite of your lack of faith?"

"I took action, Miss Courtenay, because I have a great deal of faith in my own intuition. However, neither your stepfather's accusations, nor my intuition could be proven. We have found no trace of the Cat's black stallion, and you have not been caught either leaving, or returning to Lady Beddington's house on the nights that the Cat rode."

"And that disappoints you?"

A very faint smile crossed his face. "I knew from the beginning that we were dealing with a very clever woman. I would like to know how you were able to slip past my men."

Jenny's eyes began to twinkle. "I don't recall admitting, my lord, that I am the Cat."

"You have not—yet."

"And you have not a single shred of evidence against me?"

"Not a shred, Miss Courtenay."

"Then why should I admit anything?"

The steely blue eyes warmed slightly. "Miss Courtenay, I doubt very seriously that you came to Bow Street at such an early hour of the morning simply to bandy words with me."

"No, but if I had known how enjoyable it would be to bandy words with you, sir, I would have come sooner."

Bradford smiled, and the tension in the room abated noticeably. "Would you mind telling me where you keep that stallion?"

Jenny hesitated. "In Kent. About an hour's ride from Courtenay manor."

He sighed. "I sent a man to Kent weeks ago. He couldn't find a trace of that horse."

Apologetically, Jenny said, "He's very well hidden."

Bradford smiled wryly. "Is invisibility one of your many talents, Miss Courtenay? Simmons and his partner swear that you never got past them, and yet the Cat has been at large more times than I care to remember."

Brummell, who had been an interested observer to this discussion, murmured irrepressibly, "Simmons and his dreadful cold."

Jenny cast him a shaming look, and then returned her gaze to Bradford's puzzled face. "Please don't blame your men, my lord. Simmons, who was watching the front of the house, had a very bad cold. The poor man could hardly see, and he was sneezing dreadfully. I—er—slipped past him whenever I felt that his cold distracted him."

"I see." Bradford looked thoughtful. "I can understand how Simmons could miss seeing you, Miss Courtenay, but I find it hard to understand—much less forgive—the fact that he missed seeing something the size of your horse. Or did you walk all the way to Kent?"

"No, my lord. Lady Beddington's stables have a rather well-concealed back entrance. Simmons and his partner never saw it; I myself found it quite by accident. I would slip past Simmons, then circle round to the back of the stables—which neither man could see—saddle my mare and leave the stables by the back entrance."

"And when you returned?"

"I would slip into the stables from the back, unsaddle my mare, then circle to the front of the house and get past Simmons. By then, it was usually dawn—and I have discovered that a watchman is never at his best in the hours just before dawn. Simmons never saw me."

Bradford was silent for a moment, obviously working out the time and distances involved. He looked up suddenly, a glint of admiration in his eyes. "That means, Miss Courtenay, that you were in the saddle from dusk until dawn."

Jenny nodded. "More or less."

"And yet you found the energy to continue your mad whirl of parties and balls? No one suspected that you were the Cat? I find that hard to believe, Miss Courtenay."

Jenny flushed slightly. "Nick," she murmured, "and Mr. Brummell have known for some time."

"Indeed?" Bradford looked at Spencer. "How did you discover the truth, Nick?"

"I fell in love with her the night she held up my coach," Spencer replied simply.

A twinkle lit Bradford's eyes. "And the eyes of love found no difficulty in recognizing her without her mask?"

Spencer's eyes twinkled responsively. "None, sir."

Bradford turned his gaze to the Beau. "And you, Mr. Brummell? How did you find out?"

"One or two little things at first," Brummell replied slowly, "made me suspect. Miss Courtenay's slight tension whenever the subject of the Cat was broached—"

"*Slight* tension, Mr. Brummell?" Jenny smiled wryly.

Brummell smiled at her. "Yes, Miss Courtenay. The first time we met, I mentioned the Cat, and your reaction was—odd. Then there was Lady Jersey's party."

"That *dreadful* party," Jenny murmured.

Brummell laughed softly, and turned his eyes to Spencer. "It was just before the two of you had met in society. Lady Jersey held a party, and the sole topic of conversation for everyone present was the Cat. Miss Courtenay was literally showered with remarks and speculation concerning the Cat, and was nearly frantic. However, she managed to allay my suspicions rather neatly—until I mentioned your name. Her reaction convinced me that I had indeed stumbled onto a mystery. I knew that you had been searching the features of every young lady you met for weeks, and I knew that Miss Courtenay was rather worried about meeting you."

He grinned suddenly and turned back to Jenny. "I shall confess to a bit of mischief, Miss Courtenay. I deliberately told you that I thought Nick knew who the Cat was in order to observe your reaction. When you nearly fainted, I felt that my suspicions had been correct."

Before Jenny could respond, Bradford asked, "When did you know for sure?"

"The night of Lady Jersey's next party." Brummell chuckled softly. "I overheard Nick and Miss Courtenay in the middle of a—er—a rather violent argument, during the course of which Miss Courtenay confirmed my suspicions."

There was a moment of silence. Bradford looked thoughtfully at Jenny. "I have known from the beginning," he said, "that the Cat was no common thief. I think you have what you believe is a very good reason for becoming a thief, Miss Courtenay. I would like to hear it."

"Of course, my lord. I would prefer that Simmons and his partner were also present; I think they have a right to know the truth."

Bradford nodded, rose to his feet, and went to the door. He opened it and shouted to someone to send in Simmons and Polyphant.

Jenny choked back an involuntary giggle. Avoiding the duke's amused gaze, she murmured, "Is that his name? I never knew it."

Bradford returned to his desk and resumed his seat. A gleam of amusement in his eyes, he said dryly, "Samuel Polyphant has little to say. You may have noticed."

"Yes, I—er—had noticed." Jenny's smile faded but did not entirely disappear when the two Runners entered the room. She waited for their reactions.

Simmons came in wearing a faint frown, which changed to an almost ludicrous expression of astonishment when he saw Jenny. Polyphant stopped just inside the door, carefully closed it behind him, and stood shuffling his feet and darting nervous glances around the room.

Forgetting the presence of his superior, Simmons exploded, "I knew it! You *are* the Cat!"

Jenny nodded slowly. "Yes, Mr. Simmons. I am the Cat."

After glaring at her for a full minute, Simmons suddenly burst out laughing. With a grin creasing his florid face, he asked, "How've you managed to sneak past us, miss? We never seen you—not even once."

Before Jenny could answer, Bradford spoke up. "Don't tell him, Miss Courtenay. Let him find the answer for himself." He looked sternly at the Runner. "Maybe *next* time he won't be so easily fooled."

Flushed, his expression one of chagrin, Simmons muttered, "I beg pardon, m'lord, but we never seen 'er."

"I am aware of that, Simmons. Painfully aware."

Crushed, Simmons stared at his feet. Polyphant, hoping to escape the wrath of his superior, edged toward the door, only to halt as Bradford spoke his name sharply.

Jenny took pity on the uncomfortable Runners. "Please

don't be too harsh on them, sir. You said yourself that you didn't have a shred of proof against me; I am sure they would have done better if they had know I was the Cat."

"I could argue that point with you, Miss Courtenay, but I will not." He smiled faintly. "Now that Simmons and Polyphant are here, perhaps you would be good enough to tell us your story?"

Jenny told the story simply, beginning eight years before. She told of her father's murder, the talisman ring, her decision to assume the character of a thief. She briefly told of her relationship with Jason, and how he had helped her. Her voice was without expression, her face calm. She brought forth the bald facts and let them speak for themselves.

Spencer, realizing that his love was not going to defend her, interrupted to tell Bradford of her efforts to uncover traitors, her resolve to return the money she had stolen, Carrington's decision on behalf of the War Office, and the Royal Pardon.

Bradford looked at Jenny. "Why did you leave all of these items out of your story, Miss Courtenay? You must realize they would weigh heavily in my decision."

Jenny met the steely gaze squarely. "There can be no excuse for what I have done, my lord. I have knowingly committed crimes against king and country."

"And yet you had a very good reason."

Jenny shrugged tiredly. "I was raised, my lord, to respect the laws of England. It was not easy for me to break them. But break them I did." She raised her chin, her face unconsciously proud. "I will not apologize for that. I do not regret the things I have done—I only regret the necessity of doing them. I have done what I set out to do; I have found my father's killer. I think he would be proud of me."

Bradford studied her for a moment in silence. Then,

slowly, a smile appeared. "Miss Courtenay," he said gravely, "I think your father *would* be very proud of you. And I think that all of England will be proud of you when your story is known. Bow Street will not choose to prosecute." He glanced at Simmons. "Do you not agree, Simmons?"

Simmons, who had been staring at Jenny with awe written large on his face, started and said quickly, "Yes, m'lord. Why, I told Sam from the very start that such a fine young lady must've had a good reason for thievin'—didn't I, Sam?"

Sam grunted.

# Chapter Twenty-three

Spencer surveyed the crowded ballroom grimly. The cream of London society was in attendance, and it promised to be the type of ball that hostesses dream of. Ladies and gentlemen alike were decked out in silks and satins of every imaginable color. Spencer wondered sardonically how all the lords and ladies present would look back on this particular ball.

He felt a touch on his arm, and turned to see Richard Standen's smiling face. "You're looking very satanic, my friend. Is something wrong?"

Spencer regarded him thoughtfully. "Richard, I want you to do me a favor."

His friend looked intrigued. "Name it."

"In a few moments, I am going to make a speech. I would like you to stand by the door," he gestured to the double doors leading into the ballroom, "and see that no one leaves."

"Is the speech that bad?" His smile faded as he gazed at

Spencer's serious face. "Nick, what's going on? What are you going to say?"

"I am going to expose a murderer."

"What! Nick, are you serious?"

"Very. Will you do as I ask?"

"Of course! Who is he? Do I know him?"

Spencer smiled grimly. "You will know him before the night is out." With this rather cryptic utterance, he moved away, leaving Standen to stare after him wonderingly.

Spencer stepped outside, after making sure that he was unobserved. He waited for a moment, until his eyes adjusted to the darkness, then made his way silently through the garden to the gate that opened onto the mews. Just outside stood a small group of men, all wearing red waistcoats. Spencer nodded decisively, and the men parted to reveal a small, slender, black-clad figure.

Jenny quickly stepped forward, her golden eyes glittering behind the black mask. "Is he here, Nick?"

"He's here, love. The last of the guests have just arrived. I'll go inside in a moment and set the stage. Wait outside the garden door and come in when the moment is right." He smiled down at her ruefully. "I know how important this is to you, love, but remember that the eyes of the world will be upon you. Strive to control that temper of yours."

She smiled. "Nick, I've been searching for Papa's killer for a long time. I have no intention of botching things now. I promise to be good."

All of the Runners except one had vanished into the night. The remaining man stepped forward. It was Simmons—the man who had accused Jenny of being the Cat. "My men are all posted around the house, Your Grace; he won't be able to get away." He hesitated, then said, "I hope you an' the lady are right, Your Grace, about Mr. Courtenay's killer."

Spencer nodded. "So do I, Simmons. My mother is

growing old waiting for grandchildren." While the Runner
was puzzling over this remark, the duke gazed once more at
his love. "Be careful," he said quietly.

Ignoring the Runner's interested presence, Jenny said
huskily, "I love you."

The duke struggled with his baser instincts. After a moment he responded with a hoarse, "*Now* you tell me—when
I can't do a thing about it." He turned quickly and headed
toward the house.

Jenny gazed after him for a moment, her eyes soft with
love. Then, with a businesslike air, she turned to the Runner. "It is time for us to assume our places, Mr. Simmons. I
would like you to remain outside the garden door with me.
Once I go in, you'll be able to hear exactly what goes on inside the ballroom."

Simmons nodded. "I was told to follow your orders, miss."

"Then let us go. The curtain is about to rise on our little
drama—and I don't want to miss the first scene." She began
to make her way toward the house, the Runner at her heels.

Spencer stepped inside the ballroom, leaving the door
open. The musicians were playing a waltz and the room was
filled with laughter, talk, and whirling couples. He gazed
toward the hall doors and, catching Standen's eye, nodded.
His friend immediately went to stand, arms folded, before
the doors.

Spencer then moved slowly across the room to a point
near the musicians. He saw Stoven talking to Brummell,
and felt a flicker of amusement at the Beau's bored expression. He glanced at the musicians and made an almost im-
perceptible gesture. Immediately, the music stopped. The
couples on the floor halted, bewildered, and a buzz of
protest broke out.

Spencer mounted the musicians' raised platform. "Ladies
and gentlemen, may I have your attention, please!" His
deep, commanding voice cut through the commotion, and

curious faces turned toward him. He waited for a moment, while the silence grew taut with suspense. His eyes moved over the room. Slowly, he began to speak.

"Ladies and gentlemen, I crave your indulgence for a few moments while I tell a story."

A murmur of confusion was heard, and the guests drew nearer to Spencer, their interest aroused.

"It is not a happy story, my friends. Where murder is involved, there can be no happiness." He nodded grimly at the ring of shocked faces around him. "Aye—murder."

"See here, Spencer!" It was Lord Buckham, his round face concerned. "You shouldn't talk about such things in front of the ladies! Not fitting!"

The duke smiled faintly at the agitated little man. "I have found, my lord, that the female sex is, in general, far less squeamish than we hardy males."

A titter of amusement followed Spencer's remark. Lady Catherine, a most dignified matron, stepped forward. "I believe I can speak for the ladies, Your Grace—we are eager to hear your story."

Spencer bowed to her. Again he paused before speaking. His was an imposing figure at any time, but now, dressed in black as he was and with a decidedly grim expression, he seemed positively threatening.

"My story begins some years ago, outside London. On a fine old country estate, far from the thieves and cutthroats of the city, a gentleman was murdered. The killer escaped— or so he thought. He was unaware that there was a witness to his crime."

Spencer folded his arms and continued. "The witness, my friends, was only a child—a young girl. The shock of what she had seen kept her silent, and later, when she tried to tell her story, no one believed her. But she was determined to bring the killer to justice. And so, the girl waited until she grew older. There was no room in her life for the

pleasures of other young ladies. She thought not of balls
and suitors; her only thought was to find her father's killer."

Lady Catherine again raised her voice. "The poor child."
Her blue eyes were dark with pity. "But what could she do,
Your Grace? How could she hope to find the killer?"

"A difficult problem, my lady, but the girl, now a beautiful young woman, found a solution. You see, the young
woman knew that the years had most likely changed the
killer's appearance. She was uncertain of her ability to recognize him by sight alone. But, ladies and gentlemen, she
had seen him take an article of jewelry from his victim's
body. It was this she hoped to find. And so, this young lady,
as courageous as she was beautiful, took to highway robbery in order to find that article of jewelry."

A collective gasp came from the assemblege. "The Cat!
He's talking about the Cat!" Spencer took the opportunity
to glance toward Stoven. The earl's eyes were riveted on
Spencer, his face pasty-white. He stood stock-still, his hand
gripping his cane tensely.

Spencer smiled grimly and spoke again, his words pro-
ducing instant silence. "The Cat—aye, the young lady became the Cat. She donned a man's clothes and hid her
beauty beneath a hooded mask. She became a thief. But a
very *unusual* thief. The jewelry that she took was almost
immediately returned, and the money is being kept in a safe
place—to be returned to the rightful owners as soon as the
killer is apprehended."

Lord Alver spoke, his eyes intent on the duke. "How do
you know this, Spencer?"

"My path crossed the Cat's some weeks ago," Spencer
replied. "I found myself intrigued by her. I set out to find
the reasons behind her strange career. I found those reasons;
I also discovered that she had—on several occasions—
assisted with the identification and elimination of spies
against England."

"If that is so," Alver said slowly, "then the Cat should be honored—pardoned at the very least."

"My thoughts exactly, Lord Alver. And, the Cat *has* been pardoned—fully and completely. The documents were signed only this morning. But she has one more duty to perform before she hangs up her mask."

Lady Catherine frowned. "Do you mean she must find the killer?"

Spencer bowed. "The killer, my lady, is here—in this very room."

There was a stunned silence, then the room became filled with shocked exclamations. Stoven began to edge toward the door, only to find his path blocked by a smiling Beau Brummell. "Come, Stoven," the Beau said gently, "I am sure you are as eager to learn the identity of the killer as the rest of us." Stoven, denied the chance to make good his escape, turned stiffly to face Spencer.

"Who is the killer, Your Grace?" Lady Catherine asked. "And the Cat—who is she?"

A voice came from the doors leading to the garden. "I believe I am the best person to answer your questions, Lady Catherine." The voice was cool, faintly mocking. As one, the guests turned to face the Cat. By this time, the guests were almost beyond shock; they simply stared.

The Cat moved forward slowly, her hood obscuring all but her glittering eyes and the brilliance of her mocking smile. A black cloak brushed her booted heels with every step, and one black-gloved hand rested lightly on the hilt of the sword she wore—a relic of a bygone age.

She paused and swept her cloak aside in a graceful bow. "Good evening."

Before she could utter another word, a voice spoke from the crowd. "Is it not true that you are a murderess?"

The crowd gave a gasp, and parted to reveal the pale, determined Stoven.

The Cat moved slowly to stand before him. "No, Lord Stoven," she replied calmly, "it is not true." She stared into his eyes and her own glittered with hatred. "Can you say the same?" It was little more than a whisper, but every person in the room heard her words.

Stoven fell back a step. He started to turn, and felt his arm seized by a powerful hand. It was Brummel. "The lady asked you a question," said the Beau impassively. "It would be rude of you to ignore it."

"She's mad!" Stoven exclaimed. "I've never killed anyone!"

In a flash, the Cat's hand darted out to snatch the cane from his grasp. He started forward instinctively and was once again halted by Brummell's hand.

The Cat twirled the cane and said casually, "The killer that I seek has a certain ring in his possession. Do you know anything about that ring, my lord?" Stoven was silent; sweat beaded his brow.

The Cat twisted the silver head of the cane and seemed surprised when it came off in her hand. "Why, what is this?" She slowly turned the silver head until a ring rolled out in her hand. "A ring—a talisman ring. In fact, the very ring I seek."

Stoven strained against Brummell's powerful hand. "I killed no one!" he gasped.

"Then why do you have in your possession Thomas Courtenay's ring?" Her voice was cold.

"You put it there," he said desperately, "when you took my cane! When you robbed me!"

She smiled grimly. "You will have to find another explanation, Stoven. The ring was already in the cane the night I robbed you. I have a witness to prove it."

"I'm sure you do," Stoven sneered. "Another thief—like yourself."

Spencer, who had been moving silently through the

crowd, stopped just behind the Cat. "Do you consider me a thief, Stoven?" he asked coldly.

Stoven goggled at him. "You?"

"Yes. You see, *I* am the witness she spoke of. I rode with her the night she held up your coach."

Stoven went whiter than before. "You still can't prove I put the ring into the cane."

The Cat smiled gently. "I saw you kill Thomas Courtenay. Oh, you have changed in the past eight years—I'll grant that—but you still have that peculiar little scar beneath your right ear. I took particular notice of that—eight years ago. Now, how many men do you suppose there are in England who have a scar shaped like a horseshoe beneath their right ear and who carry a talisman ring concealed in the head of their cane?"

Stoven sneered again. "Who will believe the word of a thief?"

"Well now—*there* you have a point. The Cat may not be believed." She reached up and calmly removed the hood. "But I think people will listen to—and believe—Jennifer Courtenay."

There was a gasp from the crowd. Jenny, ignoring everyone else, fixed her eyes on Stoven's pale face. "Why did you kill my father, Stoven?" she asked softly. "Was it because he was going to expose you as a traitor? Was it that?" She smiled gently at his start of surprise. "Oh, yes—I know all about that. You see, Stoven, my father always kept a journal. He wrote down everything that was important to him. And finding a traitor is certainly very important."

Stoven broke free of Brummell's restraining hand and stared wildly around the room. "It's a conspiracy! You're all against me!" He started to turn toward the door, and froze in his tracks as the point of Jenny's sword touched his throat.

"Would you like me to cut the truth out of you, Stoven?"

He stared into her deadly eyes and became suddenly calm. "All right. I killed him. I killed Thomas Courtenay. I had no choice—he was going to tell them."

Only sheer willpower kept Jenny from cutting his throat. She thought of the father she had lost, and her arm trembled slightly from the effort of holding back.

As Simmons entered through the garden doors, Jenny slowly lowered the sword. "I hope you rot in hell!" she said in a fierce whisper.

Stoven, staring into the chill of her golden eyes, felt almost relieved when Simmons took his arm and said, "Lord Stoven, I hereby arrest you for the murder of Thomas Courtenay." He was led silently away.

Suddenly, the room errupted into noisy confusion. People crowded around Jenny, congratulating her for finding her father's killer, and expressing admiration for her daring masquerade.

Brummell stepped up to Spencer, a faint smile on his face. "A fine woman you've picked for yourself, Nick. She has fire and spirit. I sincerely hope you know what you're doing—trying to tame her, I mean. Wouldn't care to try it myself."

Spencer looked at the Beau with some surprise. "I don't mean to try, George. Why should I? I love her."

Brummell watched him move away. To himself, he murmured, "That just may do it, my friend. That just may do it."

Jenny looked about her, dazed, and became dimly conscious of Spencer telling everyone that she was tired and would talk to them all later. Then he was leading her through the sympathetic crowd and out into the garden. She was unaware of the tears that coursed down her cheeks. Her only thought was that—at last—it was over.

Once in the privacy of the garden, Spencer took her into his arms and held her gently while sobs racked her slender body. Loving her as he did, he knew that the tears were a needed release from the tensions and fears of the past years.

At long last, her sobs died away, and she lifted tear-bright eyes to gaze up at him. "I—I'm sorry," she whispered huskily. "I don't know what came over me."

Spencer cupped her face in his large hands and smiled gently. "If anyone has a right to tears, love, it is you."

"I just can't believe it's over. It is, isn't it, Nick? It is over?"

"Yes, love—it's over. And now we can spend the rest of our lives together with no shadow hanging over us."

"Nick, are you—are you sure? So much has happened since we met—"

He laid a gentle finger across her lips, silencing her hesitant words. There was a glow deep in his eyes. "I am very, very sure, Jenny. Sure that I love you—sure that I want you to be my wife."

Jenny slipped her arms around his neck. With a glowing smile, she said, "I believe you mean that, Your Grace."

A laugh rumbled deep in his chest. "You require a great deal of convincing."

"Well? What are you waiting for?" There was an impish gleam in her eyes. "Convince me."

And he did.

❧ **Masquerade**

# Chapter One

A cold wind snatched at her cloak as Cassandra Eden bent forward to peer in the direction of her coachman's pointing finger. She shivered as she looked at the broken axle. It was a *very* broken axle, and she did not require the opinion of an expert coach-builder to perceive that the vehicle was not going anywhere until it was repaired. Cassandra's dismay intensified when fat white flakes of snow began to swirl through the gloom of approaching night.

"Oh, no," she said.

John Potter, her coachman, nodded glumly. "I suspicioned that axle was cracked, miss, and this godforsaken road finished it off right enough. There'll have to be a new one, and where to find aught tonight—"

"Obviously we won't be able to get it repaired tonight," Cassandra said with a sigh. "But we must have shelter. How far to the nearest inn, John?"

The grizzled coachman ruminated with a frown, then

said, "That'd be the Boar's Head, miss, and it's all of twenty miles along and back on the main road."

Even a lightweight racing curricle and team of fine horses would have required more than an hour for the journey on such a bad road, but in any case Cassandra had neither. She had a weary team of well-bred but sturdy horses and an elderly, broken coach that should have been left in her uncle's London stables. It was late January, late afternoon, and the leaden sky was a grim indication that the drifting flakes of snow were only the overture to a storm.

Cassandra glanced up at the window of the coach, where her maid's worried face could be seen, then stepped away and surveyed the countryside with considerable—though masked—worry of her own. A damaged bridge some miles back had necessitated this detour from the normal route between London and Bristol; they were presently somewhere in north Berkshire, an area that was almost exclusively patchy forests and endless acres of cultivated or pastured land.

"John, is that a manor house? There—on the edge of that forest across the field?"

The coachman squinted, then nodded slowly. "It appears to be, miss. Haven't seen another place bigger'n a cottage for miles, so stands to reason there'd be an estate of some kind in these parts. Lonesome place, though."

Cassandra agreed silently. In the fading light it was difficult to see clearly, but she thought the distant house looked lonely and more than a little desolate. But that was probably the weather, she told herself sternly.

"We shall go there, then," she said in a decided tone. "Another half mile along this road should bring us to the drive, I think."

"I'll go, Miss Cassie. I'm sure they'd be agreeable an' send a carriage—"

"Oh, nonsense, John. I would much rather walk to the

house than huddle in the coach awaiting rescue. We shall not impose upon our host any more than absolutely necessary. Come out, Sarah—we must walk from here."

Her maid, a pretty but apprehensive young woman no more than a few years older than her mistress, left the shelter of the coach reluctantly. "Walk, Miss Cassie?"

Cassandra could hardly help but smile at Sarah's consternation; town bred, the maid considered anything outside London's narrow and bustling streets the wilderness and undoubtedly quaked at the thought of walking any distance at all through this bleak landscape.

"Would you prefer to freeze, Sarah?" She didn't wait for a response but directed the groom to unstrap her smallest bag from the coach and hand it down to her. Since the horses were standing wearily with no need to be held, the lad scrambled atop the coach and did as he was bid.

"I'll carry that, miss," John Potter told her as he reached up for the bag. "Tom can stay with the coach till I bring help from the manor. An' you won't be wantin' to rap on a strange door with no more than this slip of a girl beside you."

Cassandra, who was neither a shy woman nor one who imagined herself threatened where there was no cause, was a little amused as well as resigned by her servant's determined protection. It was one of the reasons her uncle had allowed her to set out from London with only her maid; he knew very well that John Potter was a more trustworthy guard than any number of outriders and could be depended upon to defend as well as advise Cassandra in the event of trouble.

"I very much doubt the manor is filled with desperadoes," she told him in a dry tone.

"Likely not, miss," the coachman returned stolidly. "But Sir Basil would have my head on a platter was I to let you out of my sight before I was sure you'd be in good hands."

Too wise—and too chilled—to bother protesting further, Cassandra merely told Sarah to take care on the uneven surface of the road, then struck out briskly. Unlike her maid, she was country bred and enjoyed daily long walks when she was home, so this trifling distance bothered her not at all.

Her estimation of the distance involved turned out to be fairly accurate; they came upon the manor's neat driveway a little more than half a mile from the stranded coach, and Sarah had complained of sore feet only once. But the drive itself wound along for another half mile, and it was nearly dark by the time they neared the house.

John Potter seemed much reassured by the condition of the place, commenting once that care and money had been spent here right enough. Cassandra agreed silently. The estate was clearly in excellent shape, the lawns immaculate and the shrubbery pruned, and the manor house itself was neat as a pin, at least on the outside. For the first time she wondered whom it belonged to; the place was a fair distance from London—inconvenient in a country house.

Not that she was in any position to be particular as to the identity of her host, of course. She needed shelter.

With her servants half a step behind her on either side, Cassandra trod up the steps and applied the gleaming brass knocker firmly. When the door was pulled open almost immediately, she had to fight the impulse to step back, and Sarah's gasp was perfectly audible in the startled quiet.

It had become dark enough outside that the only illumination came from inside the house, and in that faint light half of the manservant's grim, swarthy face was visible. Unfortunately for the maid's disordered nerves, that side of his face bore an ugly scar that twisted from the corner of his left eye to the corner of his mouth, and the disfigurement lent him an appearance of menace virtually guaranteed to terrify an imaginative young woman.

"Yes?" he said, his unusually deep voice another shock.

Cassandra's alarm had been momentary, and when she spoke it was pleasantly. "Good evening. I am afraid I have suffered a slight misfortune on the road and require assistance."

The servant's chilly gray eyes looked her up and down swiftly, and then were veiled by lowered lids. "Indeed, miss? We don't get many travelers out this way."

A little impatient at being kept standing out in the cold and snow by a servant—hardly the kind of treatment to which she was accustomed—Cassandra's voice sharpened. "I don't doubt it. Be assured I would hardly have come this way myself had not a bridge washed out some miles back. Would you kindly be good enough to inform your master of my plight? I have my maid, as you see, and my coachman will require assistance to bring my coach and horses safely off the road."

It was not in her character to be so peremptory, particularly with a servant in a private house, but Cassandra was chilled and tired, and all she wanted was something hot to drink and a brisk fire where she could warm her hands and feet. And she was not pleased by the notion that this manservant regarded her with only thinly disguised disdain.

And, indeed, he hesitated after she spoke just long enough to subtly imply that it was his decision rather than hers to admit her to the house. He stepped back, opening the door wider, and said in a colorless tone, "If you'll step this way, miss, I'll inform His Lordship."

Cassandra came into the entrance hall, which was quite impressive and blessedly warm, and said, "His Lordship?"

"Yes, miss. The Earl of Sheffield. This is Sheffield Hall." He said it as if he seriously doubted she had not been aware of the information.

She heard a quickly indrawn breath from Sarah, and Cassandra felt a bit dismayed herself. The Earl of Sheffield?

Though she had never met him—or even seen him, for that matter—two Seasons in London had certainly exposed her to all the talk concerning one of the more infamous rakes of past Seasons.

*Stone's his name, stone his heart.* That was what they said about Stone Westcott, the Earl of Sheffield. It was always said with a sad shake of the head and an ominous frown, a warning to all young ladies of quality to stay out of the earl's path if they wished to keep their good names— and their hearts. Of course, unmarried young ladies were considered too innocent to hear what sin, precisely, Sheffield was guilty of committing, and so those interested or merely curious were reduced to piecing together whispers and overheard comments and arriving at some conclusion, however unsatisfying.

The facts Cassandra felt reasonably sure of were few. Sheffield sprang from a long line of apparently rakish earls, most of whom had treated their reputations with careless disregard and the rules of society with even less respect. Sportsmen rather than dandies, they had excelled in all the manly pursuits, and among the numerous sporting records gentlemen discussed, many were held by various Westcotts. They seemed to own the finest horseflesh and to drive their racing vehicles farther and faster than anyone else (often merely to win a bet), were famous for their punishing fists in the boxing ring, and were said to be superior marksmen.

And for generations they had seemingly held a powerful, unusual fascination for the women they encountered. Rarely handsome and never famed for their social graces, they nevertheless boasted an astonishing history filled with conquests. It was whispered that more than one lady of quality had abandoned her morals and, many times, a husband and family in order to run off with "one of those Westcotts."

From all Cassandra had heard, this particular Westcott, the current earl, was worse than all his ancestors put together.

All this flashed through her mind as the dour manservant crossed the hall on silent feet and opened the door to the parlor, where she and Sarah would wait, but her hesitation was momentary despite her misgivings. She had little choice, after all.

"What name shall I give His Lordship, miss?" the servant inquired as he held the door.

Before Cassandra could reply, her maid spoke up in a voice that was higher than usual and definitely frightened. "Wells. She is Miss Wells."

Once again, Cassandra's hesitation was fleeting. *It hardly matters, after all. With luck, the coach can be repaired tomorrow, and I will never see Sheffield after that.* So she didn't correct her maid, allowing the lie to stand.

But as soon as they were alone in the lovely, snug parlor, Cassandra took a chair near the crackling fire, held out her gloved hands toward the flames, and said severely, "Sarah, why on earth did you say such a thing? Wells is your name, not mine."

"You know very well why, Miss Cassie," Sarah retorted with spirit. "They say the earl has run through his fortune and intends to wed an heiress—and you're under his roof unprotected! He's already ruined one lady and only laughed when her brother demanded he marry her *and* nearly killed the brother in the most wicked duel the next day!"

Cassandra's surprise was momentary. Naturally, Sarah would have heard servants' gossip—which was clearly more candid than what was whispered abovestairs. But was it any more truthful?

"Duels in this day and age? Sarah—"

"It's true, Miss Cassie. It was years ago, but it happened. My cousin was groom to—to the young lady's brother, and he swears he saw it with his own eyes. How the earl stood there smiling like a *fiend* and then shot that poor young man, blood everywhere, and then he just walked away. And he was still smiling, Miss Cassie! Like a devil!" Sarah shuddered, obviously finding a ghoulish delight in the retelling of such a dramatic story.

Cassandra was unwillingly impressed but reminded herself silently that gossip—even that supposedly obtained by an eyewitness—could seldom be relied upon to be wholly truthful. Still, it seemed at least probable that a meeting had taken place between the disreputable earl and some man he had grossly insulted, though the cause as well as the meeting itself was doubtless less dramatic than Sarah's cousin had described.

"Be that as it may, you have put me in an awkward position," she told her maid firmly. "Whatever the earl may have been guilty of in his past, there is no reason to suppose he would be anything but courteous to a stranded traveler, and I very much dislike facing him with a lie."

Unrepentant, Sarah said, "Even a saint can be tempted, miss, and tempting a sinner is foolish! Bad enough you're so pretty and look so delicate—if he knew you had a fortune as would make a nabob stare, he'd be after you in a trice!"

Cassandra couldn't help laughing, but she shook her head as well and lapsed into silence as she warmed her hands at the fire. Hiding her identity had not been her doing, and it was not what she wanted, but now that Sarah had taken that step, she was uncertain if she would correct the situation.

She was not afraid of Sheffield, or of being under his roof without the protection of a family member; no matter how black the earl was painted, he was indisputably a gentleman. He might well flaunt the conventions of society, and he might even have compromised a lady and then refused to marry her, but he would no more take advantage of a young lady temporarily under his protection than he would rob a bank.

So it wasn't fear of him that made Cassandra hesitate to offer her true identity. It was, more than anything, a rather weary repugnance for the inevitable response her name evoked in so many of the men she had met. Fortune hunters had dogged her steps since the day she had come out into society, and she was very tired of weighing the sincerity of every compliment and searching each charming smile for signs of duplicity or greed.

At least if Sheffield had no idea she was an heiress, she would be able to relax that particular guard. Not that she expected him to attempt to charm her—despite Sarah's flattering words, Cassandra knew herself to be too dark for fashionable prettiness, too tall, and so pale and fine-boned that she appeared ridiculously fragile—but her social mask had become so fixed that it required a conscious effort to relax.

Which was one reason she had decided to go home for a few weeks.

Cassandra was still undecided about exposing Sarah's lie when the door opened a few moments later and a trim middle-aged woman in sober raiment entered the room carrying a tray.

"Good evening, Miss Wells. I am His Lordship's housekeeper, Mrs. Milton. He'll be down to welcome you shortly but asked that I see to your needs in the meanwhile. Your coachman has gone with some of our men to fetch your coach and horses, and I will take your maid and baggage to the room being prepared for you. We keep country hours here, but supper has been put back to allow you time to warm and refresh yourself."

As she accepted a cup of steaming tea, Cassandra said

apologetically, "I am sorry to have disrupted the routine of the household, Mrs. Milton."

Her own tone comfortable and placid, the housekeeper replied, "There's no bother, miss. We have visitors rarely enough, but His Lordship expects things to be done right. Now—I'll take your maid up and see to her, and as soon as the room is ready, I'll be back for you."

"Thank you," Cassandra murmured. Left alone in the warm parlor, she reflected wryly that the moment for confessing Sarah's lie was beginning to recede into the distance. Every time she faced someone as "Miss Wells," it would become more and more difficult to tell the truth.

She removed her gloves and untied the ribbons of her bonnet to remove it as well, having been reassured that she would remain at the Hall at least for tonight. The mirror over the fireplace told her that her dark curls were sadly crushed. She did what she could to restore them but did not worry particularly about it; she was not a vain woman and, moreover, had no desire to present any more than a neat and ladylike appearance to the earl.

She had finished her tea as well as a slice of bread and butter, and was feeling much warmer and more comfortable— and, in fact, a little sleepy—when the door opened a second time and her host strode in.

Cassandra rose to her feet in a response that had less to do with politeness than with something deeper and more basic within her, and her drowsiness vanished.

"How do you do, ma'am?" the earl said in a rather hard, abrupt tone as he came toward her. "I am Sheffield."

She did not know what, precisely, she had expected, but Lord Sheffield surprised her. She doubted he was much past thirty, which was rather young to be so infamous a reprobate. He was an unusually big man, well over six feet tall, with very wide and powerful shoulders, and he moved with an almost eerie, catlike grace. His thick hair was black, his eyes dark and brooding, his complexion tanned; he was not a conventionally handsome man, but he was quite definitely . . . impressive.

Cassandra offered her hand, having to look up to meet his eyes, which was rare for her. "Lord Sheffield. I am— Miss Wells. Cassandra Wells." She heard herself continue with the lie but was still unsure why she had.

His hand, unexpectedly well formed and beautiful, held hers for a brief moment and then released it while his frowning dark eyes looked her over with more censure than admiration—or even curiosity—and his voice was still abrupt when he spoke. "You're traveling alone? What was your family thinking of to allow a girl of your age to travel alone?"

The impatience in his tone did not disturb Cassandra; her uncle was a man of irritable temperament, and she got along quite well with him. Nor was she offended by his assumption of extreme youth; she knew only too well that, despite her height, large eyes and a childlike voice—which she had attempted in vain to mature—caused her to appear a good four or five years younger than her actual age.

If she had removed her cloak, he would have had no doubt of her maturity; slender virtually everywhere else, her breasts were well formed and generous—the envy of her friends but an attribute with which Cassandra had never been quite comfortable because of the way men looked at her. So while she might, if she wished, have added to the lie and allowed him to believe her much younger, her own body made it unlikely she would be believed.

"I am not a child, my lord, and I often travel alone," she told him, polite and perfectly composed.

He frowned. "How old are you?"

Cassandra had hoped to avoid a direct answer, but the blunt question—however rude—demanded one. Lifting her chin a trifle, she said, "I am twenty, my lord."

His brows lifted in surprise. "You don't look it—or sound it. But I maintain that you should not be traveling alone; twenty is still hardly more than a child. Sit down, ma'am." He stepped away from her to stand with one shoulder idly propped against the mantel. "Have my people seen to your comfort?"

She resumed her seat and replied only to the last rather indifferent question. "Yes, Mrs. Milton has been very kind, and I understand my coach and horses are being fetched."

He nodded, gazing at her in a very direct way that was a bit unsettling. "They are. According to your coachman, you suffered a broken axle?"

"My coach did," she murmured.

The hard stare continued for a moment, but then he smiled quite suddenly—and his harsh face was lit with warmth. "I stand corrected, ma'am."

Cassandra felt herself smiling back at him and coping with the oddest sensations. A kind of fluttering near her heart that she had never experienced before. It was deeply disturbing, almost frightening, and she was very glad when the sensation faded. She thought there was even a touch of relief in her voice when she spoke to him. "Can it be repaired quickly, my lord? I am expected home tomorrow."

"Your destination is Bristol?"

"Some miles northeast of Bristol, yes."

The earl's smile had been brief, the seemingly habitual frown quickly returning, but his voice seemed less abrupt when he said, "The broken axle is not the problem, ma'am; I would be happy to lend you one of my vehicles and send your coach along later once it is repaired. However, the weather has definitely taken a turn for the worse, and I doubt travel will be possible for at least a few days."

Dismayed, she said, "But there was only a little snow falling when we arrived—"

"There is much more than a little now; it is mixed with

sleet as well, and the wind is building steadily. Unless I much mistake the matter, we will be in the midst of a full-blown storm before midnight."

Cassandra's consternation increased, but she was too sensible to struggle fruitlessly against the potent combination of fate and nature. It appeared that her destiny included an enforced stay at Sheffield Hall. Sighing, she said, "I am sorry, my lord, but it seems I must impose upon you for the duration."

He bowed slightly with more courtesy than enthusiasm, his harsh face immobile. "It is, of course, my pleasure to offer you shelter, ma'am."

She felt one of her eyebrows rise before she could halt the indication of derision at the conventional—and obviously reluctant—offer but was able to respond politely. "Thank you very much, Lord Sheffield."

There was a sudden gleam in his dark eyes, and a faint smile played about the corners of his strong mouth, but before he could say anything the door opened and Mrs. Milton came to convey Cassandra to her room.

Sheffield bowed again, this time with a slightly mocking tilt to his dark head. "I would be honored, ma'am, if you would join me for supper. In an hour?"

Cassandra picked up her gloves and bonnet, rose to her feet, and curtsied with a brevity that held a subtle touch of her own mockery. He could deride the often stiff and formal conventions of polite society if he chose, she decided, but there was no reason why she should pretend she didn't understand his indirect ridicule; she refused to play dumb.

"Thank you, my lord," she replied sweetly. Then she followed the housekeeper from the parlor. She didn't look back at the earl, and so she didn't see his smile—or see it die as he turned his gaze to the bright fire.

# Chapter Two

The room provided by her host was lovely, and as Cassandra allowed Sara to divest her of her traveling dress, she decided that if Sheffield was indeed in financial difficulties, he had certainly not scrimped on keeping his estate up to snuff. There were no signs of economizing that she had seen: The house was neither chilly nor drafty and appeared to be in excellent repair; none of the main rooms seemed to be closed up in order to avoid having to heat them; brisk and generous fires burned in the grates; and the linens and draperies seemed in excellent condition. Still, Cassandra was completely aware that such things were not necessarily signs of a full purse. Many a noble family had kept up an appearance of prosperity while falling deeper and deeper in debt.

"The velvet gown, Miss Cassie?" Sarah inquired as she brushed out her mistress's raven hair before the dressing table.

Drawn from her musings, Cassandra hesitated. The velvet gown, while elegant and entirely suitable for a winter's evening, was also high-necked and long-sleeved, and not particularly flattering. Sarah, of course, suggested that particular gown because it was imminently *proper*, with no unseemly display of flesh—with which to tempt a sinner.

Cassandra knew she should accept her maid's sensible suggestion and wear the velvet gown, but she kept hearing the earl's brusque voice stating that "twenty is still a child," and she felt ridiculously belligerent about the matter. She was a mature and intelligent woman, and strongly disliked being viewed as a child.

"No," she heard herself say in a disinterested tone. "The blue silk, Sarah. And my lace shawl."

The brush stopped abruptly, and in the mirror Sarah's expression could only be described as appalled. "The blue silk, miss? But—"

Quite gently Cassandra repeated, "The blue silk, Sarah."

Sarah considered her mistress to be one of the kindest possible, but she understood that tone perfectly well and knew better than to argue with a mind made up. Swallowing whatever comments she wanted to offer, she murmured an obedient response, finished arranging the gleaming black hair, and then went to lay out the blue silk gown.

Some minutes later as she considered her reflection in the mirror, Cassandra knew a twinge of doubt. The gown, while perfectly proper for evening dining in a private home, *was* rather revealing. Low-cut, it left her shoulders bare and covered no more than three-quarters of her breasts. The blue silk was drawn up snug beneath her breasts and clung to the remainder of her body with every movement, glimmering slightly as silk did when light played over the material.

Though she could boast a jewel collection to rival any woman's in London, Cassandra tended to wear very little ornamentation to even the fanciest dress balls; all she wore tonight were tiny gold earrings and a wide blue velvet ribbon around the base of her throat, to which was pinned a cameo. The lace shawl, beautifully made and very old—it had been her mother's—did not so much cover her bare shoulders as it did cunningly reveal them.

The effect of the outfit was what Cassandra had hoped. While no one could have had the least doubt she was a lady of quality dressed with simple elegance, there was also no doubt she was a woman.

She knew an impulse to change into something less revealing but chided herself sternly. There was absolutely nothing wrong with what she was wearing—it was perfectly proper—and she would *not* behave like a missish female by covering herself in layers of clothing in order to thwart advances the earl certainly had no intention of making!

With that resolve in mind, she left her room with her head held high—and found the grim manservant awaiting her out in the corridor.

His name, Sarah had reported with a shudder, was Anatole. He was neither butler nor valet, but more of a head steward, responsible for making sure the earl's household was run as smoothly as possible. He was not English; Sheffield had apparently found him during a trip abroad several years before, and between the two—according to Sarah—was a relationship quite different from the usual between master and servant.

*How* it differed was something Sarah had not been able to say beyond remarking that Anatole was reportedly quite blunt in his speech to the earl and that he seemed to "take a great deal upon himself" when it came to running the household. Apparently, there were hostilities of a sort going on between Anatole and the Hall's housekeeper, a long-standing tug of war over who was in charge.

All that flitted through her mind as Cassandra left her room and found Anatole waiting for her, and she couldn't help wondering if there had been a tussle to determine who would escort her down to supper.

The manservant, his scarred face expressionless, bowed to her with more politeness than he had yet shown. "I am Anatole, miss. Most find the Hall difficult to negotiate at first; I will show you the way."

She had a good sense of direction and was confident she could find her own way, but Cassandra didn't object. Composedly she said, "Thank you, Anatole," and followed him down the hall.

The Hall *was* both unusually large and laid out rather peculiarly, she thought as they made two turns and traversed three short hallways before reaching the main staircase. But there were candles aplenty to light the way, most in sconces, and by the time her escort had bowed her into a pleasant drawing room, Cassandra was confident she had memorized the way.

Lord Sheffield was in the drawing room. He, too, had changed, from the country buckskins he had worn earlier to knee-britches and a long-tailed coat. His coat was cut so that he could shrug himself into it without the aid of his valet, and his cravat was neatly rather than beautifully arranged, but the less dandified dress suited him admirably, Cassandra thought. He was a physically powerful man and would have looked a trifle absurd decked out in the affectations of a town tulip.

"Good evening, ma'am." He bowed as she came toward him, but he did not leave his position by the fire and move to meet her. "I trust your room is—"

Cassandra felt heat rise in her cheeks as his impassive query broke off abruptly. His dark gaze was every bit as direct as it had been earlier, unnervingly direct, and she had the doubtful satisfaction of knowing that the blue silk gown had chased all notions of childishness out of his head.

"My room is quite lovely and entirely comfortable, my lord, thank you," she replied as if he had completed the question, her own voice sedate. She sat down in a chair near the fire, forcing herself to continue meeting that unsettling stare. However, she had not fully considered the earl's characteristic bluntness, and so his next words caught her by surprise.

"I see I am to stand corrected a second time, ma'am. Twenty is not always a child, after all. You have a magnificent figure."

For a brief moment Cassandra debated whether she should take offense or else pretend he had not said anything that was certainly frank beyond the bounds of what was appropriate; those *were,* after all, the only two acceptable ways of handling such disgraceful bluntness. But as she gazed into his dark eyes, she felt a surge of recklessness inside her. After two Seasons of polite conversation and genteel advances from gentlemen, she found the matter-of-fact admiration in the earl's words and tone curiously refreshing.

"Thank you." Her voice was a bit dry but calm. She frowned slightly. "Though I suppose I am hardly responsible; I am told I very much resemble my mother."

The earl seemed amused, whether by her clear acceptance of his scandalous manners or by her response she could not be certain.

"Indeed? Then I envy your father."

She had asked for the outrageous response, Cassandra decided ruefully. Unable to hide her amusement, she merely said, "Do not be so quick to envy him, my lord; my mother was also infamous for her temper. She was half French, you see, and prone to throw things when she became enraged."

"And do you throw things, ma'am?"

Thoughtfully she replied, "I have not so far become more than irritated, I should say. So there is really no telling what I would do when thoroughly enraged."

The earl was definitely smiling. "While I have no wish to enrage you, I confess I am most curious. I have never seen a lady throw things."

It was most improper, but Cassandra could not help offering him a hint of her sophistication by casually responding, "Perhaps not, but I am sure you have, in the course of your life, seen *some* female in the throes of passion."

"One or two," he retorted without hesitation.

Cassandra felt another blush rise in her cheeks as she suddenly recollected that the word *passion* had many meanings, but she refused to allow the unintended blunder to cause her to retreat back into conventional politeness.

With dignity she said, "I should be much surprised, my lord, if you had *not* observed some female enraged enough to throw things at you. You seem to me a man at whom any female would frequently become *infuriated.*"

He laughed suddenly, and she felt once again that mysterious and alarming flutter insider her. His whole face changed when he laughed, from something hard and rather forbidding into something warmly and unexpectedly attractive. She was curiously breathless for an instant and knew an impulse to rise and touch him—an urge as shocking as it was incredible.

"That is probably quite true, ma'am," he said, concurring somewhat wryly with her charge. "I have a blunt character and a thoughtless tongue—and both have led me into difficulties with the female sex on more than one occasion."

Having recovered her composure, Cassandra said, "As I said, my lord, I cannot have any doubt of that."

Whatever he might have said then was prevented by the opening of the door. Anatole stood there, his gaze on the earl, and bowed slightly before retreating. Cassandra assumed from this that their meal was ready to be served, a guess confirmed when Sheffield stepped toward her and offered his arm.

"Shall we? I understand my cook has exerted himself, delighted by the prospect of a more appreciative audience than I provide."

"So you are a man of plain tastes, my lord?" Cassandra rose and took his arm, very conscious of his nearness and the contact as he escorted her toward the dining room. She was far more accustomed to being on eye level with most gentlemen; the earl's height and evident strength made her aware of him in a way she had never known before.

"When it comes to what I find on my table, yes, ma'am. I have no liking for heavy sauces, and that preference is apparently a knife to the heart of any fine cook."

That may have been so, Cassandra thought much later, but the earl seemed to enjoy his cook's efforts as much as she did herself. The food was excellent—and the company was even more so. After her exhausting day she had thought herself too weary either to care what she ate or to be much interested in conversation, but both beliefs were in error.

When the meal was finished, Sheffield suggested that she forgo the custom of withdrawing while he enjoyed his port in lonely splendor, and she was pleased to accept; in her uncle's house that practice was confined to evenings in which there were no guests present, and she had always enjoyed the relaxed and casual conversation with her aunt and uncle.

In the earl's snug dining room it seemed to her just as comfortable. He drank his port, she leaned her elbows on the table, and they talked on in the frank manner so quickly established between them, discussing subjects ranging from the treacherous unpredictability of the weather this time of year to the war with France.

He seemed quite interested in her opinions even when they disagreed with his, and never once treated her as anything other than an equal with an intelligent mind fine enough to challenge his own. Cassandra had encountered that unusual attitude in only one other man, her uncle, and she responded to Sheffield with a pleased freedom from constraint that made her virtually glow.

The conversation turned eventually to the social scene. The earl laughed often, much entertained by her perceptive and pungent descriptions of society, particularly when she became somewhat indignant on the subject of young girls "married off to the highest bidder"—that being her opinion of London's glittering social Season.

"When did you come out, ma'am?" he asked her.

"Last Season. I was presented at Court, of course, and *that* was interesting enough, but the rest tried my patience sorely."

"Balls and routs? Dancing at Almack's? Theater parties?" His voice was matter-of-fact.

Cassandra, who knew that the earl was welcome at any private social event as well as Almack's should he happen to grace London with his presence, felt curious as to why he had for years—to her knowledge—avoided such events. While many in society clearly still disapproved of him, and mothers of marriageable daughters quailed at the mere mention of his name, he undoubtedly had friends and connections who urged him to attend their social gatherings.

But she shied away from asking the question, reluctant to bring up the subject of his place in society both because she did not want to betray what knowledge she had and because she was afraid the discussion would change the frank and easy manner between them. So she merely answered his questions.

"Yes. And visits of ceremony, and rides in the park

where one cannot even shake the fidgets out of one's mount with a brisk gallop. The necessity of changing one's clothing half a dozen times each day. Having one's toes crushed at least twice each evening by an unwary step, and being forced to suffer both the sly digs of matchmaking mamas with daughters to settle and the measuring scrutiny of gentlemen silently debating one's attributes and possibilities."

Sheffield chuckled. "I daresay you encountered quite a number of the latter, ma'am."

Since she wanted to avoid any mention of the fortune hunters who had dangled after her, Cassandra merely said briskly, "According to the current standards of beauty, I am both too dark and too tall to be accounted any more than passably attractive, my lord, as you well know. However, I must say that a number of gentlemen seemed to believe that my possibilities were worth their interest."

"Yes, there must be a few intelligent men among the town bucks," the earl stated casually. "Doubtless you have received several offers. Then why are you unattached, ma'am? If this has been your second Season, you must be conscious of the usual pressure brought to bear upon young ladies expected to become betrothed quickly to a suitable candidate."

Cassandra hesitated, but then answered truthfully. "I have a blessed advantage most of my contemporaries lack. My uncle—who had been my guardian for fifteen years— has the novel idea that I might like to decide my own future. To that end, he has left the decision of marriage—whom I wed and, in fact, whether I choose to do so at all—up to me."

"And so far, no aspirant to your hand has persuaded you to abandon your independence?"

Surprised at his understanding, she nodded a bit hesitantly. But then, lest he believe she was boasting of conquests, she said with a touch of wry humor, "My aunt tells me that I have stuffed my head with too many romantic notions, but I must say the thought of accepting a sensible and cold-blooded arrangement to spend the rest of my life with a virtual stranger is something I simply cannot support."

"Then you're holding out for a love-match?"

Cassandra was surprised again, this time that there seemed to be no mockery in his question. And her surprise led her to reply more honestly than she might otherwise have done. "I—I suppose that is what I want. Perhaps it is a foolishly romantic desire, but I know myself too well to believe I would be happy with anything else." She looked at him curiously, bothered by an elusive note in his voice that she couldn't define. "Do . . . you believe in love-matches, my lord?"

For the first time that evening, his gaze fell away from hers, and he studied his glass of port as if the shimmering liquid held secrets. His mouth was hard, a little twisted, his voice suddenly bored and yet a bit harsh when he answered.

"I believe, ma'am, that whatever the wishes of we mere mortals, the pressure of those around us is often impossible to resist. As I have no doubt you will discover—the first time someone refers to you as an unmarriageable spinster."

Cassandra felt a twinge of hurt, yet at the same time she had the odd idea that he was telling her something far more important than his words indicated. Was his absence from the social scene these past years less a matter of his supposed sins than his animosity toward society? And, if so, what had caused it? Was there more to the tale of a young lady's good name scandalously ruined than Cassandra knew or could imagine?

She wanted to ask, but the earl's closed, brooding expression warned her that this was not the time. Instead, suddenly weary and aware of how late it had grown while they had sat talking, Cassandra pushed back her chair and rose to her feet.

"If you will permit me, my lord, I will retire. It has been a very long and eventful day."

He rose as well, and his voice remained bored, the earlier relaxation and enjoyment completely gone. "Of course, ma'am. If you require an escort—"

"No, I believe I can find my way. Thank you very much, my lord, for your aid and hospitality as well as a very pleasant evening. Good night."

"Good night, ma'am."

She felt his gaze on her as she left the dining room, but Cassandra did not look back at him.

The port decanter is empty, my lord. Should I refill it?"

The emotionless voice roused Sheffield, and he thrust his empty glass away from him in a gesture of controlled violence. "No," he replied shortly.

"Very good, my lord."

"What's the time?"

"Nearly midnight, my lord."

"As late as that?" The earl frowned down at the polished table but made no move to rise.

Silent, Anatole removed the decanter and glass. He then knelt to put more wood on the fire, which leapt up eagerly to snatch at the new fuel and brightened the snug room with its renewed energy. With that task completed, the manservant rose and pinched out a guttering candle, then polished the gleaming sideboard and adjusted two of the chairs at the table.

The earl scowled at him. "Would you have the goodness to leave me in peace? Your endless fidgeting would try the patience of a saint!"

Anatole stood by the table, still expressionless. "Of course, my lord." He did not move.

Sheffield, staring broodingly down at the gleaming table once again, muttered, "She is very young."

"If I may say so, my lord, not in her self-assurance and manner. Quite an intelligent young lady, and not at all flighty unless I miss my guess. It was pleasing to hear Your Lordship so enjoy the evening."

"She has a—an engaging frankness. And amusement rather than missish dismay when I respond in kind."

"An excellent attribute, my lord."

"She's lovely as well. 'Too dark and too tall to be accounted more than passably attractive,' indeed! As if any man with a particle of sense would prefer some ordinary female with pale hair and washed-out eyes to her glorious raven curls and smoky eyes. And however childlike her voice, her splendid shape proclaims her most definitely a woman."

Anatole preserved a diplomatic silence.

Sheffield swore beneath his breath. "I am being a fool even to entertain thoughts of . . . We met only hours ago, I cannot possibly feel . . ." He stopped, then said stolidly, "In a day or so the weather will improve, and she will be gone."

"I believe, my lord, that the storm will be a severe one, and native members of the staff agree. Travel may not be possible for a week or longer."

"A week." There was a silence, and then the earl said, "I have been alone too long."

"Perhaps it would be more accurate, my lord, to say that you have been alone long enough."

After a moment the earl looked up at his manservant. He was frowning once again. "If you for one moment suppose that I am so lost to all sense of decency as to take advantage of a young lady under my protection—"

"No, of course not, my lord," Anatole soothed. "But to spend time with the young lady here, where all is peaceful and where there are no . . . difficulties . . . surely that is a *situation* of which to take advantage."

Sheffield's scowl faded but did not entirely disappear, and he did not reply to the comment. Instead, he pushed back his chair, rose, and spoke abruptly. "Have we supplies enough to weather the storm?"

"Yes, my lord."

The earl nodded, hesitated, then sighed a bit wearily. "I am going to bed. See that I am awakened at first light."

Scarred face still impassive, Anatole bowed. When his master had gone, he banked the fire for the night and began extinguishing candles. The building wind of the storm outside made itself heard for the first time, and as he paused to listen to the eerie sound, Anatole smiled to himself.


Cassandra slept well, though when she awoke the next morning, she had the discomfiting awareness that her dreams had been highly sensual ones. She did not remember specifics, but found it oddly embarrassing that she woke smiling.

Sarah did not seem to notice anything amiss. While Cassandra drank her morning coffee, Sarah chattered on as usual, commenting on various members of the household staff and offering her opinion that Anatole would win the conflict with Mrs. Milton, because the housekeeper had stated her intention of leaving the post she had held since the earl was a boy.

"Leaving?" Cassandra frowned at her maid. "When?"

"By spring, she said, Miss Cassie. She's all upset about it but says she can't have Anatole taking over her job and still hold her head up."

Cassandra thought about that as she finished her coffee. It wasn't her place, of course, and the earl would probably not thank her for interfering, but she had experience directing a large household staff and was reasonably sure she could soothe Mrs. Milton's territorial spirit. She was less certain of Anatole but thought shrewdly that he would not object to her suggestions so long as he remained head of the household staff.

She rose and dressed, choosing today a subdued dress of gray merino that was rather plain but suited her coloring and figure most admirably and which was one of her warmer dresses; though the temperature inside remained comfortable, the wind could be heard from time to time, and its howling had a chilling effect upon the mind. She had ventured a look outside her bedchamber window, only to find a white world in which swirling snow hid all else, and resigned herself—with a lack of regret she knew she should find appalling—to an extended stay at the Hall.

It was still early morning when Cassandra left her room and, armed with directions from Sarah, found her way to the second-floor linen closet, where Mrs. Milton was at work sorting out pieces needing repair.

"Mrs. Milton, I am sorry to disturb you, but I just wanted to thank you for providing me with such a lovely and comfortable room."

Her sincere appreciation had the desired effect, and after no more than five minutes of casual conversation she was seated in a small parlor while the housekeeper poured out her woes to a willing and sympathetic ear. The situation was much as Cassandra had suspected; though Anatole had not, in fact, deliberately trespassed upon the housekeeper's territory, the rest of the staff recognized in him a stronger personality and a higher authority and had been going to him for their orders. Mrs. Milton had done little to remedy the matter except to complain to some of the other staff members— which had served to lower her even more in their eyes.

Cassandra was careful to keep her suggestions thought- ful and tactful, basing them, she said, on a similar situation that had occurred in her uncle's house. By the time she was finished speaking, the housekeeper was nodding happily, convinced that only a minor adjustment or two would solve her problem.

Less than an hour after she had left her room, Cassandra found her way to the dining room where breakfast waited on the sideboard, kept warm in silver serving dishes. She helped herself, and when Anatole appeared to pour her coffee, she thanked him serenely and carried her plate to the table.

"His Lordship is doing his business accounts in his study, miss."

She hadn't asked—but she had wondered. Still composed, she merely said, "Thank you, Anatole. Pray do not disturb him on my behalf. I shall do quite well on my own. I believe I shall explore that splendid library I caught a glimpse of last night."

"An excellent idea, miss."

Cassandra was a little amused by his approval. Her first impression of him had not been good, but she was beginning to revise it—not so much because he was more polite to her now, but because she had the idea he was totally devoted to the earl—and she thought he would prove a valuable ally. . . .

Ridiculous thought. Why on earth would she need an ally in this house?

"I would like to speak to my coachman this morning," she told Anatole before he left the dining room.

He bowed. "I will bring him to the library when you have finished breakfast, miss."

He was as good as his word, delivering John Potter to the library some half an hour later and before Cassandra could do more than begin scanning the shelves. Her coachman came in, hat in hand, explaining that he was preparing to make his way to the stables where the coach had been taken.

She frowned. "It is still storming, John."

"Yes, Miss Cassie, but we've strung ropes down to the stables so nobody'll get blown away or lost—it's that bad, you can't see your hand in front of your face, I swear—an' His Lordship's man has a fire going in the stove, so we'll be snug enough. He says as how there's an old coach no longer useful, but the axle's stout enough to replace our broken one; we're going to change 'em over."

"With His Lordship's permission, I trust?"

"Oh, yes, miss."

"Excellent, John." She kept her voice cheerful. "Then we'll be able to start forward again once the storm is over and the roads are passable?"

"The coach should be repaired by the end of the day, miss. But as to the storm—I'm told it's expected to last at least another day or two, an' maybe longer. With the wind we'll have drifts as much as two or three feet deep in places."

"What are you saying, John?"

He turned his hat in his hands and sighed heavily. "I'm sorry, miss, but I wouldn't want to try pushing ahead for at least a few days after the snow stops."

"Then . . . we may be here a week?"

John Potter mistook her careful question for one of anxiety and hastened to reassure her. "As soon as the snow stops, I'll ride out an' check the roads, Miss Cassie. Maybe they'll be clearer than I expect—"

"It's all right, John, I quite understand. If we must remain here a week, then so be it." Cassandra smiled, hoping that he saw only resigned forbearance rather than the (really quite appalling) lighthearted pleasure she felt.

When she was alone once again in the library, which

was a marvelous room with enough books to delight any reader, she took a more careful look around and was even more pleased by what she saw. The room was airy and more than spacious, yet as warm and snug as the rest of the house. The two tall windows were heavily curtained, effectively shutting out the sight of the storm and permitting very little of its wailing to be heard.

Cassandra, who had been raised to be self-reliant and independent and for whom reading was a particular pleasure, sighed happily and went to explore His Lordship's shelves. She quickly discovered a treasure: a recent novel she had not yet read by one of her favorite writers. Obviously, the earl also enjoyed adventurous fiction—or, at least, considered it worth adding to his library.

Ten minutes later she was comfortably seated in a chair by the fire and completely engrossed in the exciting activities of pirates sailing the high seas.

In the normal way, once Cassandra was involved in a book, it required either a loud noise or a shake to get her attention. But it appeared that she was particularly sensitive to the earl's presence, because even though the opening door made almost no sound at all, she looked up as if someone had shouted her name.

"Forgive me, ma'am—I didn't intend to disturb you." Back in his country buckskins, he looked unnervingly powerful as he stood in the doorway. His dark gaze was direct as ever and seemed to search her face.

"Not at all, my lord," she returned politely, using a finger to mark her place as she closed the book. "I hope you do not mind, but I took the liberty of exploring this wonderful library."

He came into the room rather slowly. "Of course I do not mind, ma'am—please feel free to explore any room you wish." His deep voice was a little abrupt.

Cassandra was oddly unwilling to allow a silence to

develop between them. "My coachman tells me you have supplied an axle with which to repair my coach."

He shrugged, standing now near the fireplace and looking down on her with a very slight frown. "It is little enough, ma'am, and useless to me."

"Then why are you frowning, my lord?" She hadn't realized she was going to ask that until the question emerged.

"Was I?" His brows lifted, effectively altering his expression. "I beg your pardon. Business accounts are sometimes tiresome, ma'am."

"As are household accounts; I understand perfectly, my lord." She hesitated, then said diffidently, "Please don't feel yourself obliged to entertain me while I am here. I have no wish to disrupt the routine of the household—or your routine."

He smiled suddenly, crooked and slightly rueful. "Even if I wish it?"

Cassandra felt herself smiling back at him. It was doubtless the storm, she thought, making him feel restless and in need of companionship. That was all. But it was difficult to hide her own pleasure when she asked, "What did you have in mind, my lord?"

She felt the now-familiar fluttering sensation deep inside her for a moment, because there was something in his dark eyes she had never before seen in any man's gaze, something heated and hungry. She was suddenly conscious of her clothing touching her flesh, of the dim wail of the wind outside, and the nearer crackle and pop of the flames in the fireplace. She could feel her heart beating as if she had run a long way, and it seemed difficult to breathe all at once.

It was as if all her senses had . . . opened up. As if all her life she had seen and felt everything through a gauzy curtain until that moment when he looked at her.

There was a part of Cassandra, a rational, sensible part,

that urged her to be on her guard. This, then, was his charm, it had to be—this ability to make a woman feel that no one else had ever looked at her, *seen* her. It was utterly compelling. This was the seductive power the men in his family were known to possess, the ability to enthrall a woman until she threw morals and scruples aside to do anything he wished her to do.

The sensible part of Cassandra offered that warning, but before she could make an effort to—to what? save herself?—his dark eyes were unreadable once again, and he was smiling in a perfectly polite and casual way.

"Do you play cards, ma'am?"

The written adventures of pirates held no appeal for her now, and Cassandra was barely aware of laying her book aside. "Yes," she heard herself say with astonishing calm. "Yes, my lord, I play cards."

# Chapter Three

He taught her a particularly intricate, often perplexing, and sometimes downright Byzantine card game which he had learned from a colorful ship's captain on a journey across the Mediterranean, and she astonished him by not only grasping the rules but soundly defeating him in only the third hand dealt.

"How on earth did you do that?" he demanded.

Briskly shuffling the cards, Cassandra showed him a mock frown and laughing eyes. "You should know, my lord. It was you who taught me the game."

"Yes, but it's the devil of a game to win," he told her frankly.

"Then we shall call it beginner's luck, sir. Did you say you learned it from a ship's captain?"

"I learned it from a rascally pirate who called himself one," the earl replied dryly. "And the bas—the ruffian emptied my pockets three nights running."

Cassandra picked up her hand and regarded him in amusement. "Does it have a name, this game?"

"None that I ever heard. In fact, I rather doubt it existed before Captain Bower invented it in order to fleece those of his passengers raw enough to sit down with him."

"I cannot imagine you being raw, my lord."

Ruefully he said, "Oh, I promise you I was. Hardly older than you are now, and not at all up to snuff. It was more than ten years ago." He looked down at the cards he held, the light of amusement in his eyes dimming and his mouth hardening just a bit as his thoughts obviously turned painful or bitter.

Before Cassandra could respond to what he had said, Anatole came into the library where they were playing cards and asked the earl if luncheon at twelve-thirty would be satisfactory, and by the time he left the room, the earl's abstraction had vanished and he was once more relaxed. What might have been a brief opening through which she could have learned more about his past was now firmly closed again.

The card game continued until lunchtime, with Cassandra winning once more and then playing the earl to a draw. Which meant, he said, that they were "evenly matched in terms of possessing labyrinthine minds." Whether or not that was true, it was obvious that each enjoyed the other's company far beyond what was merely polite.

After luncheon they played chess in the earl's study, and it proved another game in which they had like minds and tendencies, both employing shrewd tactics and alert strategy. And so they whiled away the stormy afternoon, pausing from time to time in their conversation to listen to the wind reach a crescendo and then fade away only to shriek once again and send sleet rattling against the windowpanes.

"Nasty," Cassandra observed.

"Very. Check, ma'am."

"Now, how did you . . . Oh, I see. White must resign, my lord, for I can see you mean to pursue my king across the board."

"I would never be so unhandsome as that, I promise you. Another game, ma'am?"

But the clock on the mantel chimed the hour just then, and Cassandra excused herself in order to go upstairs to change and freshen herself before supper. She had thoroughly enjoyed the day, and she returned to her room with a smile she didn't think about hiding until Sarah greeted her with anxious eyes.

"Sarah, he is a complete gentleman," she assured her apprehensive maid.

"Just be careful, Miss Cassie, that's all!"

But Cassandra only laughed, certain that her maid's fears were completely unfounded. Indeed, it seemed her own instincts were to be trusted, for the earl's behavior during the next two days was so exemplary that even Sarah seemed reassured (or, at least, she stopped issuing dire warnings). He was an entertaining and appreciative companion, forthright without being in any way offensive, and though she did not want to admit it to herself, Cassandra knew she was drawn to him in a way she had never known before.

That moment when he had looked at her with naked intensity was something she remembered far too often for her peace of mind, but it was not repeated during those days. He made more than one flattering observation, but since his comments tended to be quite casual and matter-of-fact, she could be sure of nothing except that he considered her attractive—and for all she knew he would have been just as appreciative of any personable young woman appearing on his doorstep.

It did not occur to Cassandra that the severe isolation of the storm had created a kind of refuge for both of them, and that the return of good weather might change that. All she knew was that the glittering but restrictive world of London society seemed very far away.

The storm raged outside, with a fierce wind blowing the existing snow about even when no fresh precipitation fell, and those inside the house became so accustomed to the sounds of fury that their cessation in the early evening of Cassandra's third full day at the Hall was something of a shock.

She came downstairs after dressing for supper and found that she was early; the earl was not waiting for her. Restless, she wandered into a small salon near the earl's study, a room she had not so far explored except to note the presence of a pianoforte. There was a fire burning in the grate, though it had been allowed to die down a bit, and though the room was comfortable, it was not really warm. A candelabra set upon the pianoforte provided light that was only adequate, leaving the corners and much else of the room in shadows.

Cassandra sat down on the bench and sorted through several sheets of music until she found something familiar. She considered herself a fair musician without being in any way exceptional, and since she had had little opportunity to practice during recent weeks, her fingers felt a bit awkward on the keys. But it did not take many minutes for her to relax and find her touch, and the first tentative notes of a sonata soon became easier and more confident.

Nevertheless, due to her lack of patience, the piece required all her concentration, and she had no idea she was not alone in the room until the final notes faded into silence and he spoke.

"You play beautifully."

Startled, she half turned on the bench to find the earl

standing only a few feet away. He was turned so that the light of the candelabra flickered in his eyes, making them glitter with a strange intensity.

Trying to collect herself, struggling with a curiously compelling awareness of him, she said, "Thank you, my lord." She wanted to go on, to make some innocuous comment about the excellent instrument or something equally as nonchalant, but she could not. Her throat seemed to close up, and she could feel her heart thudding.

Sheffield took a step toward her, then another, and quietly said, "It is cool in here, ma'am, and your shawl has slipped. Permit me."

Cassandra did not move as he lifted the lacy edge of her shawl to cover her bare shoulders. The gesture was more than courtesy; his hands rested on her shoulders briefly, and she felt his fingers tighten just a little before they were removed. Then he offered his hand, silent, and she took it, turning toward him as she rose to her feet.

He didn't release her hand as he should have done, or tuck it into the crook of his arm casually. He held it and looked down at her with an expression she could not quite read in the shadows of the salon.

Cassandra did not know what was different, but she knew something was. In him or in her, or perhaps both, there was a change. The intensity of the moment lay heavily in the very air of the room, and she had the odd notion that if she moved too suddenly or spoke too hastily, something terribly rare and valuable could be destroyed.

Then Sheffield drew a quick breath, and when he spoke his voice was low and husky in a way that seemed almost a caress. "I think . . . I cannot go on calling you ma'am. Would it displease you very much if I called you Cassie?"

She shook her head just a little, unable to look away from his intent gaze. "No. No, of course it would not." Her own voice sounded so shaken she hardly recognized it.

His fingers tightened around hers, and he lifted her hand until his warm lips lightly brushed her knuckles. "Thank you, Cassie."

It wasn't the first time a man had kissed her hand, but it was the first time she had felt heat shimmer through her body in a shocking, exciting response. She knew he could feel her fingers trembling, and would not have been surprised if he could actually hear her heart beating like a drum. And the way he said her name, something in his voice, pulled at her.

Absurdly, she murmured, "You're welcome, my lord."

His mouth curved in a slight smile. "My name is Stone, Cassie. A ridiculous name, I agree, but mine. If you could bring yourself to use it, I would be most pleased."

Almost imperceptibly, she nodded. "Stone."

He raised her hand to his lips again, the touch a lingering one this time as heavy lids veiled his eyes, and Cassandra felt another wave of heat when he whispered her name. Her name had never sounded like that before, tugging at all her senses and perhaps something even deeper and more basic inside her. And how odd it felt, the sensations he evoked. They seemed to spread all through her body, yet settled more heavily deep in her belly and in her breasts, until she ached.

She didn't know what, if anything, she would have said, but they heard the soft chimes of a clock in one of the nearby rooms proclaiming the hour just then, and the earl carried her hand to his arm.

"If we don't go to the dining room," he murmured, "Anatole will only come in search of us."

A bit dazed, she allowed herself to be guided toward the door, vaguely surprised that her unsteady legs could support her weight. And it was only then, as they reached the door, that she realized what was different, what had been different from the moment she had turned to find him in the room. It was a silence, a hush so absolute it seemed to have a physical presence.

"I—I don't hear the wind," she said.

He was holding her hand against his arm, and his fingers pressed hers. He looked down at her. "I know. I believe the storm is dying."

It was such a casual and ordinary thing to say, Cassandra thought, a perfectly reasonable thing to say—why did it sound so very ominous? So very disturbing? Why did she want to cry out a protest, or insist fiercely that he was wrong? Why did she suddenly feel almost frantic with anxiety?

She did not comprehend the answer to all those questions until she looked across the dining table at Sheffield some minutes later and remembered that once the storm was gone, the roads would soon be clear enough for travel . . . and she would have to leave the Hall. Her good name was already at risk because she had stayed here with him unchaperoned; if word of that should spread, the storm would probably be an acceptable justification—for now, at least, and for all the most suspicious and cynical members of the *ton*. But nothing would protect her if she remained here once the weather cleared.

She would have to leave very soon. And perhaps it should have horrified her to realize that she was more than willing to risk her reputation by remaining here—but it did not. It did not even surprise her very much.

Not after he had whispered her name.

Their conversation during supper was quieter than usual, desultory; she thought they were both very conscious of how quiet it had become outside as the storm died away. Cassandra could not seem to keep herself from stealing glances at his face, her gaze falling away swiftly whenever he chanced to look at her. He seemed somehow changed,

she thought, his features not so harsh, the expression in his
dark eyes direct as ever but warmer now and . . . tender?

Her imagination, most likely. She wanted to be sensible,
to keep her head and not indulge in such foolish . . . imaginings. That was dangerous. She knew the pain of romantic
flights of fancy brought cruelly to earth, knew that she had
in the past more than once failed to judge a man accurately
until his true character was revealed by his own actions.
She had more than once seen her worth to a man measured
in the cold mathematical accounting of her fortune.

But Sheffield—Stone—did not know who she really
was. Odd how she kept forgetting that. Or perhaps it was
not so odd, after all; she could not recall anyone in the
house addressing her by the name Sarah had offered since
that first evening. No one ever called her Miss Wells. She
was "miss" or "Miss Cassie," with nothing else added. And
"ma'am" to Stone, until now.

She had never discussed her background in anything but
the vaguest terms, and he had not questioned her even to
ask the name of the uncle she mentioned, so she had not
been forced to choose between the truth and more lies.
But the one great lie she had told was now weighing heavily on her.

It was when she was thinking of that during supper that
Cassandra almost confessed the truth. She even opened her
mouth to do so, but the words would not come. Not because
she feared that Stone was a fortune hunter, but because she
felt so guilty about lying.

When they left the table—earlier than usual—she had
not managed to confess and was unhappily aware of her
duplicity. She murmured an assent when the earl asked her
to play the pianoforte, but it was not until they went into the
salon serving the Hall as a music room that a flicker of
amusement lightened her mood. The room that had been so
dim and shadowed earlier was now much more inviting,

with several sconces and candelabras alight and the fire burning briskly.

"Did Anatole know we would return here?" she asked the earl, sitting down on the bench.

"He seems to know everything that goes on in this house," Sheffield replied, then smiled as he leaned against the side of the pianoforte. "I believe I have you to thank for ending the feud between him and Mrs. Milton."

"I merely made some suggestions." Cassandra played a few notes idly, then began to pick out a soft tune from memory. "All she really needed was a sympathetic ear and someone to advise her to reclaim those areas in which she excels. After all, I doubt that Anatole *wants* to be responsible for the care of linen and the training of the housemaids—and so on."

"Very wise of you. And very much appreciated, Cassie."

She watched her fingers tremble over the keys but managed not to strike a sour note. What *was* the magic of his voice saying her name? Keeping her own voice casual, she said, "My pleasure. I must admit, I am most curious about Anatole."

"In what way?"

"He is not English, is he?"

"No, Greek." His attention caught by a smoldering log that had fallen half out onto the hearth, the earl went over to the fireplace to nudge it back into place. He remained there, leaning a forearm on the mantel and looking down at the flames. "I encountered him on that ship I told you about, the one with the rascally captain. He was the first mate."

"And you offered him a position?"

Sheffield smiled oddly as he looked across the room at her. "Nothing so ordinary, I'm afraid. Shortly after we docked in Italy, he saved my life."

Cassandra stopped playing abruptly. "He—?"

"Yes. I was set upon by thieves, and there were too many for me to handle. If not for Anatole, I would have been knifed in the back and left to bleed to death. It was the first time he saved my life—but not the last."

Obeying her instincts, Cassandra rose and went to him, halting so that they faced each other. "You must have been very young," she ventured, remembering that Anatole had been with the earl for a number of years.

"I was twenty-one." He gave her a twisted smile. "Wild and bitter and bent on getting myself killed because I was convinced life had nothing more to offer me. God knows why Anatole chose to follow me across half the world, but he did. He kept me alive until I'd the sense to look out for myself, and after that he made himself useful—in fact, indispensable."

Cassandra studied his hard face curiously. "And you returned here—?"

"Four years ago. It took the next two years and more to get this place in some kind of order. The house had been closed up since I left England, and had been allowed to virtually fall into ruins, so I had my work cut out for me."

Which, she thought, was a fair explanation of why he had vanished so completely from the London social scene; he had been either out of England or else very much occupied here for the past ten years.

"I see," she said.

"Do you? I have not been what anyone of sense would call a suitable match for a young lady, Cassie." Matter-of-factly, Sheffield added, "I had succeeded to the title when I was nineteen, and found myself the possessor of a vanished fortune, useless properties, and a name painted black going back five generations. Naturally, it did not take long for me to add to the sins of my ancestors. I left England very much under a cloud and not quick enough to avoid the scandal I'd caused."

Cassandra had certainly been curious about his background and, in particular, the sin that had earned him the condemnation of society, but in that moment all she wanted to do was to ease the strain in his low voice.

"Stone—I heard all the rumors about you when I first came out."

He was obviously surprised, and not a little wary. "Good God, are they using the sins I committed more than ten years ago to frighten debutantes?"

She kept her voice solemn. "Oh, yes, and it's quite effective. They never explain what, exactly, you were guilty of, but then it never seems to be necessary. All those horrified whispers and sad shakes of the head are enough to cause any girl to think twice if she is contemplating some reckless act." Pondering the matter, she added thoughtfully, "I daresay you have saved any number of parents from the consequences of rash daughters. I shouldn't doubt it if they were not actually eager to welcome you back to society."

The earl smiled slightly, but his gaze was very intent on her. "I was not ostracized, you know. I can return if I choose to do so."

"I know."

"I suppose I should go back from time to time—if only to prove I lack horns and a tail."

Cassandra smiled. "Don't forget the cloven hooves."

"Has there been no other scandal in England since I sinned?" he demanded a bit ruefully.

"Not really. *I* believe it was because of the war."

"The war?"

"Yes. You see, so many of the young men were occupied with the war for so long that they simply had not the time or energy to get much tangled in scrapes and scandals."

In a grave tone he said, "I begin to see that the sin I was most guilty of was one of bad timing."

*Sin.* She wondered if he was fully conscious of his use

of the word. "And you could hardly be blamed for that. After all, you were very young."

"Older than you are now," he retorted.

Cassandra laughed but said, "In any case, you should probably return to London society at least long enough to show that you have become perfectly respectable."

"For all you know, that might not be the case at all," the earl warned her in a voice that was not *quite* humorous. "They say some things are in the blood, and mine is certainly wicked enough to give any rational young lady pause—even without tales of my dissolute past. Perhaps I am only biding my time for my own amusement."

"Until?" she said, interested.

"Until I have . . . won your trust. It is the classic method of rakes, you know."

"Perhaps." She was smiling.

He looked into her big gray eyes and then shook his head a little in wonder. "You are not the least bit afraid of me, are you, Cassie?"

"Should I be?"

"Virtually alone with me in my house, cut off from the outside, no chaperon—"

"Should I be?" she repeated steadily.

He reached up and touched her face very gently, the very tips of his fingers tracing the delicate arch of her brow, the curve of her cheek, and the clean line of her jaw. "I would not harm you for the world."

Cassandra wondered if she was breathing, but it did not seem important. She felt feverish, yearning, vulnerable, and yet enthralled. His touch was like something she had felt in a dream, and if it was a dream, she did not want to awaken. She heard her voice and was not surprised that it was husky. "Then I have nothing to fear."

For a moment it seemed that he leaned toward her, but

then his hand fell to his side and he smiled at her, only the intensity of his dark eyes hinting at something not nearly as calm as his voice when he said, "You promised to play for me."

"So I did." She turned and went back to the pianoforte, and when she began to play, she was not much surprised to realize that her fingers had selected a love song.

It was like a wonderland. Cassandra stood at the top of the front steps of Sheffield Hall and gazed around in utter delight. Snow had turned the bleak winter landscape into something so beautiful it made the heart ache. The brown grass had vanished beneath a blanket of pristine white, and the bare branches of trees seemed dressed now with their mantle of snow.

Already, the earl's servant had been at work, for the steps were swept clean of snow, and Cassandra had no fear of her footing as she closed the door behind her and set out. She was warmly dressed—and very glad of it when a sudden gust of wind snatched at her cloak as she was making her way cautiously through the uneven drifts of snow along the carriage drive toward the stables. Though the storm was apparently over, this was still winter and winter's name might have been caprice; the occasional wind was urgent in its warning that spring was far away.

Cassandra had awakened early and with the most amazing sense of energy. She had had her coffee in bed but had not yet breakfasted; Anatole had reported that the earl had gone down to the stables before his own meal, and she had instantly decided to go in search of him. She needed fresh air and the chance to get a bit of exercise, she told herself—and nearly laughed out loud at the absurdity of this attempt to delude herself.

If Sheffield had vanished into the depths of a dungeon or sallied forth to drive over a cliff, it was more than likely that she would have followed him without hesitation.

She saw her breath mist before her eyes as she did laugh out loud, and shook her head at this odd, bewitched creature she had become. It should have been appalling, she thought, or at the very least shocking, but she could not seem to summon those negative emotions. She was too happy. She wanted to smile all over, to laugh again and throw a snowball at someone.

Most of all, she wanted to see the earl.

She heard his voice only moments later when she reached the stableyard and followed her ears to find him standing before a row of stables talking to a spare, middle-aged man who was no doubt the head groom or coachman.

"Watch his leg to make sure it doesn't swell, Flint, but if he's all right by afternoon, turn him out."

"Yes, my lord."

The earl turned then and saw Cassandra approaching, and his smile was instant as he stepped forward to meet her. "Cassie, I would have waited for you if I had known you wished to come down here."

She was only vaguely aware that the groom had gone away, all her attention focused on Sheffield. He was holding her hand, and she felt a flicker of annoyance that she was wearing gloves. "I had no notion where I would end up," she confessed. "Is it not beautiful out here? Who has hurt his leg?"

With a chuckle, the earl said, "Yes, it is beautiful—even more so now. And my favorite hack made a spirited attempt to kick down the door of his stable earlier; he dislikes storms *and* being confined for any length of time, and wants to kick up his heels in his paddock."

"Impatient as his master, I collect?"

"Now, when have I ever shown you impatience?" he demanded in a voice of mild surprise.

"That first evening," Cassandra replied promptly. "You looked at me in *such* a way, and spoke very brusquely."

"If I was brusque, I beg your pardon." He lifted her hand to his lips and kissed it. "As for how I looked at you, I can only say I was charmed and delighted to find a smoke-eyed beauty quite unexpectedly in my house."

Cassandra promised herself she was never going to wear gloves again, even if her fingers froze. She drew a breath and said rather uncertainly, "I—I see. Then I suppose I must forgive you."

"Thank you, ma'am."

"You are laughing at me," she said suspiciously.

He kissed her hand again, and there was a gleam in his dark eyes that was something more than laughter. "Never. Are you warm enough? May I show you my horses before we go back to the house?"

"I am quite warm enough, and I would love to see your horses." She smiled up at him.

He continued to hold her hand instead of tucking it into his arm, an arrangement Cassandra was delighted by. She did not even feel self-conscious when Sheffield introduced her to his head groom, Flint—but she was rather glad to be told that her coachman had borrowed a hack and ridden out first thing to check the condition of the roads just as he had said he would.

She was glad that John Potter was not confronted by the sight of her and the earl holding hands most improperly—but her coachman's eagerness to check the roads was an unwelcome reminder of time ticking away. The roads were not passable today, she knew, but what of tomorrow or the next day?

With that in her mind Cassandra's pleasure in being

with the earl during the casual tour of his stables was even more precious to her than it would otherwise have been. She could not seem to get enough of hearing his deep voice or watching the changing expressions of his face (had she once thought it harsh?), and every time he said her name it was as if the sound of it touched something deep inside her.

Still, perhaps nothing irrevocable would have happened if Sheffield's favorite hack had not betrayed his native impatience by trying to ascertain if Cassandra had a lump of sugar hidden somewhere on her person. The big bay gelding nudged her so hard with his Roman nose that she stumbled back away from the stable door and would have fallen had not the earl caught her.

"Oh! My goodness, you—"

"Clumsy brute! Cassie, love, are you—"

They had spoken in the same moment, and she stared up at him as both their voices broke off. Had he said what she thought he had? He was holding her so close . . . even with his greatcoat and her cloak she could feel the hardness of his body, the warmth of him. Her hands had somehow landed on his chest, gloved fingers spread, touching him. Both his arms were around her, and then only one because he had lifted the other hand to push the hood of her cloak back and touch her face with his fingers the way he had last night in the music room.

"Cassie . . ."

It did not occur to her to push herself away, to make some attempt to stop this. It simply did not occur to her. Instead, she offered her lips in the most natural way imaginable, and when his mouth covered hers, she heard an unfamiliar little purr of pleasure in the back of her throat.

She had been kissed by boys—those eager young swains with whom she had shared country dances before her first Season—but never by a man, and the difference was shocking. His mouth was not awkward or wet and she felt absolutely no desire to burst out in giggles at the absurdity of lips pressed together; his mouth was skilled and sure, hard yet silken, and a shimmering heat ignited inside her at the first touch.

Cassandra thought she was melting. All the strength was flowing out of her legs, and the burning inside her intensified until it was a wild fever consuming her. She should have been shocked when the possessive invasion of his tongue turned the kiss into something more intimate than she had ever imagined was possible, but instead what she felt was pleasure and desire, and a dim wonder that he could make her feel this way. . . .

When Sheffield lifted his head at last, Cassandra opened her eyes dazedly, hardly aware that she had uttered a faint sound of disappointment. His eyes had a heavy, sensual look that made her pounding heart skip a beat, and she wished once again that her gloves were off so that she could touch his hard face.

He drew a slow breath, then said huskily, "I have wanted to do that since you walked toward me dressed in blue silk that first evening, so beautiful I could hardly bear it. Must I beg your pardon?"

She should have said yes, she knew, but propriety was beyond Cassandra. Far beyond her. She shook her head, unable to tear her gaze from him. "No." It was almost inaudible, and she cleared her throat to try again. "No, of course not."

His already black eyes seemed to darken even more, deepen somehow, until they were bottomless pools into which she knew she could lose herself. Into which she wanted to throw herself, body and soul. Then he bent his head again and rubbed his lips over hers in a brief, almost rough caress that was even more stirring to her senses than the prolonged kiss had been.

"For that?" he murmured.

Cassandra had the dazed notion that he was teasing her, but she was also aware that he was hardly unaffected; there was a tension in his body she could feel, and there was no disguising the hunger of his taut expression.

Her lips trembling and tingling, she whispered, "I am shameless, I know . . . but please don't beg my pardon, Stone."

Her tremulous words and guileless pleasure seemed to affect him most oddly. He moved slightly as if to kiss her again, but then his mouth firmed and he put his hands on her shoulders to ease her back away from him. A muscle flexed in his jaw, and there was a note of disbelief in his voice when he spoke.

"I must be out of my mind."

She blinked, the fingers clinging to his greatcoat beginning to slacken, but her sharp pang of hurt vanished when he continued grimly.

"A cold, drafty stable through which anyone might pass—and probably has—and I want nothing more than to find a pile of reasonably clean straw and make a bed for the two of us."

Burning color rose in her cheeks, but Cassandra was not nearly so shocked by his blunt desire as she should have been. Instead, she felt a hollow ache deep in her loins, a wild urge to cast aside every vestige of breeding and every principle of ladylike behavior by pleading with him to make that bed and carry her to it, and that shocked her more than anything.

He laughed, a low, raspy sound. "Have I shocked you?"

She caught her underlip between her teeth and felt the sensual tenderness left by his ardent kisses. "No—yes—I don't know. I cannot think."

His rather fierce expression softened, and his hands

lifted to frame her hot face. "My poor darling—so bewildered." His thumb caught her bottom lip and pressed gently until it was free of her small white teeth, and the pad of his thumb rubbed back and forth slowly. "And so damnably young. I ought to be shot for taking advantage of you this way."

"Ought you?" She met his eyes steadily despite the virginal blush. "Even if—if it is what I want?"

He did not move for an instant, just looked down at her as if her honest response had stolen his breath or stopped his heart. Then, very slowly, he took his hands off her face, lifted her hood carefully to cover her raven curls, and then took one of her hands and tucked it into his arm. He was frowning slightly as he did all this, but it seemed to her a frown of concentration rather than anger, as if it required all his resolution.

"Come," he said. "We must return to the house."

"Must we?" she ventured regretfully.

"Yes," he said, his voice very rough, "we must. Before I forget you're a lady."

Stealing a glance up at his face as they walked, Cassandra wondered for the first time if being a lady might prove a definite stumbling block for a girl who wanted to become a woman.

# Chapter Four

It was not to be expected that their earlier relaxed companionship could remain unaffected by what had happened in the stables. Indeed, the awareness between them was so potent that Cassandra discovered only a glance from him had the power to stop her breathing, while his dark eyes instantly lit with the now familiar hot glow of desire when they met hers and his voice changed almost imperceptibly when he spoke to her.

She had the suspicion that the dusting of pink across her cheekbones that was all that remained of her blush in the stables had become a permanent thing; when she retired to her room late that evening, the face in her mirror wore it like a muted banner of sensual awakening. And her eyes seemed different, larger and more brilliant, she thought, gazing at her reflection as Sarah took down her hair and brushed it. *Smoke-eyed* he had said. A smoke-eyed beauty.

He *had* called her love. And his poor darling. And for the

rest of the day, that note in his voice, husky and caressing whenever he spoke to her.

Normally a young woman who was very sure of herself, Cassandra was both excited and bewildered by the earl and by her own feelings, and though she felt few doubts or hesitations when she was with him, alone in her bed that night she tossed and turned restlessly. Her body was feverish, her mind troubled.

They had gone for a long walk in his snow-covered garden after breakfast, taking care in the drifts and attempting to guess what plants lay beneath odd-shaped humps of snow. He had held her hand, and once caught her when she would have slipped, but there were no more kisses or thrillingly blunt statements of desire.

John Potter found them there when he came to report the impassable condition of the surrounding roads, and though Cassandra tried hard, she was afraid her voice betrayed the relief she felt at knowing they could not leave just yet. Sheffield did not comment on the information other than to say calmly that it would likely be another day or two before travel was possible, and when they were alone together again he talked of other things.

The remainder of the day was much as the previous ones had been, with amusing card games and conversation and chess to occupy them—but when Cassandra went upstairs to change for the evening, he stood in the entrance hall and watched her go up; she could feel his eyes on her. And just before she retired to her room much later, she had accidentally (she assured herself) brushed against him as she rose from her chair; he had caught her in his arms and kissed her almost violently, and Cassandra had melted against him with a murmur of pleasure.

"This must stop," the earl told her fiercely, giving her bare shoulders a little shake and then kissing her again.

"Must it?" Her fingers clung to his lapels, but she

wanted to burrow closer to his hard body, to slip her arms around him and press herself against him. The urge was shocking, and she did not care.

Sheffield half closed his eyes as he looked down at her, his face a hard mask. "Yes, dammit." But instead of shaking her once more, his fingers probed at the delicate bones of her shoulders, then followed the graceful length of her neck upward until his hands cradled each side of her face and his thumbs gently smoothed the heated skin over her cheekbones.

Without thought she moved her head a little so that she could feel the slightly rough texture of his palms. She was dizzy, excited, yearning, and half-frightened all at once, *wanting* without being able to put a name to what it was she craved so terribly.

"Cassie . . ." He bent his head to kiss her, his tongue sliding deeply into her mouth, stroking hers in a secret, erotic duel that made the fever inside her burn even hotter. Learning rapidly, she responded with a swift and total abandon, and his mouth was wild on hers for a moment before he jerked his head up and ground out a curse so savage it cut through the daze of her need.

She blinked at him uncertainly. "Stone?"

He gave her a fierce look that seemed to her to hold reluctance but something else as well. Anger? Bitterness? Whatever it was, she had little opportunity to try and understand it. He took his hands off her and stepped back until they were no longer touching. Then he drew a breath and said politely, "Good night, Cassie."

So she had left him, retreating to her room in some confusion, and now she tangled the bedclothes with her restless tossing and turning. Her body ached, and she could not stop thinking, suddenly worrying.

After all that had happened between them, Sheffield had not uttered a single word about the future. He had called her love, yes, and his poor darling—but did it signify anything? How could she be certain, after all, that what he said to her and the way he kissed and touched her was important to him? She had heard it said that, for a man, there could most certainly be passion without love. According to the discreet murmurs of older women, many men were held to make love with ease and without real meaning—what if Stone Westcott was such a man?

He certainly had the blood of rakes in his veins—as he had warned her himself—but did that automatically mean he could feel nothing but passion for her?

She did not know. But he had not so much as hinted there might be a future for them together, and Cassandra was very much afraid that *did* mean something.

He greeted her quietly but with shuttered eyes and an impassive expression at breakfast, and Sheffield spent that morning and much of the afternoon closeted in his study with his estate agent. That was neither unusual nor unexpected, since storms tended to cause problems on any large estate, and those would need to be reported to the earl and remedies planned. Cassandra did not resent the duties that occupied him—but she wished they could have been postponed a few days.

Even one day might have made a difference, because she was much afraid that was all the time she had left. The temperature had warmed during the afternoon so that the snow was already beginning to melt, and John Potter had offered his opinion that travel might be possible as early as the following day. The main roads were clearing rapidly; the mail had gone through, and the Bristol Light Post Coach as well, so that was strong evidence of improving conditions.

John had the coach repaired; the horses were rested; the weather was breaking. She would have to leave.

From the astonishing, dizzying pleasure and excitement of the previous day to the anxiety and fears of this day was such a plummeting drop Cassandra felt almost ill with reaction. She managed to keep herself occupied during the day but acknowledged to herself the uselessness of it when she realized she had read the entire pirate adventure and could not recall a single word of the story.

The earl was still shut in his study when she went disconsolately upstairs to change for the evening, and when the tall case clock on the landing chimed the hour cheerfully, she wanted to kick it. There were clocks *everywhere* in this dratted house, and all of them insisted on reminding her of the passage of time.

"Miss Cassie—will we be leaving soon?"

She thought that Sarah's voice was just a trifle too disinterested (considering her worries earlier), but Cassandra was putting tiny diamond drops in her earlobes and didn't look at her maid when she replied calmly, "I believe so. The roads are clearing, and so we should be on our way."

"To Bristol, miss?"

"Perhaps. Or back to London." She had lost her desire to continue on and felt the need to return to her uncle's cheerful house in Berkeley Square.

Sarah said no more, and Cassandra tried not to think of tomorrow as she went back downstairs. She had rather defiantly chosen to wear the blue silk dress again, her lace shawl draped across her shoulders, but when she went into the drawing room where they met before supper, he was not there.

Sighing, she went to stand before the fireplace, head bent as she gazed down at the flames, and when she heard his voice a few minutes later, it required every ounce of her control to keep from flinging herself into his arms.

"Good evening, Cassie." He closed the door behind him

as he came in, then moved to stand at the fireplace so that they faced each other.

No one else had ever made her name sound that way, and she felt an absurd prickle of tears that she fiercely blinked away before meeting his gaze. "Good evening." Her voice was calm; what an actress she seemed to be! "I trust the storm did no lasting damage to your estate?"

"No, nothing that cannot be repaired." He was frowning a bit, obviously preoccupied, and his eyes were still shuttered.

Cassandra wondered if he had even noticed the blue silk dress he had said made her look beautiful. She made her voice light and careless. "I believe I may be able to travel by tomorrow. John Potter reports that the main road is in quite good shape, so we shall only have to take care until we reach it."

"On to Bristol?" The earl spoke slowly, and his frown appeared to deepen.

"Oh—back to London, I think. I am promised to at least three balls after next week, and might as well return in time to attend them."

He nodded. "It is just as well you mean to go, Cassie," he said in a very deliberate tone. "These past days . . . shut off from outside contact and thrown together as we have been—"

However he might have finished what he meant to say, Cassandra was left with only painful conjecture when a sudden bustle of noise from the entrance hall caused Sheffield to break off abruptly and start toward the drawing room door.

"What the devil?"

Cassandra was feeling numb, hardly interested in visitors, but when the drawing room doors were thrust open before the earl could reach them and a woman swept in still speaking over her shoulder to Anatole, she could not help arriving at the forlorn conclusion that she was being punished.

"Oh, don't be absurd, Anatole—we hardly need announcing in my own brother's drawing room!" Lady Harleston, the wife of the vague but amiable Lord Harleston, sailed into the drawing room as if it were her own, with her much quieter husband following. She was a tall woman in her late thirties, quite handsome in a decided rather than pretty way, several years older than her brother, and it was immediately apparent that between them flourished a somewhat bristly tolerance rather than warm affection.

"Althea, what the devil are you doing here?" the earl demanded grimly.

"A fine welcome, I must say! When we took the time and trouble to get off the main road—on our way back to London, you know—only to make certain the storm left you and the Hall still standing!"

"As you can see, we stand," Sheffield retorted. "Hello, Jasper."

"Evening, Stone. Sorry to drop in on you like this, but Althea would have it you was frozen in a drift and needed to be dug out." Lord Harleston smiled, as good-natured as his wife was sharp-tongued.

"It would have suited me better," the earl said, "if she had waited until the spring thaw to look for me."

Lord Harleston's responsive chuckle broke off abruptly as he saw Cassandra—who had stood perfectly still and hoped she would pass unseen. His mild blue eyes widened, and he looked at the earl in some surprise, but before he could speak, Lady Harleston also took notice of her brother's guest.

"Why, is that you, Miss Eden?" she demanded, striding forward to shake hands briskly.

"How do you do, Lady Harleston," Cassandra murmured, hoping wistfully that all this would—somehow!—turn out right.

"How do *you* do is the question I want answered," Her Ladyship replied with all her brother's bluntness and none of his humor or charm. "Were you not supposed to be fixed at Bristol until next week? What on earth are you doing here at the Hall?"

It was the earl who replied, his voice unusually flat. "The lady's coach broke down, Althea."

"Today?" Her Ladyship demanded to know.

Deliberately he replied, "No. A few days ago at the beginning of the storm."

Cassandra had stolen one glance at Sheffield's face, and that had been enough. He had not missed his sister's use of the name Eden, and obviously realized he had been lied to; his expression matched his name, and his eyes were completely unreadable. Cassandra wished the floor would open up and swallow her, and be done with it.

Lady Harleston, shocked, exclaimed, "Days ago? And she has been here unchaperoned? Stone, what can you have been thinking of? A child of her age—with a man of your reputation! Do you for one moment think anyone would believe it innocent? When word of this reaches London—"

"Althea," her husband warned softly.

But Lady Harleston finished her warning defiantly: "—she will be ruined!"

There was an awful silence that seemed to Cassandra to last an eternity. Then she squared her shoulders and, without looking at the earl, said quietly, "If our society believes that a lady may not take shelter from a vicious storm in the home of a gentleman without sacrificing her reputation and marring his, then it is not a society of which I wish to be a part."

Lady Harleston glared at her brother. "Say something!"

The clock on the mantel chimed. Unemotionally the earl said, "Will you join us for supper, Althea? Jasper? I am sure Anatole has set two more places."

By the time Cassandra retired to her room several hours later, her nerves were so strained by the effort of preserving a composed front before the earl and his guests that all she wanted to do was crawl between the covers and indulge in a passionate bout of tears. *He* had seemed perfectly calm, of course, fielding his sister's insistent questions by simply refusing to discuss Cassandra's presence in his house, but Cassandra was exhausted.

Sheffield had made no effort to speak to her alone; in fact, he had hardly spoken to her at all. Whether he was furious over her using a false name, disturbed by the unexpected arrival of Lord and Lady Harleston, or simply impatient with the entire situation was not clear. He had retired behind a wall of remoteness, and what his thoughts were behind that impenetrable barrier was very much his own secret.

Now, in her bedroom, Cassandra changed from the blue silk dress into her nightgown and wrapper and allowed Sarah to take her hair down. But she did not want to be fussed over tonight and was about to dismiss her maid when there was a soft knock and Lady Harleston came in. She was not yet dressed for bed and seemed to take no notice of Cassandra's attire.

"May I speak to you, my dear?" she inquired briskly.

It was the last thing Cassandra wanted, but common courtesy forced her to dismiss Sarah with a nod and murmur, "Of course, Lady Harleston."

The earl's sister sat down on a chair near the dressing table and, as soon as the maid had gone, said, "I know we are barely acquainted, but this *is* my brother's house, and since you have no older female to advise you in this situation—"

"My lady, I thank you for your concern, but I assure you I require no advice." Cassandra kept her voice steady and met the other women's eyes as directly as she could manage. "I took shelter here because there was no place else I could go under the circumstances, and I remained during the storm because I had no other choice. Lord Sheffield has been a most kind and hospitable host, for which I am most grateful."

Lady Harleston nodded but with an expression that said she had expected to hear such platitudes. "I have no doubt that *you* considered the circumstances innocent, Miss Eden, and I am perfectly aware you had little choice in the matter. However, the fact remains that you have spent several nights unchaperoned under my brother's roof."

Evenly Cassandra said, "During which time I had no need to lock my bedroom door, my lady. We may have been alone together upon occasion, but there were always servants about." Tactful servants. Not that she cared what they may have seen. She shut from her mind the aching memory of soul-wrenching kisses and forced herself to go on speaking what was nevertheless the literal truth. "I have not been compromised, and I refuse to behave as if I have. I cannot believe any right-thinking person could possibly condemn me, or blame the earl, for a situation which was not of our making."

Lady Harleston shook her head. "My dear, you've *been* in London this last year and more, and I've the suspicion you have more sense than most, so let us speak frankly."

Just the possibility of the earl's sister speaking more frankly than she already had was rather terrifying, and Cassandra tried to stem the flow. "My lady—"

She was ignored.

"It's never been forgotten that he ruined a girl more than ten years ago; I know you've heard the tales."

"Yes, but—"

"She was an heiress, did you hear that? And him with mortgaged estates and a borrowed coach he carried her off in, as well as the reputation of a rake, even though he was hardly more than a boy himself. Her brother was hours behind them, and when he caught up to them at an inn on the North Road, well . . . it was too late."

"Too late?" Cassandra assumed Lady Harleston meant that the couple had spent an unchaperoned night at the inn. "To travel together, even so far, and spend a night in the same inn—"

"In the same bed," the earl's sister said bluntly.

Cassandra stared at her for a moment, not as shocked as she should have been because she herself had learned firsthand just how effortlessly a Westcott man could seduce. She drew a breath and murmured, "And he refused to marry her."

"No."

"But—the tales—everyone believes—"

"I know what everyone believes." Lady Harleston's voice was matter-of-fact now. "My brother had too much pride and was too much a gentleman to set the wagging tongues aright, and I was already married with a household of my own and didn't find out the truth until much later."

"Then—what happened?" Cassandra was too curious not to ask.

"Stone was head over heels in love with that chit, didn't care a button about her fortune. He was wild then, quick-tempered and tempestuous like all the Westcott men when they're young, and I have no doubt the girl was carried away by all the high drama of being pursued by such a romantic figure. In any event, Stone offered for her, and though I don't know what precisely passed between them, I do know that her brother refused the suit harshly. It seemed he preferred something other than an impoverished earl for a brother-in-law. A likely guess is that he wished to control her fortune himself and had no intention of handing her over to a husband in need of money."

Lady Harleston sighed. "Naturally, Stone was enraged by the refusal. He managed to convince the girl to run away with him, and they set out for Gretna Green in a borrowed coach. Very bad, of course, but he *did* fancy himself in love and certainly would have married the chit, so if it had ended as planned the scandal wouldn't have been so bad. But it did not end as planned."

Obviously less prim than most ladies of the *ton*, the earl's sister added thoughtfully, "I suppose they were both of them carried away by the high drama of it all, and since they expected to be married right afterward, it must have seemed foolish to wait to have each other. Or perhaps he seduced her—though, to her credit, the girl never made that claim, at least not publicly."

Slowly Cassandra said, "Her brother found them— together?"

"No, for Stone had gone to a nearby livery stable to arrange for a better team of horses. What the brother found was his no-longer-innocent sister in a tumbled bed. She confessed quickly enough, and tearfully I imagine—but what I can't be sure of is whether he took her away by force or if she went willingly. When Stone followed them back to London—more high drama!—he was told the girl was betrothed to a nabob friend of the brother's twenty years her senior."

"How could she—?"

"I don't know. Nor do I know why the nabob overlooked her rather profound indiscretion—unless, of course, he had no idea she had actually given herself to Stone. I suppose the girl was swayed by her brother, or even forced by him, to turn Stone away, but he has always refused to talk about it, and only the two of them and the brother likely know the whole truth."

Cassandra swallowed hard. "I heard . . . there was a duel."

Lady Harleston nodded. "The brother would have preferred to avoid more doings sure to reach the ears of the *ton*, I'm sure, but Stone was past reason. I believe he offered what the gentlemen consider unpardonable offense, and they met a few days later. Both were wounded—Stone only slightly, but the brother nearly bled to death. Of course, gossip was rampant, and with the brother badly wounded and the girl sent off with telling speed to marry her nabob and go abroad to live, Stone was the only principal upon whom society could pile its condemnation. The brother left soon after to live abroad himself."

After a silent moment Cassandra said, "Stone—the earl left England after that?"

Lady Harleston did not appear to notice the slip. "Yes, that summer. I believe he has seen much of the world in his travels. He returned only a few years ago, and since then he has worked to restore the Hall." She paused, then said, "He should have reappeared in society, of course, and quieted if not silenced the wagging tongues, but he did not. So the tales grew wilder, and in them he was painted blacker. You know as well as I that he is still seen as a rake at the very least."

Cassandra drew a breath. "Even so, I refuse to behave as if I have done something wrong."

"My dear, you know word of your stay here will reach London eventually. Jasper and I can be trusted to keep silent, you may be sure, but servants talk. Tradesmen come to the door, deliveries are made, gossip is exchanged—and before you can say scat, garbled bits of information take on a life of their own. What was, in fact, understandable and perfectly innocent will never be seen as such. If Stone cares a jot about his reputation I have never seen it, but you must care for yours. Your fortune and standing in society may protect you from open hostility, but you will be called upon to pay some price for this, my dear."

*I already have.* But Cassandra did not say those words, of course. Instead, she said steadily, "What would you have me do, my lady? Insist that your brother make me an offer so that we may forestall vulgar speculation?"

"Why not?"

Lifting her chin, Cassandra said, "Because it is very obviously not what he wishes to do, ma'am!"

"What about what you wish him to do?"

Cassandra felt heat sweep up on her face but managed to keep her voice calm. "He has been very kind, but—"

"Oh, don't talk such nonsense! I believe it is said that love and a cough can't be hidden—and I am neither blind nor stupid. You watched him all evening, and if ever I saw her heart in a woman's eyes, I saw yours!"

Shaken, Cassandra could only murmur, "Whatever I may feel, my lady, I nevertheless refuse to force any man to marry me."

"He is not a fortune hunter," his sister declared, "so you need not worry about that. I don't understand how it came about, but Jasper says Stone turned his West Indian properties to the good after years of neglect, and so recouped much of the fortune our father ran through."

Cassandra was glad of that for his sake but shook her head slightly. "You have no need to tell me that, my lady. But I will not marry to protect my reputation. Tomorrow I will return to London, where I will tell my aunt and uncle the circumstances of my stay here."

"Sir Basil won't like it," Lady Harleston said shrewdly.

Conjuring a smile, Cassandra said, "Perhaps not, but I

manage my own life. If there is talk, I will deal with it in
my own way. And that does not include marrying any man
to suit society's notions of propriety."

The older woman eyed her for a moment, then rose with
a gusty sigh. "It's a great pity, Miss Eden; I believe you and
my brother would deal extremely well together."

Cassandra felt the sting of tears and blinked them away.
Quietly she said, "Good night, Lady Harleston."

"Good night, Miss Eden."

When she was alone in her bedroom again, Cassandra
sat there at her dressing table for a long time gazing at nothing. She thought she understood a few things now, the information supplied by Lady Harleston having drawn a
clearer picture for her.

Sheffield must have loved that girl very much. Perhaps
he still loved her; he certainly felt some bitterness or anger
about that episode of his life. It hardly mattered. His attitude toward Cassandra today, as well as what he had said
just before Lord and Lady Harleston had arrived, demon-
strated his true feelings for her quite clearly.

*"It is just as well you mean to go, Cassie. These past
days . . . shut off from outside contact and thrown together
as we have been—"*

She really did not need to hear the rest. He did not want
another chit of a girl losing her head and ruining his life a
second time, obviously. And who could blame him for that?
She had lied to him about her identity, had virtually thrown
herself at him in the most wanton, unprincipled way . . .
He had known how she felt, of course, even his *sister* had
seen it, and this older earl, with his experience of flighty
girls with fickle hearts, had decided to take no chances that
Cassandra's foolishly romantic imaginings could cause
him trouble.

Desire was one thing—love quite another.

Cassandra let herself cry a little, but not for long. She

had too much to do, and very little time in which to do it. She dried her eyes and rang for Sarah, and when her maid appeared, said, "Sarah, can you contrive to get a message to John tonight without alerting the Hall staff?"

Bewildered, Sarah said, "Yes, Miss Cassie, but—"

"I want you to do so. Tell him we are leaving here at first light and returning to London. Ask him to bring the coach around to the front, as quietly as possible, and *not* to rap on the door if we are not already waiting. You and I will carry what baggage we can—the rest can be sent."

Sarah was staring at her.

Cassandra passed a hand across her brow and sighed. She was so very tired. "I am sorry to keep you working so late, Sarah, but we shall have to pack tonight, and we must be ready before dawn."

"It's quite all right, miss," Sarah said mechanically.

"Thank you. Go and talk to John now, if you please—we have a great deal to do."

While her maid went to advise the coachman, Cassandra found paper and ink and concentrated fiercely on composing a suitable note for the earl.


The snow crunched softly but otherwise muffled the sounds of the coach and horses, and in the gray light of dawn Cassandra left Sheffield Hall. She looked out the coach window until the huge house was lost to sight, then settled back against the cushions with a weary sigh.

How strange it was to know that her life had been forever changed in less than a week. That *she* had been changed. A broken axle and a winter storm—fate's tools.

And now it was past. She had done the best thing possible by leaving this way. She would return to London, and if there should be talk about her stay at the Hall, she would hold her head up and reply calmly to any remarks addressed to her. And if, after the Season was done, she was unable to bear it any longer, she could retreat to either her uncle's country home or her own and have the satisfaction of knowing she had stood firm.

When Cassandra heard a miserable sniff, she thought at first it was her own. But then she turned her head to find Sarah was trying to inconspicuously blot her damp cheeks with a square of equally damp linen.

"Sarah? Why, what is wrong?"

Her gray eyes red-rimmed, Sarah blinked several times, then blew her nose fiercely and very nearly wailed, "Anatole!"

Blankly Cassandra repeated, "Anatole?"

Sarah nodded.

"Oh, Sarah—do you mean to say that you and Anatole—"

With another watery sniff, the maid said, "I didn't mean for it to happen, Miss Cassie, but I just couldn't help it."

"But I thought you were afraid of him."

"Only at first, miss. But that scar isn't so bad once you get accustomed to it, and he has the *kindest* eyes. And such a deep, strong voice."

"I see."

The maid smiled somewhat mistily. "I was stiff with him at first, but he didn't let *that* go for long. With the Hall closed up against the storm and you and His Lordship spending so much time together, we just seemed to keep meeting each other here and there, and so we'd talk. He told me the most wonderful stories about places across the oceans. And it seemed so natural somehow, the way I felt . . . and the way he did . . ."

"Sarah, you haven't—you didn't—"

"Oh, *no,* miss! I'm a good girl—and he never treated me like anything else. Never. I think—I believe he would have asked me to marry him, but . . ."

"But I had to drag you away. I am sorry, Sarah, truly. I

had no idea." She sighed, wondering why she was so surprised. If she could fall in love in less than a week, then
why not Sarah?

"Miss Cassie? Do you think His Lordship might have a
notion to come to London?"

Cassandra looked into that hopeful face and couldn't
find it in her heart to say what she believed—that Sheffield
would very likely avoid London at all costs. "I . . . don't
know, Sarah. Perhaps."

But as the coach reached the main road and picked up
speed, Cassandra gazed out the window at the passing
landscape and wondered if it was only Sarah whose hopes
she was so reluctant to dash. Did she—*could* she—still
have hopes of her own? Could she possibly imagine that
Stone would leave his restored estate and return to the society that had denounced him only because she was there?

Could she possibly be that foolish?

# Chapter Five

"Excuse me, Miss Cassie, but there is a gentleman to see you." Cassie looked up from the stack of invitations and notes in her hand and frowned at her uncle's butler, Gargary. "I told you I am not at home—"

"Yes, miss, but the gentleman was most insistent," Gargary said with a slight bow, keeping to himself the knowledge of the very handsome sum bestowed on him by this insistent gentleman.

"Who is he?"

"He did not give his name, miss."

Cassandra felt her heartbeat quicken and wondered with despair if she would go on forever reacting this way to no more than the possibility of seeing Sheffield. Back in London for nearly two weeks now, she had tensed at the first step of every caller and searched every face she saw on the streets, but there had been no sign of him.

Now she realized she was rising and nodding mechanically to the butler. "Very well, then. I will—I will see him."

"In the front parlor, miss."

She paused to check her appearance in the mirror beside the door of her sitting room and was surprised to find that the dusting of pink across her cheekbones had returned. She had believed that she had left it at Sheffield Hall, that evidence of awakened sensuality, but now the delicate color bloomed, making her eyes sparkle and diminishing the wan look she had worn for so many days. She smoothed her hands down the bodice of her simple morning dress of dove gray, aware that she had lost a few pounds she could ill-afford to lose since returning to London.

Not that her visitor would notice, of course, because it would not be him. It was never him.

She went downstairs, her pace deliberate, and paused before the parlor door for an instant to gather herself. Then she opened the door and went in. "Good after—" Her voice broke off, and suddenly it seemed almost impossible to breathe.

He turned from the window, where he had been gazing out into the street, and something flared in the depths of his black eyes when he saw her. Immediately he came toward her, an unnervingly powerful man who seemed to fill the room with his presence. When he reached her, he held out a hand imperatively, and without a thought she put hers into it.

He bent slightly to brush his lips against her knuckles in a gesture far too intimate for a social greeting, but his voice was calm when he said, "Hello, Cassie."

Since it didn't seem he was going to release her hand, Cassandra pulled it gently away. She did not want to, and she felt bereft when the contact was broken, but she could not think when he touched her, and she needed to think. She eased past him and walked to a chair near the fireplace; she did not sit down, but rested her hands on the back as she looked at him. "I—am surprised to see you here, my lord," she said formally.

Sheffield closed the door she had left half open, then leaned back against it and met her gaze. Those dark, direct eyes were fixed on her face. "Are you? I came to deliver the baggage you left behind at the Hall," he said.

"Oh." She saw him smile at her deflated syllable, and fought a sudden wild urge to throw something for the first time in her life. Apparently, her mother's half-French temperament was alive in her—and had needed only this utterly maddening man to bring it to the fore.

"And for a few answers," he added, pushing himself away from the door and coming to stand at the fireplace. He eyed the chair she had placed between them like a shield, and his mouth quirked again in the smile of amusement.

Cassandra lifted her chin. "Answers?"

"Well, I have a number of questions," he said casually.

"Oh?" She tried to make her voice haughty.

"Certainly. For instance, I would like to know why you had to carry off your maid just when Anatole was fixing his interest with her."

Cassandra blinked. "You knew?"

"Didn't you?"

"No. That is—"

Sheffield shook his head. "Well, never mind. Now that I plan to be settled here in town for a while, I depend upon you to allow Sarah to see Anatole. He was a confirmed bachelor, you see, and fell very hard for her. I believe that is usually so whenever one has . . . given up all hope for love."

Her throat seemed to close up, and Cassandra hardly knew what to say. "I—I would never stand in their way if—"

He bowed slightly. "Thank you, on behalf of Anatole."

She nodded. "Um . . . you said you had questions?"

"You left the Hall so abruptly we had no opportunity to talk," he reminded her. "In fact, you slipped away at dawn, without a word."

"My note—"

"Yes, your note—shall I tell you what it said? I have it memorized, you know." He leaned his powerful shoulders back against the mantel and crossed his arms over his chest, gazing at her unreadably. "It said: 'My Lord, thank you very much for your hospitality and your kindness in providing shelter from the storm. I am most grateful. I regret being unable to say goodbye to you in person, but I feel sure you agree that it is best I return to London immediately.' And it was signed: Cassandra Eden."

He *had* memorized it. Cassandra cleared her throat. "Well, then? What questions could you possibly—"

"I think we can begin with your name. Why did you give me a false one?"

That was a question she had expected, and she answered it honestly. "Sarah gave it, because Anatole frightened her when he first opened the door and because she knew your reputation. I kept up the lie because . . . oh, at first because I was weary of—"

"Fortune hunters?"

She nodded. "The longer I kept up the lie, the more impossible it seemed to tell the truth, so I just put it out of my head."

It was impossible to tell if he believed or disbelieved her, or even if he felt anything at all about the matter; he merely nodded and said matter-of-factly, "Did you believe I was a fortune hunter?"

Cassandra hesitated. "No, not really—not after I got a good look at the Hall. It seemed to me you had no need to dangle after an heiress."

He nodded again. "I see. That seems reasonable enough. Now for the next question. Why, Cassie?"

"I beg your pardon?"

"Why?" His voice was infinitely patient. "Why did you feel it necessary to bolt for London at dawn?"

This was an answer that was more complicated. "The storm was past, the roads clear. I—I had told you I meant to go. There was—there was no reason for me to remain any longer."

"Was there not?"

Cassandra struggled silently for a moment, then blurted, "You did not discourage me when I said I meant to go! In fact, you said—"

"I know what I said," he interrupted. "And what you obviously do *not* know is why I said it. It is a pity we were interrupted before I could explain myself."

Back in control, she said stiffly, "I believe the reason is clear, sir, and required no further explanation. You as good as said that the—the attraction we felt for each other was due to the circumstances of our being thrown together by the storm."

"And did you believe that was true?" he asked politely.

Staring into his eyes, she saw a flicker of something she dared not try to define. But it roused a tiny spurt of hope in her, and it forced her to say hesitantly, "I—I thought you believed it."

In a very deliberate tone he said, "What I believed was that you should leave as soon as possible for three reasons. Because you were unchaperoned. Because the storm *had* isolated us and quite possibly led you to believe you felt more for me than you actually did. And because I no longer trusted myself not to accept what you offered me so passionately with every look, every touch, and most especially every kiss."

She blinked at that last candid statement, knowing without a doubt that she was blushing furiously. But before she could either deny his words or somehow defend herself, she found herself caught by his intent gaze. The flicker in his night-black eyes had become the heated look that was achingly familiar to her, like the sensual curve of his lips and the faint rasp in his low voice. She felt her heart skip a beat and then begin to pound unevenly, and heat was rushing through her body even before he came to her and pulled her into his arms.

All the long days without him had only sharpened the need he had created in her, and Cassandra molded herself to him instantly, her mouth wild and eager under his, her arms slipping up around his neck in total surrender. He crushed her against his powerful length, his arms fierce and his mouth ruthless as it plundered hers. And when he jerked his head up at last, his eyes were brilliant with fire and ferocity.

"Do you understand now?" he demanded roughly. One of his hands slid down her back to her hips, and he pressed her lower body hard against his. "Do you?"

Cassandra caught her breath, dizzy from his kisses and the shockingly intimate awareness of his blatant arousal. Her body was trembling and she thought all her bones had melted. She could only stare up at him, mute, electrified, and enthralled.

His embrace gentled, his hands stroking up and down her back slowly, and his lips feathered over her flushed, heated face. "I wanted you so badly I knew it was only a matter of time before I lost my head," he muttered.

When he drew back just a bit to look down at her again, she touched his cheek with wondering fingers, and a tremulous smile curved her kiss-reddened lips. "That was why you were so—so distant that last day? Why you said I should go?"

"Yes." He turned his head to kiss her palm lingeringly. "Cassie, you were under my protection. I may spring from a long line of rakes, but only a monster would take advantage of a girl under such circumstances. And—"

"And?" she prompted.

He hesitated, then said, "At twenty-one I fancied myself

in love, but what I discovered was that to one so young, powerful emotions are often something entirely different from what one supposes. I wanted to make certain you had the time to consider what you felt, Cassie, before anything irrevocable happened between us."

She frowned a little. "Is that why you waited all these days, leaving me to wonder if I would ever see you again?"

He bent his head and kissed her in apology, leisurely this time but with unmistakable hunger. When he raised his head, she was trembling again, and his voice was hoarse. "Can you forgive me for that? I promise you, it was the most difficult thing I have ever done in my life to stay away from you."

Cassandra drew a shaky breath. "I—I suppose I shall have to forgive you."

He chuckled, then gently drew her arms down and stepped back, holding her hands in his. Reluctance was clear in his eyes. "If I do not leave you now, I will not be able to."

"I suppose you . . . could not stay," she ventured.

Bluntly Sheffield said, "However willing your uncle is to allow you to manage your own life, my darling, I doubt very much that he would be sympathetic if he found me making love to you under his roof."

She found herself both smiling and blushing, pleased by his frank talk of his desire for her even as she was a little embarrassed—or thought she should be.

He smiled at her. "Do you attend the St. Valentine's Day Ball tomorrow night?"

"Yes."

"Good. Save all the dances for me."

She nodded without hesitation, but couldn't help saying, "I won't see you before then?"

Sheffield smiled but shook his head. "There are things I

must attend to. Remember, it has been quite a few years since I've been in town during the Season."

Cassandra nodded reluctantly in understanding, and she managed not to throw herself back into his arms when he kissed each of her hands and then released them. She didn't object when he said goodbye, but when he reached the door, she said, "Stone?"

One hand on the knob, he turned to look at her.

Burning her bridges, Cassandra said steadily, "I am very sure of how I feel—I want you to know that. I fell in love with you that first night."

She had no idea what was in her eyes when she said it, what expression she wore, but whatever the earl saw caused him to release the doorknob and take a jerky step back toward her—and his face was taut with hunger.

He stopped, struggled visibly with his baser instincts, then muttered, "My God, Cassie—you'd tempt a saint," before jerking open the door and striding from the room.

Sir Basil, who had received the news of Cassandra's stormbound stay at Sheffield Hall philosophically, reacted to the news of the earl's return to London with characteristic perception. When Cassandra very casually mentioned after supper that evening that Sheffield had called upon her in the afternoon (since the earl had not stated his intentions in so many words, she was hesitant to inform her uncle that she was being courted), Sir Basil looked very hard across the dining table at his niece.

"I somehow doubt Sheffield's come to London to be measured for a new pair of boots, not when he's avoided the place for the better part of ten years. Should I expect a visit from him, Cassie?"

She hesitated, then replied, "I don't know."

His brows flew up. "You don't know if he means to offer for you?"

Candidly she said, "I don't know if he would ask your permission to offer for me."

Lady Weston, who sat opposite her husband, said, "Dear me," quite placidly and looked at Cassandra with interest. "You never seemed to wish to discuss it, dearest, but we gathered you had formed an attachment for the earl. You were so careful to barely mention him, you know, and that is always a dead giveaway. And then, naturally, we've noticed your low spirits since you came back to town."

Sir Basil, dryly, said, "Quite different from tonight, in fact. A blind man could see how you feel about the man, so I hope you don't intend to try keeping it a secret."

Cassandra smiled on them both, immensely grateful for their love and trust in her judgment. "People will probably talk," she said ruefully. "Even if there is no gossip about my stay at the Hall, I have a notion that Stone has no intention of being . . . circumspect in his attentions. And since he has been away from society for so long—"

"He will definitely be under observation," Sir Basil finished. "Some will call him a fortune hunter, you know; even a man with adequate funds risks that when he pays his addresses to an heiress."

"They may just as easily reproach me and say I wished only to be a countess," she commented in a dry tone.

"Very true, I suppose. But more likely to go the other way. Will that disturb you, Cassie?"

Cassandra smiled faintly. "No, why should it? I know he is indifferent to my fortune."

Sir Basil eyed her thoughtfully. "You do, do you?"

"Oh, yes." There was something of her aunt's utter placidity in that response, and her uncle looked satisfied; when Eden women had at last made up their minds and were certain of something—of anything—they were invariably right.

It was a family trait that Sheffield would no doubt soon discover, Sir Basil mused. If he had not already.

It was an old English belief that birds chose their mates on February fourteenth, and out of that conviction had sprung up in London society the yearly event known as the St. Valentine's Day Ball, which was held on the evening of the thirteenth of February. It was a masquerade ball like any other, where the ladies wore costumes or dominoes with masks, and the gentlemen costumes or merely evening dress with masks. Dancing and conversation were exactly as usual, with the only difference being the Midnight Waltz.

At midnight the final waltz would be announced, and gentlemen were invited to choose their partners. Those gentlemen who did so were, by tradition and accepted practice, announcing publicly their choice of life mate.

Naturally, most of the couples who took the floor for the Midnight Waltz were either married or betrothed; for all its air of impulse and romance, the tradition offered few surprises because it was a rare gentleman who risked public rejection in the event his chosen lady refused him, and a rare lady willing to announce her engagement in such an impromptu manner.

In all honesty, Cassandra had forgotten the significance of the Midnight Waltz. She had certainly enjoyed the evening, not in the least because Sheffield had come to her within five minutes of her arrival and had not left her since.

To the astonished members of society, as yet still ignorant

of Cassandra's stay at Sheffield Hall, it must have appeared the most startling and incredible romance of the Season—perhaps of many Seasons. The scandalous earl, after many years of travel and (it was said) adventure that had left him older and wiser and much more flush in the pocket (a pirate's treasure was alluded to, though no one seemed to know by whom) had returned to London society and, the very day after his arrival, become instantly smitten with the lovely but elusive heiress, Cassandra Eden.

While she was *masked*, for heaven's sake!

More than one former suitor of Miss Eden's, glumly watching the dangerous earl obviously delight and enchant her with apparently little effort, longed wistfully for the cachet of a mysterious and/or wicked past. And more than one scandalized debutante could nevertheless not help but think how thrillingly romantic it must be to know those black eyes followed one's every movement, and with a light in them that was really . . . quite extraordinarily amorous. . . .

"We are the talk of the ball," Cassandra informed the earl solemnly late in the evening. She had chosen to wear a blue dominoe rather than a costume, but her gray eyes, framed by the gleam of her black mask, seemed fittingly mysterious.

Sheffield, who had scorned a costume and early disposed of his mask (like many other gentlemen), could only agree with her. He knew most of their observers were scandalized—but in a relatively mild way. Not that he cared. Except where it concerned Cassandra—as when he had worried she might be wary of him because of the tales she had heard—he was indifferent to his reputation.

"I suppose they must talk of something," he allowed.

Rueful, she said, "Well, we have certainly given them something."

"Do you regret it?"

Cassandra smiled up at him. "Of course not."

Sheffield was about to speak again when the musicians struck up a flourish of drumrolls, and the dance floor began to clear of couples.

"The Midnight Waltz!" the lead musician announced.

Smiling, the earl reached up and untied the ribbons holding Cassandra's mask. "I believe this is my dance, ma'am," he said.

It took a moment for Cassandra to remember the significance of this particular dance. When she did, she murmured, "But, Stone—they think we have only met tonight, and that this is the first time you have seen me unmasked—"

"And now they will believe I fell in love with you at first sight—which is perfectly true."

Cassandra thought her heart would burst, it pounded so rapidly. "You—you did?"

"Certainly, I did." He tucked her mask carefully inside his long-tailed coat as one would a keepsake, then bowed low before her as the musicians struck up the Midnight Waltz. "May I have your hand in marriage, Miss Eden? Will you dance with me?"

Without hesitation she placed her hand in his and curtsied, her eyes glowing with happiness. "If you please, sir."

He kissed her hand and then led her out onto the dance floor, and it was only then that Cassandra realized they were the first couple to begin—because every other eye in the room had been fixed upon them in fascination.

"We have shocked them all," she murmured as, slowly, other couples joined them on the floor.

He was smiling down at her, his mouth both tender and sensual, and his black eyes heated. "We will shock them still further if I am able to persuade you to marry me quickly, my love."

"How quickly?" she asked, solemn.

"By the end of the week—if I am able to wait that long. A special license, a private ceremony—and a very long honeymoon."

Still solemn, she said, "I believe I would like that of all things, my lord."

And her lord, inflamed by the love and desire shining in her gray eyes, waltzed her out of the ballroom and onto a dark and private terrace, under the shocked, scandalized, and wholly envious eyes of society.

# Kay Hooper

is the *New York Times* bestselling, award-winning author of many suspense and romance novels. She lives in Bostic, North Carolina. Visit her website at www.kayhooper.com.

Now Available

# Kay Hooper

*New York Times*
**Bestselling Author**

## Enchanted

Together for the first time—three beloved romance classics: *Kissed by Magic, Belonging to Taylor, & Eye of the Beholder*

A Jove Paperback

0-515-13714-6

*New York Times* bestselling author
**Kay Hooper**

*The Haviland Touch*

A brand-new edition of the classic novel
of romantic adventure!

It's been years since Spencer Wyatt jilted Drew
Haviland for another man. Now she is free—and
Drew will do anything to get vengeance and take
what's been promised to him. But closer inspection
shows him that Spencer is in dire trouble—and in
desperate need of his help.

"KAY HOOPER WRITES A WONDERFUL BLEND
OF WIT, WHIMSY AND SENSUALITY...
SHE IS A MASTER OF HER ART."
—LINDA HOWARD

0-515-14040-6

penguin.com